TEXAS!
Sage

TEXAS!

Sage

Sandra Brown

Doubleday

New York • Toronto • London • Sydney • Auckland

PUBLISHED BY DOUBLEDAY
a division of Bantam Doubleday Dell Publishing Group, Inc.
666 Fifth Avenue, New York, New York 10103

DOUBLEDAY and the portrayal of an anchor
with a dolphin are trademarks of Doubleday,
a division of Bantam Doubleday Dell
Publishing Group, Inc.

Book design by Patrice Fodero

Library of Congress Cataloging-in-Publication Data
Brown, Sandra, 1948–
     Texas! Sage / by Sandra Brown.—1st ed.
         p.   cm.
     I. Title.
PS3552.R718T49   1991
813.029.54—dc20   90-33463
                              CIP
                   ISBN 0-385-41581-8

5   7   9   10   8   6   4

TEXAS!
Sage

Chapter ONE

*H*er lips were soft and inviting against his as she sighed, then whispered, "Merry Christmas."

"Merry Christmas to you, too, Sage."

Smiling, she folded her arms around his neck and placed her lips on his again, putting more passion into their kiss . . . or trying to. "Travis!"

"What?"

"Kiss me."

"I did."

"I mean, really kiss me," she said and growled sexily. "You're allowed to kiss sexy, you know, even though it is Christmas."

"Sage, please." Nervously the young man glanced toward the windows. A party was underway inside the house. "Somebody might see us."

She removed her arms from around his neck and

blew out a gust of air. "Oh, for heaven's sake, Travis, you're so damn proper! Nobody is looking. And if anyone is, who would care if we're out here necking?"

"Mother would care. Do you like your bracelet?"

Temporarily distracted, she replied, "Of course I like the bracelet. What woman wouldn't? It's beautiful."

Raising her arm, she shook the heavy gold bangle around her wrist. "I'm glad you let me open my present tonight instead of waiting for Christmas Day."

"This way you can enjoy it over the whole holiday."

"That was very thoughtful of you. Thank you."

"I still sense that you're disappointed."

Sage Tyler looked up at him through her dense lashes and made a softly spoken confession. "I thought you might give me my engagement ring for Christmas."

Before he could say anything, she rushed on. "But it's not as though we've already picked out rings. Who knows? I might not even want a traditional engagement ring. I'll probably flaunt convention and choose something radically different. Maybe a colored stone instead of a diamond."

Travis cast his eyes down to the white leather pants she was wearing. Her sweater was appropriate enough—white angora with a tasteful amount of glittering studs and rhinestones sprinkled over the shoulders and upper bodice. The pants, however, were definitely a fashion risk.

He smiled weakly. "Nobody ever accused you of being conventional, Sage."

"Thank heaven for that." A movement of her head sent her mane of dark blond hair swinging over her shoulders. "I thought your mother was going to have heart failure when I came downstairs and joined the party wearing these pants."

"Well, she, uh, associates leather clothes with Hell's Angels and rock stars, I guess."

"Hmm. Maybe I should have worn something in a nice pastel taffeta."

He frowned in disapproval of her sarcasm. "Mother is Mother. She and her friends are more or less alike. They do the same things, go to the same places, wear basically the same kind of clothes. She's accustomed to certain things."

"If I'm going to be her daughter-in-law, she had better get accustomed to me, hadn't she? I hope she doesn't expect me to start wearing long plaid skirts and respectable navy flats when I become your wife. All I'll be changing the day we get married is my last name. Speaking of which," she added on a burst of inspiration, "Valentine's Day would be such a romantic date to get officially engaged. Even better than Christmas."

Sage had dragged Travis outside for a breath of fresh air on the long, wide veranda of the Belcher home. The redbrick Georgian structure was strung with twinkling Christmas lights. In the living room behind them, an enormous Christmas tree, arranged by a decorator who favored lace, pearls, and butterflies, commanded attention from one of the wide windows overlooking the veranda.

Three evergreens had been temporarily transplanted in the front lawn and decorated for the benefit of passersby who came from all points of Harris County to view the elaborate Christmas displays the residents of this affluent Houston neighborhood put up each year. A trail of bumper-to-bumper cars snaked along the street, their headlights blurred by the mist.

Though the temperature was relatively mild, Travis hunched deeper into the collar of his dark suit coat and slid his hands into his pants pockets. This belligerent stance never failed to irritate Sage who thought it made him look like a sulky rich kid. It usually meant he had something unpleasant on his mind that he dreaded discussing.

"The fact is, Sage, I'm wondering if we're not jumping the gun to announce our engagement."

The statement caught her off guard, but instantly captured her full attention. "What do you mean?"

Travis cleared his throat. "Well, after the spring semester, I've still got internship and my year of residency ahead of me. After that, there's all the specialty courses in dermatology to get through."

"I know exactly what's required before you can open

a practice, Travis. We'll be all right. Now that I've got my master's degree, I'll find a good job."

"I'm not worried about money. My parents will support me until I set up a practice."

"Then what are you worried about? Lighten up. It's Christmas!"

He glanced at the line of cars crawling past the house. "I don't think you understand what I'm trying to tell you, Sage."

Her wide smile faltered. "Apparently not, but it must be something terrible. You look like you're about to throw up. Don't torture yourself any longer or keep me in suspense. If you've got something to say, let's hear it."

He scratched his head, he coughed behind his fist, he shuffled his feet. "I've given this a lot of thought lately, and . . ."

"And?"

"And I don't think . . . It's not that you're . . . Sage, we're just not . . ."

"Not what?"

He floundered, opening and closing his mouth several times before blurting out, "Suited. We're just not suited to each other."

Having said that, his shoulders relaxed. He exhaled a deep breath. By all appearances, he had relieved himself of a tremendous burden.

Dumbfounded, Sage stared at him. She couldn't believe her ears. She had been dating Travis exclusively for more than a year. It had been understood that they would get married when she earned her master's degree. The semester was ending, and she had been expecting an engagement ring and a formal announcement of their impending marriage during the holiday season. It was preposterous to think he was dumping her. Her! *Sage Tyler!* Surely she had misunderstood.

"You can't mean you're breaking our engagement?"

He cleared his throat again. "I think we ought to think about it some more."

"Don't beat around the bush, Travis," she said testily. "If you're dumping me, at least have the guts to come right out and say so."

"I'm not dumping you. Exactly. Mother thinks—"

"Oh, 'Mother thinks . . .' Mother thinks that I'm not good enough for her little boy."

"Don't put words in my mouth, Sage."

"Then spit it out."

"Mother thinks, and I agree, that you're, well, a little too rowdy for me."

"Rowdy?"

"Showy."

"Showy?"

"Flamboyant."

"Because I wear leather pants?"

"Sage, be fair," he protested.

"Fair be damned. I'm mad."

"You've got no right to be."

"No right?"

"If you'll think back, I never officially asked you to marry me. Did I?" he asked uncertainly.

"Of course you did!" she cried. "We talked about it all the time. My family—"

"Will be delighted if it never comes off," he interrupted. "Your brothers think I'm a wimp. Your mother only tolerates me because she's nice to everybody. That sheriff who's always hanging around harrumphs and shakes his head with what appears to be disapproval every time he looks at me."

"You're imagining all of that," she averred, though she knew he wasn't.

"Well, whatever," he said impatiently, "I think we need a rest from each other."

Her anger gave way to hurt. "I thought you loved me."

"I do."

"Then why are we having this conversation? I love you, too."

He looked earnestly miserable. "I love you, Sage. You're beautiful and sexy. You're the most unpredictable, fascinating woman I've ever met. You make my head spin. You're exuberant. You like pushing people around, bending them to your will."

"You make me sound like a longshoreman!"

"I don't intend to. You've got a zest for life that I can't

match. I'm tired of trying. You're spontaneous and impetuous. I'm methodical and careful. Your politics are liberal. Mine, conservative. You believe wholeheartedly in a personal God. I have my doubts. All things considered, I'd say our differences are irreconcilable."

"Opposites attract."

"I'm beginning to think not."

"This is all crap, Travis. You're trying to sugarcoat it, aren't you? You're lining up your justifications. If you're going to jilt me, at least dignify it by not being so mealymouthed."

"Don't make this harder for me than it is," he complained.

Hard on him? Sage formed a fist as though preparing to sock him. "You don't love me anymore. Isn't that what this is really about?"

"No. Everything I said before is true. I do love you, Sage. But, damn, it takes so much of my energy just keeping up." He gave a helpless laugh. "You're like a playful puppy. You require constant attention and affection."

"I haven't noticed you complaining about my affectionate nature before," she said coolly. "In fact you've begged for more on numerous occasions."

He had the grace to look chagrined. "I deserved that. The fact is, Sage," he said, sounding dispirited, "I've run out of steam. You've drained me. I can't keep up with you and devote the time and attention to my studies that they demand. I think we should take a break from each other and give ourselves time to reassess the situation before we jump into marriage."

He touched her for the first time, placing his hands lightly on her shoulders. "When you've had time to think about it, I'm sure you'll agree with me. I'm no more right for you than you are for me. You might believe you love me, but I think you've only talked yourself into it."

She jerked her shoulders free. "Don't start doing my thinking and believing for me, Travis." This must be a bad dream, a nightmare, she thought. Soon she would wake up, call Travis, and tell him about the bizarre dream she had had and warn him never to make it come true.

It was too real, however, to be a dream. Holiday lights twinkled all around her. She could smell evergreen boughs and hear carols playing over the stereo system inside the house. She could feel the pressure of tears behind her eyelids. Humiliation had a brassy taste. She had always been the one who told admirers when it was over. If there was any breaking off to be done, she was the one to do it.

Travis, even tempered and ambitious, had been positively crazy about her. She couldn't believe he was dumping her. Why several months ago, he had pleaded with her to share an apartment with him, which she had declined to do. After sulking for a few days, he claimed to love her all the more for her strong moral fiber.

They rarely quarreled. He had his moments of pique when he could stubbornly take a position and refuse to give way. Like now. When backed into a corner, however, he usually surrendered to her stronger will.

"To tell you the truth, Travis, I'm not big on postponements. Either you love me and want to marry me, or you don't." She tossed back her hair and confronted him challengingly. "Make up your mind. It's now or never."

He looked pained as he studied her determined expression and the belligerent angle of her chin. Finally, he said, "If you put it that way, I guess it's never, Sage."

That knocked the wind out of her, though she managed to maintain a proud posture. Such bald rejection was inconceivable. He couldn't do this to her!

When he had time to think about it, he would regret it. He would come crawling back on hands and knees, begging her to share his bright future as a successful dermatologist. Until then, she'd be damned before she would show him how much he had hurt her. Not a single tear would he see.

Mrs. Belcher was no doubt behind his unheralded decision. His mother could cow Travis with one imperious glance, but Sage wasn't afraid of her. Her hauteur only made Sage want to provoke her further—by doing things like wearing leather pants to her dinner party.

When Travis finally came to his senses and crawled back, she would marry him and have six children, evenly spaced ten months apart.

In the meantime, she wasn't going to let Travis off easily. Defiantly she said, "That's fine with me. I'll get out of your life as soon as I pack my things."

"Now?" he exclaimed. "But you can't go now, Sage. Your car's in Austin. Where will you go?"

"I'll manage."

He shook his head with diminishing patience, as though he were dealing with a willful child. "You can't leave now."

"The hell I can't," she fired back, knowing that Laurie Tyler would cringe if she could hear her daughter's language.

"Look, Sage, there's no reason why we can't enjoy the holidays together as we planned. As friends. I still want to be friends."

"Go to hell."

"If you don't come back inside, it'll spoil Mother's party. There'll be an odd number at dinner."

"I don't give a damn about your mother's dinner!" she shouted. "Those stupid little chickens she serves every year are always stringy and tough. I wouldn't go back in there if my life depended on it. It was a stifling, dull, boring party to begin with. I should thank you for giving me a good excuse to get out of it."

Uneasy with the volume of her voice, he glanced over

his shoulder. Formally attired guests were milling around the opulent living room, nibbling canapés served by white-coated waiters and toasting the season and each other with highballs and spiked eggnog.

"Sage, be reasonable. I . . . I wasn't going to discuss this with you until after the holidays, but you, well, you sort of forced the issue tonight. I don't want you to feel badly."

"Badly?" she scoffed. "I feel marvelous. Now I can enjoy Christmas without wondering if a society grande dame is going to approve of my wardrobe. Not that I give a fig."

"Don't behave this way," he pleaded.

One of her brows arched malevolently. "What way?"

"Like a high-strung brat."

"First you make me sound as pushy as a Roller Derby queen, then you compare me to an annoying pet, then a simpleton who doesn't know her own mind, and now I'm a high-strung brat. And you claimed to love me!"

"There's no reasoning with you when you get like this." Travis cursed beneath his breath and turned away from her. "Mother will start missing us. I'll see you inside after you've thrown your little temper tantrum." Righteously indignant, he went through the front door.

"Don't hold your breath," she called after him.

The door was decorated with a wreath that in Sage's opinion was extravagant to the point of vulgarity. So was the Christmas tree in the living room. Where were the Santas and candy canes and tinsel they decorated with at her home?

She glared at the gaudy artificial tree through the sparkling windowpanes. The lights placed at precise intervals along its perfect branches began to blur. The tears that had threatened before, now filled her eyes, making the shiny decorations look crystalline.

As her initial anger abated, she began to feel the impact of what Travis had done. Someone whom she loved, whom she believed had loved her, had rejected her.

All that he'd said could be paraphrased in four simple words: "I don't want you." She might be cute and cuddly and capricious, but the bottom line was, he didn't want her. Her zest for life, as he had called it, was irksome to him.

She placed her arms around one of the six fluted white columns supporting the balcony over the veranda. Hugging it, she laid her cheek against its cold, ridged surface. What was she going to tell everybody? How could she hold her head up when word of this got around? What would her own family think? About the only thing they expected of her was to marry someone who loved her as much as she loved him. Well, she had blown that. Like everything else.

How could Travis do this? She loved him. They were perfectly compatible. Couldn't he see that? She liked to maneuver; he would rather be maneuvered. He plodded; she was good at prodding. He was so stolid, he needed someone exuberant in his life—to quote him.

He must be suffering from temporary insanity, she decided. He would come around. Eventually. Her guess was that it wouldn't take too long. He would miss her terribly. Without her, his life would be like his parents', tepid and colorless.

When he did come slinking back with his tail tucked between his legs, and his pride a big goose egg caught in his throat, she would be slow to forgive him for hurting her this way. He had ruined her holiday. They were supposed to be celebrating her earning her master's degree, something neither of her brothers had done. Travis had put a blight on that as well. She would never forgive him.

Stepping away from the column, she wiped the tears off her face, refusing to indulge in them. As a child, whenever her feelings were hurt she had brazened out the situation rather than let her real emotions show. That only tended to invite more ridicule. If she had been a crybaby in front of her brothers, she never would have survived childhood. Not that they would have harmed her; she would have died of her own shame over crying.

Now, she had no choice but to tough it out until Travis realized how foolish he was being. It was absolutely unthinkable that she run home to her family, a jilted woman, tearful and dejected.

First on the agenda was finding a way out of this place. Hell would freeze over before she'd return to the Belchers' party. Nor would she ask for their help, although she knew Mrs. Belcher would gladly see her on her way. Taking a deep breath of determination, she turned toward the corner of the veranda.

She took only one step before drawing up short.

He was loitering against the ivy-covered wall, partially hidden in the shadow thrown by a potted evergreen. There was, however, enough light spilling through the windows for Sage to see him well. Too well.

He was tall and lanky, even thinner than her brother Lucky. Although much of his hair was hidden beneath a damp, black felt cowboy hat pulled low over his brows, Sage could see that the hair above his ears was dark blond, shot through with streaks of pale ivory. Long exposure to the outdoors had left him with a deeply baked-on tan and sunbursts radiating from the outer corners of electric blue eyes, which were regarding her with unconcealed amusement.

He had a firm, square jaw that suggested he wasn't to be messed with, and a lean, wiry musculature that justified the arrogant tilt of his head and his insolent stance.

He was wearing a pale blue western shirt, with round, pearl snap buttons. His jeans had a ragged hem. The faded, stringy fringe curled over the instep of his scuffed boots, the toes of which were wet and muddy. His only concession to the chilly evening was a quilted, black vest. It was spread open over his shirt because he had the thumbs of both hands hooked into the hip pockets of his jeans.

He was about six feet four inches of broad-shouldered, long-legged, slim-hipped Texan. Bad-boy Texan. Sage despised him on sight, particularly because he seemed on the verge of a burst of laughter at her expense. He didn't laugh, but what he said communicated the same thing.

"Ho-ho-ho. Merry Christmas."

Chapter TWO

In an attempt to hide her mortification, Sage angrily demanded, "Who the hell are you?"

"Santy Claus. I sent out my red suit to be dry cleaned."

She didn't find that at all amusing. "How long have you been standing there?"

"Long enough," he replied with a grin of the Cheshire cat variety.

"You were eavesdropping."

"Couldn't help it. It would have been rude to bust up such a tender scene."

Her spine stiffened and she gave him an intentionally condescending once-over. "Are you a guest?"

He finally released the laugh that had been threatening. "Are you serious?"

"Then are you part of that?" She indicated the sightseeing traffic. "Did your car break down or something?"

While shaking his head no, he sized her up and down. "Is that guy queer or what?"

Sage wouldn't deign to retort.

The stranger smacked his lips, making a regretful sound. "The thing is, it'd be a damn shame if you ever got rid of those leather britches, the way they fit you and all."

"How dare—"

"And if you'd squirmed against me the way you were squirming against him, I would have given you the sexiest kiss on record, and to hell with whoever might be looking."

No one, not even her most ardent admirers, had ever had the gall to speak to her like that. If she hadn't shot them herself, her brothers would have. Cheeks flaming, eyes flashing, she told him, "I'm calling the police."

"Now why would you want to go and do that, Miss Sage?" His usage of her name stopped her before she could take more than two steps toward the door. "That's right," he said, reading her mind, "I know your name."

"That's easily explainable," she said with more equanimity than she felt. "While rudely eavesdropping on a conversation that obviously went way over your head, you heard Travis call me by name."

"Oh, I understood everything that was said, all right. Y'all were speaking English. Mama's Boy dumped you, plain and simple. I thought I'd politely wait until he finished before delivering my message to you."

She glared at him with smoldering anger and keen suspicion. "You're here to see *me*?"

"Now you're catching on."

"What for?"

"I was sent to fetch you."

"To fetch me?"

"Fetch you home."

"To Milton Point?"

"That's home, isn't it?" he asked, flashing her a white smile. "Your brother sent me."

"Which one?"

"Lucky."

"Why?"

"Because your sister-in-law, Chase's wife, went into labor this afternoon."

Up to that point, she'd been playing along with him. She didn't believe a word he said, but she was curious to learn just how creative a criminal mind like his could get. To her surprise, he was privy to family insider information.

"She's in labor?"

"As of two o'clock this afternoon."

"She's not due until after the first of the year."

"The baby made other plans. Didn't want to miss Christmas, I guess. She might have had it by now, but she hadn't when I left."

Her wariness remained intact. "Why would Lucky send you after me? Why didn't he just call?"

"He tried. One of your roommates in Austin told him you'd already left for Houston with Loverboy." He nodded toward the windows behind which the guests were being ushered into the dining room.

"All things considered," he continued, "Lucky reckoned it would take me less time if I just scooted down here to pick you up." He pushed himself away from the wall, gave the dripping skies a disparaging glance and asked, "You ready?"

"I'm not going anywhere with you," she exclaimed, scornful of his assumption that she would. "I've been driving to and from Milton Point since I was eighteen. If I'm needed at home, my family will contact me and—"

"He said you'd probably be a pain in the butt about this." Muttering and shaking his head with aggravation, he fished into the breast pocket of his shirt and came up with a slip of paper. He handed it to her. "Lucky wrote that for me to give you in case you gave me any guff."

She unfolded the piece of paper and scanned the lines that had obviously been written in a hurry. She could barely read the handwriting, but then no one could read Lucky's handwriting. Lucky had identified the man as Tyler Drilling's new employee, Harlan Boyd.

"Mr. Boyd?"

One corner of his lips tilted up. "After all we've been through together, you can call me Harlan."

"I'm not going to call you anything," she snapped. His grin only deepened.

Her brother had instructed her to accompany this man back to Milton Point without any arguments. The last two words had been underlined . . . for all the good that would do.

"You could have forged this," she said accusingly.

"Why would I do that?" he asked, giving her that taunting grin again.

"To kidnap me."

"What for?"

"Ransom."

"That wouldn't be too smart. You're family's broke."

That much was true. Tyler Drilling Company was barely making expenses and then only because Marcie Johns had made Sage's older brother Chase a loan when they got married. Because of the sagging oil industry, drilling contracts were few and far between. Presently, the Tylers were among the genteel impoverished. These days that was almost like wearing a badge of honor.

It stung her pride, however, that this reprobate knew about her family's financial difficulties. Her light brown eyes narrowed. "If the company is in such bad financial shape, why did Chase and Lucky put you on the payroll?"

"They didn't. I'm working strictly on commission. Occasionally I get a bonus. Like tonight. Lucky offered me fifty bucks to come fetch you."

"Fifty dollars?" she exclaimed.

He tipped back his cowboy hat. "You sound sur-prised. Do you figure that's too much or too little?"

"All I know is that I'm not going anywhere with you. I'll drive myself to Milton Point."

"You can't, remember? You left your car in Austin and drove down here with Hot Lips." The lines around his eyes crinkled when he smiled. "I guess you could ask him to take you home. Although his mama would probably have a conniption fit if her little boy wasn't home at Christmastime. But you're not going to ask him, are you, Miss Sage?"

He knew the answer to that before he asked it, and she hated him for it.

While a group of carolers strolled down the sidewalk, harmonizing about peace on earth, Sage stewed. She weighed her options and considered the advisability of leaving the relative security of the Belchers' veranda with a man who looked as though committing felonies was his favorite pastime.

On the other hand, her family was the most impor-tant thing in the world to her. If she was wanted at home . . . The note from Lucky looked authentic, but if a crook were clever enough to track her to her fiancé's house. . . .

"What time did you say Sarah went into labor?"

His slow, easy grin could have basted the Christmas turkey better than melting butter. "This is one of those trick questions, right? To see if I'm legit."

Unruffled, she folded her arms across her middle and stared back at him as though waiting.

"Okay, I'll play," he said. "Chase's wife's name isn't Sarah, it's Marcie. Maiden name, Johns. She's a realtor and, every once in a while, Chase affectionately calls her Goosey, his nickname for her when they were in school."

Throwing his body weight slightly off-center and relaxing one knee, he assumed a stance that was both arrogant and pugnacious. His thumbs found a resting place in his hip pockets once again. "Now, Miss Sage, are you coming peaceably, or are you going to make me work for my fifty dollars?"

She gnawed on her lip. He was correct on several points, chiefly that she was stranded at Travis Belcher's house. She wasn't about to throw herself upon Travis's mercy. Even though Harlan Boyd was a lowlife and her brothers had consigned her to spend time with him— something she intended to take up with them at her earliest possible opportunity—her pride wouldn't allow her to turn to a single soul in that house.

"I guess you don't leave me much choice, do you, Mr. Boyd?"

"I don't leave you any choice. Let's go."

"I've got to get my things."

She tried to go around him, but he sidestepped and blocked her path. Tilting back her head, she glared up at him. It was a long way up. She had inherited the Tyler height from her daddy, just like her brothers.

There were few men she could really look up to. It was disquieting. So was the heat radiating from his eyes. So was his voice, which was soft, yet tinged with masculine roughness and grit.

"Given the chance you gave Loverboy, I'd've lapped you up like a tomcat with a bowl of fresh, sweet cream."

She swallowed with difficulty, telling herself it was because her head was tilted back so far. "My sister-in-law once had a phone freak who called her and talked dirty. Now I know just how disgusted she must have felt."

"You're not disgusted. You're scared."

"Scared?"

"Scared that you'd like it if I kissed you."

She scoffed. "I'd like to see you try."

"I was hoping you'd say that."

Her face was still taut with the dire warning she had issued when he cupped the back of her head and drew her up to his mouth for a searing kiss. In less time than it took for her brain to register what was happening, his tongue was inside her mouth, exploring inquisitively.

Bug-eyed with astonishment, she could see beyond his shoulder through the window into the formal dining room. The waiters were moving around the long, elegantly set table, serving Rock Cornish game hens and candied yams to the Belchers' guests while their former-future daughter-in-law's mouth was being scandalously ravaged out on the veranda by a man with a larcenous grin and muddy boots.

If she hadn't been frozen with shock, she would have been laughing hysterically.

Within seconds, however, she regained her senses. Giving his chest a push with all her strength behind it, she shoved him away. Breathing didn't come easily. She gulped oxygen and swallowed air several times before wheezing, "You try another trick like that and you'll wish you hadn't."

"I seriously doubt that, Miss Sage. And so do you." He gave the skies another worried glance. "Before the weather gets any worse, we'd better skeedaddle. Go get your stuff. I'll be waiting for you right here when you come back."

Too infuriated to speak, she marched off.

"This is the lowest, sneakiest trick you've ever played on me," Sage said into the telephone receiver. It stank of tobacco breath and was sticky with God-only-knew-what.

"Sage, is that you? Devon's got her tongue in my ear. You'll have to speak up."

"I know you can hear me, Lucky," she shouted. "I also know my sister-in-law wouldn't neck with you in a hospital corridor. By the way, has the baby come yet?"

"No. Can't be long now though. Better not be. Chase is driving us all crazy."

While her brother apprised her of Marcie's condition and Chase's expectant-father antics, something dark and furry scuttled among the packing crates only a few yards away from the pay telephone. Sage shivered and would have raised her feet off the concrete floor, but there was nowhere to go.

This had to be the worst night of her life. First her fiancé had dumped her, then she was "fetched" home by a smart aleck whose manners were intolerable.

The Belchers' maid had accompanied her up the back staircase to the guest room, where she had helped to pack Sage's belongings. As he had said, Harlan Boyd was waiting for her when she returned. He had placed her in the passenger seat of a car that was surprisingly clean and reasonably new.

However, no sooner had she become resigned to making the long car trip with him, than he took an exit off the interstate highway and turned onto a narrow road that was virtually unmarked and totally unlighted.

"Where are we going?"

She wouldn't panic, she had told herself. These people could sometimes be talked out of their misdeeds if only the victim kept cool. She promised herself she wouldn't reach for the door handle, open it, and hurl herself into the gloomy night until she was certain that his plan was to demand from her family a high ransom in exchange for the whereabouts of her brutally beaten body.

Sounding far more sane than her own thoughts, he replied, "This is the road to the airstrip."

"Airstrip?"

"Where I landed the plane."

"Plane?"

"Are you hard of hearing or what? Stop repeating me."

"You mean we're flying home?"

"Sure. What'd you think? That we were going to drive?"

"Exactly."

"Just goes to show how wrong a person can be. Kinda the way you were about Casanova back there."

She had let that remark pass without further comment and lapsed into hostile silence for the remainder of the trip. It was quite a comedown from the earlier part of the evening when she'd been rubbing elbows with the upper crust of Houston society.

Now she found herself standing in a drafty, damp, rodent-infested airplane hangar, waiting for a man who kissed like he made his living from it and who teased and insulted her every chance he got. He was currently outside, putting the aircraft through a pre-flight check.

She took out her frustration on her brother, whom she had had paged at the hospital in Milton Point.

"Lucky, what were you thinking of to send this . . . this person . . ."

"Are y'all about to leave?"

"Yes, we're about to leave, but I'm furious with you. How could you send a person like him after me?"

"What's wrong with Harlan?"

"What's wrong with Harlan?" She was repeating herself again. "This is a long distance call," she said, trying to massage the headache out of her temples, "and it would take too long to enumerate his bad qualities. Why did you send him? Why didn't you just call the Belchers' house and tell me to come home?"

" 'Cause I knew you'd taken Travis's car to Houston and left yours in Austin. Your roommate told me. You had said that Travis's folks weren't too pleased that y'all were coming up here early Christmas morning, so I knew they wouldn't want him to bring you two days early and miss Christmas Eve at home, too. So—"

"Okay, okay, but you could have warned me that I was going to have an escort."

"I'm sorry, Sage, but there hasn't been time. Chase is tearing his hair out and gnashing his teeth. He's worried because Marcie's thirty-six and this is her first baby."

"She's all right, isn't she?" Sage asked, instantly concerned for the woman she admired.

"Basically, yeah. But she's not having an easy time of it. It's all Mother can do to keep Chase civilized, much less calm. You know what this baby means to him. Lauren's fussy because she's cutting a tooth."

"Oh! Her first?"

"Right. Smart little dickens can already bite with it, too. Anyway, Devon's got her hands full with our baby, so it's been kinda wild and hairy."

Sage could imagine the scene at the hospital. Nobody could keep the Tylers away when one of their own was in need. She recalled the night Devon had given birth to Lauren. It had been chaotic. Of course, there had been extenuating circumstances. That night, one of Marcie's clients had assaulted her. Sage had arrived after Marcie had been rescued and hospitalized, but she had empathized with Marcie's terror. It was crises like that that bonded families.

A lump formed in her throat. For all the pandemonium, she longed to be there with them now. "I could have rented a car," Sage said sulkily.

"We didn't want you to. The cold front hasn't reached Houston yet, but it blew through here around noon and it's cold. Wet, too. We didn't want you driving in the bad weather and knew you'd argue about it. So we decided not to give you the opportunity and sent Harlan after you."

"I'd be safer with the weather than with Harlan."

"What was that? I didn't hear it. A cart was wheeled by."

"Never mind." She didn't want to malign Harlan to

her brother, who obviously trusted him. It would serve no purpose now but to worry everybody until she arrived safely in Milton Point. Once there, however, she intended to give them a full account of his outrageous behavior. "I'll see you when I get there. Give everyone my love. Especially Marcie."

"Will do. See ya, brat."

Wistfully she replaced the receiver. She was trying to wipe the yuck off her hand when Harlan sauntered up. "Has the baby come yet?"

"Not yet. Soon, Lucky said."

"Plane's ready whenever you are."

"Is there a place I could wash my hands first?"

"This way. Better take care of any other necessities before we leave, too. This is a nonstop flight."

She didn't find him in the least amusing and showed it by sweeping past him when he pushed open the restroom door. When he switched on the light, she drew up short, her back coming into contact with his chest.

"Good Lord." It was a disgusting facility that hadn't been tended to in ages.

"Everything you need," Harlan said, laughter underlying his words.

Sage, tamping down her revulsion, marched into the room and slammed the door in his face. She did only what was necessary, being careful not to touch anything. After washing her hands in the rusty sink, she shook them dry.

Emerging from the corrugated tin building, she found Harlan waiting for her on the tarmac. "Where are my suitcases?"

"Already stowed, ma'am. May I see your boarding pass, please?"

She shot him a drop-dead look. "Can we please get on with it?"

"Don Juan shot your sense of humor straight to hell, you know that?"

Taking her elbow, he ushered her toward a single engine plane. The closer she got to it, the more dismayed she became. It was a wreck, a relic of years gone by. The skin of the fuselage had been patched and repainted so many times, it looked like a quilt. The propeller was whirling, but the engine knocked, whined, and rattled. She pulled her arm free of his grasp and turned to confront him.

"Did you build this heap yourself?"

"It's not mine. I only borrowed it."

"You don't really expect me to fly in it, do you?"

"Unless you've sprouted wings."

"Well, forget it. I've heard ancient sewing machines that ran smoother than that motor. Did my brothers know what you were flying in?"

"They trust my judgment."

"Then I mistrust theirs."

"It's perfectly safe." Taking her arm again, he all but dragged her across the cracked runway. When they reached the passenger side of the aircraft, he palmed her fanny and gave her a boost up to the step on the wing. "Up you go."

She clambered into the tiny cockpit. When he was seated in his pilot's chair, he reached across her chest and made sure the door on her side was fastened securely. His arm slid over her breast. It could have been an accident, but she didn't risk looking at him to find out. She stared stonily through the windshield and pretended that she wasn't tingling all over.

"Seat belt fastened?"

"Hmm."

"Comfy?"

"Fine."

"You might want to take off your jacket," he said, nodding at the short, fitted jacket that matched her pants. The outfit had been her Christmas present to herself. It had been in layaway since August. So far, Harlan Boyd was the only one besides herself who had liked it. That didn't say much for her taste.

"Will you please hurry and take off so I can stop dreading it?" she said crossly.

For the next several minutes, Harlan was busy clearing his takeoff with the "tower," a room on the second story of the large building. He taxied to the end of the runway, waited for clearance, then rolled forward. Sage was tempted to pedal her feet in an attempt to help out.

Long before it seemed to her they had sufficient ground speed, the small craft lifted into the air. Harlan put it into a steep climb that had her reclining in her seat like it was a dental chair.

Gripping the edge of her seat cushion, she risked looking out the window. "I can't see the ground anymore!"

" 'Course not. We're in the clouds."

"What are we doing in the clouds?"

"Will you relax? I flew choppers out to oil rigs in the Gulf for a year or two. This is duck soup."

"This is pea soup. You can't see a thing. How do you know you won't run into something?"

"I know, okay? Once we get above this low ceiling, it'll be smooth flying straight into Milton Point."

"Are you sure you'll know where to find it?"

"I hit the right spot every time. I've got a fail-safe instrument." He glanced at her and grinned.

"Cute," she said shortly. "If you value your job, you'd better cut that out."

"What?"

"The sexual innuendoes."

"Why? Are you going to tattle to Chase and Lucky?"

"They won't think you're near as clever as you obviously consider yourself to be."

He eased back in his seat and stretched his long legs as far as they would go in the tight confines of the cockpit. "Bet you don't tell them a damn thing about tonight."

"Why not?"

"Because I know a better story. The one about you and Hot Lips." His eyes caught the reflection of the instrument-panel lights. "I don't think you're going to give them that story straight, are you?"

"Whatever happened between Travis and me is my personal business," she said indignantly. "How I deal with it, what I tell my family about it, is private. Certainly no concern of yours, Mr. Boyd."

He chuckled. "Nope, you're not going to tell it to them straight. You're not going to tell them that he dumped you. That's okay, Miss Sage." He winked at her. "It'll be our little secret."

She muttered something wholly unladylike and turned her head to gaze out the window. All she could see below the plane was a ghostly, gray blanket of clouds. Looking down made her nervous, so she rested her head on the top of her seat and closed her eyes.

"How long will it take?"

"An hour. There 'bouts. Depending on the turbulence."

Her head sprang up. "Turbulence?"

"Just kidding, to see if you were really asleep. Want some coffee?" He reached between his knees to the floor and came up with a shiny chrome thermos. He passed it to Sage. "Sandwich?" He let go of the wheel in order to open a brown paper sack and peer inside.

At the mention of food, her stomach growled indelicately, reminding her that she'd missed Mrs. Belcher's Rock Cornish game hens. "You concentrate on flying. I'll unwrap the sandwiches."

He handed her the sack. She placed the thermos between her thighs. "Bologna and cheese with mustard," she said, investigating the contents of the first sandwich. She unwrapped the second and lifted the top slice of bread. "Two bologna and cheese with mustard."

She handed him one and bit into the other. Around vigorous chewing, she said, "Mother is usually more creative when she packs a lunch."

"Laurie?" he mumbled around his first bite. "She didn't fix these."

"Where you'd get them?"

"Catering by Moe."

"Who's Moe?"

Harlan swallowed and pulled off another big bite. "Moe. I took his car to the Belchers' house. Guess you didn't meet him. That's right, when he came downstairs, you were in the john. Moe runs the landing strip back there. I asked him to throw together whatever he had handy."

Sage spat the bite of food into her palm. "You're kidding, aren't you?"

"Nope. Say, if you don't want the rest of your sandwich, I'll take it."

She practically threw the remainder of her sandwich

at him. It landed in his lap, directly over the faded fly of his jeans. "You don't like Moe's cooking?"

"No! You knew I wouldn't eat anything that came out of that rat motel."

Her fury amused him. "You would if you got hungry enough. Pour me some coffee into the lid of that thermos, will you?"

"Pour your own coffee."

"Fine. But I'll have to let go of the wheel. And I'll have to reach for the thermos."

The thermos was still held securely between her thighs. Harlan smiled at her guilelessly, one of his eyebrows raised into an eloquent question mark.

Sage poured his coffee.

Chapter
THREE

*T*en minutes after Sage's arrival at the hospital, Marcie delivered her baby. Sage had barely had time to hug everybody when Chase barged through the double swinging doors.

"It's a boy!" His face was drawn and haggard, his hair was standing on end, and he looked silly wearing the blue scrubs, but he was beaming a thousand-watt smile.

He had suffered tremendously after the death of his first wife, Tanya. His unborn child had died with her in an auto accident, which had also involved Marcie Johns. Last year, to everyone's surprise, he'd married Marcie.

The details of their courtship and sudden decision to marry remained a mystery to Sage. It wasn't until several months after the civil ceremony that she became convinced they were in love and that the marriage was going to work.

By all appearances it was working exceptionally well. Chase had never look so tired, or so happy. "The baby's perfect," he proudly told them. "Nine pounds seven ounces. Marcie's fine. Real tired though."

"Nine pounds plus? Hmm? Pretty big for a preemie," Lucky said, digging his elbow into his brother's ribs.

"James Lawrence, behave," his mother remonstrated.

"Before y'all go counting it up, I'll admit that Marcie got pregnant on our wedding night."

"You didn't waste any time, big brother."

"I sure as hell didn't," Chase said to Lucky, winking. "By the way, my son's named after you. We decided on James Chase."

"Damn," Lucky said, swallowing hard. "I don't know what to say."

"That's a switch." Chase slapped his brother on the shoulder; both looked embarrassingly close to tears. To prevent that from happening, Chase quickly looked elsewhere and spotted Sage. "Hey, brat, glad you made it in time."

Chase was ten years older than Sage. He and Lucky were barely two years apart. Her two rowdy brothers had been her tormentors when she was growing up, but she had always adored them. She wanted to believe her affection was reciprocated.

She derived a lot of comfort from Chase's strong hug. "Yes, I made it. Barely," she added, shooting Harlan a dirty look.

"Congratulations, Chase," he said, stepping forward and extending his hand.

"Thanks." After they shook hands, Chase said, "Y'all excuse me now. I want to get back to Marcie."

"Do you want to stay at the house with us tonight?" Laurie offered.

"No thanks. I'll be here as late as they'll let me stay, then I'll go on home."

He began backing toward the swinging doors. Even though he had been eager to share the news of his son's birth with them, Sage could tell he would rather be at his wife's side. She felt a pang of envy at their happiness. No one else was as important to them as they were to each other.

Sage doubted she would ever be so essential to another person, so much the center of someone's universe, a source of light and love. Travis's rejection had reinforced her doubt.

Within a few minutes, a nurse carried James Chase Tyler to the nursery window and held him up for their inspection. "He's dark like Chase," Laurie said, her eyes misting. "He looks like Chase did when he was born. Remember, Pat?"

Pat Bush, the county sheriff, was a lifelong friend of the family. Sage didn't remember a time when Pat wasn't around to lend support if the Tylers needed him. When her father had died several years earlier, he'd been indispensable to them. In Bud Tyler's absence, he'd been a staunch ally, protector, guardian, and friend.

He nodded down at Laurie now. "Sure do. Young Jamie here looks the spittin' image of his daddy."

"Jamie!" she exclaimed. "Oh, I like that. Pat, I think you've just nicknamed my first grandson."

Shortly the nurse withdrew with the squalling newborn. "Guess that's our signal to go home," Lucky said. "Besides, Lauren needs her own bed."

His seven-month-old daughter was asleep in her mother's arms, but the excitement had partially awakened her. She was beginning to fret. "I need my own bed, too," Devon said with a weak smile. "I've been wrestling her for hours."

"Let me hold her." Sage reached for her niece, whom she didn't get to see often enough. It was just as well. Devon had said that if Sage had her way, Lauren would be spoiled rotten. "You take a break," she said to her sister-in-law. "I'll hold her on the way home—that is, if you don't mind giving me a ride."

She refused to travel another step with Harlan Boyd, especially since the pickup truck waiting for them at Milton Point's small landing strip had been in no better condition than the airplane they'd flown in from Houston.

It wasn't that she was snobbish about the make and model of vehicles she rode in. Her brothers drove company trucks that looked like they'd come through a war. Travis teased her about her car because it rattled. She was driving the same one she'd taken to Austin her freshman year at U.T. She did, however, expect a few small frills, like windows and ignition keys. Harlan had started his pickup by touching two bare wires together. For all Sage knew, it could have been stolen. The passenger-side window was gone. The opening had been plugged up with a square piece of cardboard, which hadn't kept out the cold, damp wind.

Harlan didn't appear to be offended because she chose not to ride with him again. "See y'all," he said, and moved toward the elevators.

Sage was annoyed to notice that as he passed the nurses' station, several pairs of female eyes were distracted from business. They watched his loose-jointed swagger all the way down the corridor. Sage conceded that his hair was an attractive mix of brown, blond, and platinum shades, and that his eyes were spectacular, and that ordinary Levi's did extraordinary things for his rear end, but she hated herself for thinking so.

"I'll take Laurie home," Pat offered.

"We've got plenty of room in our car, Pat," Lucky said. "Save yourself the trip."

"No problem."

They left the hospital en masse. As Lucky pulled out of the parking lot, Sage glanced through the rear window of his car to see Harlan climbing into the cab of his pickup.

"I hope he remembers to deliver my suitcases to the

house," she remarked. At the landing strip he'd placed them in the bed of the truck and slung a tarpaulin over them. It was still raining. Hopefully the covering hadn't blown off.

"Who? Harlan? You can count on him."

"Apparently you do."

Lucky glanced up at her through the rearview mirror. "Do I detect a note of snideness?"

He'd given her a golden opportunity to express her opinion of his new employee, and she was going to give it to him. "Either you have an inexplicably high regard for him, or no regard at all for your little sister."

"I hold Harlan in high regard. And you're okay," he said, deliberately trying to get a rise out of her.

In the rearview mirror, she could see the mischief twinkling in his eyes—which she had always thought were the bluest in the world until she met Harlan. Lucky's charm failed him this time, though. Sage had had all the ribbing she could take for one evening.

"Who is this person, Lucky?" she demanded. "He appears out of nowhere, I've never heard of him, you give him a job in the company business, and entrust him with your only sister's life. What's the matter with you?"

"In the first place," Lucky began, curbing his famously short temper, "he didn't appear out of nowhere. Chase met him last year in Houston."

"Oh, well, why didn't you say so?" she asked sarcastically. She shot him a fulminating glare in the mirror. "Houston's crawling with criminals and cutthroats. Don't you read the newspapers? Having met him in Houston hardly makes him instantly trustworthy."

"Chase trusted him."

"Based on what?"

"Gut instinct."

"Then I'm beginning to doubt Chase's judgment. Did Harlan just show up here one day unannounced?"

"About six weeks ago."

Because she'd been studying so hard, she hadn't come home at Thanksgiving. Otherwise she would have met him then. In recent weeks there had been little time to spare on anything except writing her thesis. Her phone calls home had been brief and to the point. During those short conversations, no one had mentioned the new hired hand, by name or otherwise.

"He wanted to sponge off Chase, I suppose," she said.

"Not sponge. He was looking for work. His last job had run out."

"I'll bet. He looks like a vagrant. A sly, shifty no-account who'll probably abscond with the company's profits."

"There aren't any profits," Lucky said dismally.

Devon, who had wisely stayed out of the quarrel, now placed a reassuring hand on her husband's shoulder. "They're hoping some of Harlan's ideas will save the business, Sage."

Sage divided her gaping stare between them. "What? Are you kidding me? *Him*? *His* ideas? Did I miss something? Did he drop out of the sky? Hatch from a golden egg?"

"Enough, Sage," Lucky said tetchily. "We get your drift. Apparently Harlan didn't make a very good first impression on you."

"That's putting it mildly."

"What did he do that was so terrible, track mud into the Belchers' marble foyer?"

"Much worse than that. He—"

He had eavesdropped on a conversation she didn't want her brothers to know had taken place.

He had said things to her she didn't want to repeat to her brothers because there might be bloodshed.

He had kissed her with a carnality that had stolen her breath. She wanted to pretend that both the kiss and her surprising reaction had never happened.

"Well?" Lucky prompted from the front seat. "He what?"

Quashing every word she had been about to say, she substituted, "He's rude and obnoxious."

"Harlan?" Devon asked, sounding surprised. "He's usually very polite."

Having hoped that at least Devon would share her impressions of him, Sage now felt abandoned. Curtly she said, "I don't like him."

"Well, just steer clear of him, then," Lucky said.

"You've got nothing to do with the business, so what do you care who works for it? Soon you'll be married and outta here anyway. Speaking of which, how's the future zit doctor?"

The insult to Travis went unnoticed. Sage's attention had snagged on Lucky's reference to her disassociation from the family business. His offhand, but painfully correct, remark cut deeper than he or anyone else would ever guess.

Naturally she had nothing to do with Tyler Drilling. She was the baby girl of the family. An afterthought. Probably an accident. A hanger-on. Hadn't she come along eight years after her parents' second strong, healthy, overachieving son? The boys were a team, a pair. Whenever anyone in town mentioned the Tyler boys, there was no doubt who they were talking about. She was the Tyler boys' little sister.

Her brothers hadn't been too crazy about the idea of having a baby sister. For as far back as she could remember, they had teased her unmercifully. Oh, she knew they loved her. They would protect her from any and all harm and give her anything she asked of them.

But they were very close to each other, best friends and confidants, as well as brothers. She had never been a part of that special male bonding and was always secretly jealous and resentful of it. It was something she hadn't outgrown.

Quelling her deep-seated hurt, she moodily responded to Lucky's question. "Travis is fine."

"Is he coming up Christmas Day as planned?"

"Uh, I doubt it. He's . . . he's bogged down with his studies. It was going to be inconvenient for him to make the trip in the first place. Now, with Jamie's arrival, Christmas is going to be so hectic. . . ."

At the risk of painting herself into a corner, or telling an outright lie, she let her explanation trail off. The unvarnished truth was that Travis wouldn't be joining them on Christmas Day, period. They didn't need to know anything beyond that.

Once Travis and she were reconciled, she might tell them about the "spell" he'd taken at Christmas, but probably not. It would be a long time before his rejection would qualify as one of those episodes in life that one could look back on and laugh about.

"Damn shame he won't be here," Lucky said with affected sincerity. Devon gave his shoulder a hard nudge.

Any other time, Sage would have lit into Lucky for poking fun at Travis, but, again, his comment went virtually unnoticed. She was experiencing a twinge of conscience and arguing with herself that she hadn't actually told a lie.

Lucky hadn't asked her point-blank, "Are you still engaged to Travis, or did he break it off earlier tonight?" Sage reasoned. She had avoided mentioning it, that's all.

Then why was she haunted by Harlan's gloating grin?

Why could she hear the echo of him saying, "I don't think you're going to give them that story straight, are you?"

All her life she'd managed to hide her hurt feelings and screen her disappointments by bluffing. It was unsettling that an imperfect stranger, a tramp like Harlan, had seen straight through her bluff.

Laurie Tyler was never happier than when bustling around her kitchen, the house full of family. She had been a housewife since marrying Bud Tyler when she was eighteen. She made no apology for never having had a career outside the home. It would never occur to her to regret her life because she had always been blissfully happy with all the choices she had made.

She was active in civic and church work and could be depended on to handle either a leadership position or the most menial and thankless task. She was quite comfortable in either capacity.

But in her kitchen, with her noisy, rambunctious family seated around the large table, she was in her element. Tonight she was especially happy because she had been blessed with another grandchild . . . and Sage was home.

Sage had been conceived long after Bud and she had thought their family was complete. The baby girl was an added bonus, like a gorgeous gift wrap on a very special present. Her blond prettiness had dressed up the family. Her personality had given it spiciness.

Laurie entertained no illusions about her daughter, anymore than she did her sons. Sage had many attributes. She also had flaws. She was headstrong and stubborn and had the same trait as Chase of being very hard on herself. Like Lucky, she had inherited the Tyler temper.

She wasn't demure and soft-spoken, qualities some might use to typify the ideal daughter. Not Laurie, who was glad that Sage was more passionate than proper. She preferred vivacity to vapidity, and Sage had plenty of the former.

Laurie loved her daughter in a special way, even though Sage herself sometimes made loving her difficult. She didn't accept or express love easily. As though fearing a rebuff, she always kept a part of herself protected. In that way, too, she was much like Chase and very unlike Lucky, who often let his emotions run away with him.

"Would you like something to eat, dear?" Laurie asked her daughter, unable to resist the impulse of lovingly smoothing her hand over Sage's mane of hair.

"Please, Mother, if it's not too much trouble." Momentarily she rested her cheek on the back of Laurie's hand. Then, as though embarrassed by the childish gesture, she pulled away. "Hmm, Christmas cookies."

"Yes," Laurie replied, laughing as she surveyed the

mess on the kitchen countertop. "Marcie went into labor while I was right in the middle of frosting them. As you can see, I dropped everything and ran. We'll finish them tomorrow."

"I'd like that," Sage said, giving her a swift hug before taking a chair at the table.

"I'm so sorry we had to interrupt your holiday plans with Travis." Laurie dropped a pat of butter into a hot iron skillet and began building a cheese sandwich.

"Don't worry about it."

"Secretly I'm glad you're going to be home tomorrow."

"Me, too."

"Christmas Eve just wouldn't be the same without you here, snooping around all the presents."

"I never snooped!"

"Like hell." Lucky sauntered in and dropped into a chair. "Remember the Christmas that Chase and I unwrapped your presents and replaced what was inside with dead crickets? You wished you hadn't snooped that Christmas."

"Infidel." Sage threw a Frito at him. Grinning, he caught it and ate it.

"I remember that," Pat said. He was leaning against the countertop, snitching raw cookie dough and sipping the coffee Laurie had poured for him. "Bud had to paddle you both on Christmas Eve. Hated like hell to do it. Laurie, you tried to talk him out of it."

"Though Lord knows they needed it for that stunt. Where's Devon, Lucky?"

"She said to tell everybody good-night. She was exhausted."

"For all the tricks you and Chase played on me, it's a wonder I'm not psychotic," Sage remarked.

"I think you are."

She threw another Frito at her brother. This one he threw back. She threw another one. He threw it back too. Soon corn chips were flying.

"Children! I swear, you're worse than three-year-olds."

They were all still laughing when Harlan came through the back door, carrying Sage's suitcases, one in each hand. Whenever Laurie saw him, no matter how briefly or how long it had been since the last time, she was always a little surprised by how handsome a young man Harlan Boyd was.

Quite objectively, she thought her sons were the handsomest men around. That opinion was borne out by the number of ladies they had squired before falling in love and getting married. For his age, Pat, too, was a heartthrob. Plenty of women in and around Milton Point were jealous of his devotion to Laurie.

Harlan, however, was movie-star handsome. Some matinee idols might even envy the angular bone structure of his face and the provocative shape of his mouth. And his eyes . . . One look into those eyes could steal the breath of even an old woman like herself, Laurie thought.

"Thank you, Harlan," she said to him now. "Set those suitcases down there. We can take them up later. Would you like something to eat?"

"No thanks." He removed his damp hat and raked his hand through his thick, tousled hair. "Just some coffee, please."

Laurie poured him a cup. When she turned around to hand it to him, she caught Sage looking at him with such disdain, he could have been one of the crickets her brothers had replaced her Christmas presents with.

Granted, Harlan was a little rough around the edges, but she was disappointed that Sage couldn't feel more charitable toward him.

Then she saw Harlan smile at Sage and wink. No wonder Sage was in a snit. Laurie could barely suppress her smile. He was barking up the wrong tree if he was trying to flirt with Sage. Unless her strong-willed daughter could lead a man around by the nose, the way she did Travis, she wasn't interested.

Harlan, however, seemed unfazed by her condescension. To Laurie's amusement, he continued to stare at Sage while she methodically ate her grilled cheese sandwich and drank two glasses of milk. About the time she finished, Lucky stood up and stretched.

"Guess I'd better check and see if Devon got Lauren

SANDRA BROWN

to bed okay." He said his good-nights and left the
kitchen for upstairs.

"I'm beat, too," Sage said, coming to her feet. "I had a
harrowing trip," she added, looking pointedly at Harlan
who continued to nonchalantly sip his coffee, though a
betraying grin played around his mouth. "Good night,
Mother. We'll get on those cookies first thing in the
morning." She kissed Laurie's cheek. "Good night,
Pat."

Harlan stood up when she went for her suitcases. She
waved him back into his chair. "I can get them."

"No problem," he said, lifting the suitcases off the
floor.

Sage wrested the handles from his hands and marched
from the kitchen without another word. Pat looked at
Laurie inquisitively. She shrugged with puzzlement. Harlan returned to the table to finish his coffee.

"It's late. I need to get back to town," Pat said.

"I'll walk you out." Laurie reached for her jacket
hanging on the rack just inside the back door and threw
it around her shoulders.

Once Pat and she were out of earshot and away from
the pools of light coming from the windows, he pulled
her into his arms and kissed her. His mouth was warm
and mobile over hers. Their kiss was giving, loving, and
sexy. He drew her closer, and, for a moment, she
submitted to having his hands on her hips before self-
consciously stepping back, her cheeks flushed.

"You sure as hell don't kiss like a grandma," he teased.

"You make me behave in a scandalous way," she murmured, nuzzling his neck.

They nibbled on each other before falling into another deep, lasting kiss. Pat placed his large hand inside her jacket and rested it lightly on her ribcage, just beneath her breast. She moved enticingly, letting him know she longed for his touch as much as he longed to touch her. He covered her breast, massaging it gently through her clothing.

Moments later, he released her, making a low groan in his throat. "Laurie, have you thought about it some more?"

She didn't have to ask what he was talking about. Most of their evenings together ended on this subject. "It's all I ever think about, Pat."

"Don't you want to?"

"You know I do."

"You asked me to give you until the holidays. Well, the holidays are here."

"But I didn't know that Jamie was going to arrive early."

"What difference can that make? That's no excuse," he said shortly. "Look, I'm getting fed up with all this sneaking around, stealing kisses, and groping in the dark like a couple of kids. I'm too old for this."

"I don't like it any better than you do."

"Then let's go ahead and do it. Nobody's going to be shocked. Chase already knows about us. They all probably suspect."

"I don't know, Pat," she said uncertainly.

"Laurie, I'm dying," he said, then groaned again. "I want to sleep with you, dammit. I've wanted to for forty years. Why are you making me wait any longer?"

"Sage, for one thing."

"Sage?"

She could tell by his tone that she'd surprised him. "Soon she'll be making wedding plans. I don't want my romance to take any gilt off hers. That would be awfully selfish of me, wouldn't it?"

"It's about time you were selfish. You've spoiled those kids rotten."

"And you've helped me spoil them," she fired back.

"Sage is a modern-thinking young lady. She'll understand."

Indecisively, Laurie gnawed her lower lip. "I'm not sure how she'll take the idea of us being together. She was Bud's sweetheart, a real daddy's girl."

"She was no more devoted to Bud than you or I were." His mouth turned grim. "I want an answer, Laurie. Soon. I won't go on like this indefinitely."

His harsh tone of voice didn't intimidate her. It didn't fool her either. She placed her arms around his neck. "Are you issuing an ultimatum, Sheriff Bush?"

"Take it any way you like."

She moved closer to him. "Don't even think of leaving me, Pat. If you ever leave me, I'll hunt you down and shoot you."

"Damn. I believe you might."

"I would. Count on it."

A smile tugged at his lips for several seconds before he gave into it. "Aw, hell. I ain't going to leave you and you damn well know it." He lowered his head again and kissed her meaningfully. They finally parted reluctantly. He ambled toward his squad car. "I'll be out tomorrow evening to drive you to church."

Laurie waved him off and dreamily moved back toward the house. She had just made it through the kitchen door when a terrible, crashing racket came from upstairs.

"What in the world?" she exclaimed. Her first concern was for Lauren in her crib.

"Sounds like the house is falling down."

Harlan bolted from his chair at the table and ran out of the kitchen, headed for the staircase in the hall. Laurie was right behind him. They scrambled upstairs. Lucky and Devon stumbled from their bedroom. Lucky was in his briefs. Devon was pulling on a robe over her nightgown.

Across the hallway from their room, Lauren had set up a howl from the nursery. Devon went in to calm the baby and get her back to sleep. Lucky scratched his chest and glared darkly, asking, "What the hell was that?"

"*That,*" Sage enunciated, "was your baby sister entering her room and finding that it's been taken over by somebody else." At the end of the hallway, she was standing with both hands on her hips, tapping her foot and bristling with rage.

"Oh, dear," Laurie said with a sigh. "I forgot."

"I reckon there's going to be hell to pay," Harlan said.

"Let me handle it."

"Be my guest," he muttered.

"Sage, dear—"

"Mother, what is this *person's* stuff doing in *my* room?" she pointed her finger at the center of Harlan's chest.

"That's what I was about to explain," Laurie said calmly. "We invited Harlan to stay with us. He lives here now."

Chapter FOUR

"Lives here? He lives here? In my room? You took in a vagabond and gave him *my* room?"

"Sage, if you'll calm down—"

"I can't believe this!" Sage cried, cutting Laurie off in midsentence. "Has everyone in this family except me gone daft?"

Devon slipped out of the nursery and quietly closed the door behind her. "Lauren's gone back to sleep."

"Good," Lucky said. "Pipe down, will you, Sage? That shrieking could wake the dead."

He shackled Devon's wrist with his long fingers and drew her across the hallway and into their bedroom, giving her bottom an affectionate pat. "But I sure do appreciate your waking Devon up." Lecherously bobbing his eyebrows, he closed their bedroom door behind him.

Sage glowered at the closed door and muttered, "Animal." Then she returned her attention to her mother and the man who had not only intruded into her life, but had apparently seized control of her home and family. She had never heard of him before tonight, now he was the bane of her existence. What was more, he seemed to be enjoying it.

"What's his stuff doing in my room?" She had lowered her voice only a few decibels in deference to the sleeping baby. "Where are my things, Mother? I can't believe you just moved me out and moved him in without even consulting me."

"Sage, that's enough! Calm down this instant."

When her mother used that tone of voice, it was time to hush up and listen. By an act of sheer willpower, Sage reined in her anger. The way things were going, if she didn't mind her p's and q's, she'd be kicked out into the cold while Harlan Boyd basked in the warmth of her family's love and adoration.

"I *did* ask your permission to rearrange the rooms," Laurie said. "Remember, several weeks ago, I called and asked if I could move some of your things into the guest bedroom?"

"Oh." Reminded of that particular conversation, Sage's accusatory gaze lost some of its angry sheen. "I vaguely remember something like that. I was working on my thesis. I barely listened. But I'm sure you didn't tell me that you had taken in a boarder who was going to reside in my room."

"I sensed your distraction," Laurie explained. "I ended the conversation because I knew your mind was on your studies. I didn't think it was necessary to tell you about Harlan at that time."

"You didn't think I'd want to know that somebody had taken over my room?"

"Sage, you haven't lived in that room since you went away to college almost seven years ago!" Laurie's maternal patience had finally been expended. "You have an apartment in Austin. Soon you'll be married. You and Travis will have a home of your own."

Harlan noisily cleared his throat. Folding his arms over his chest and crossing his ankles, he braced himself at a slant against the wall. Sage saw his struggle to keep a straight face and could have murdered him with her bare hands.

"Married or not, I thought I'd always have a room in the house where I grew up." In spite of her best efforts not to, she sounded wounded and plaintive. Well why not? Without her knowledge, somebody must have declared this Let's-kick-the-slats-out-from-under-Sage Day.

Laurie's expression softened and she drew Sage into an embrace. "Of course you have a room in this house," she told her gently. "You always will. And when you're married and bring your family here, I'll find room to sleep everybody.

"But from now on, Sage, this house will be a stopover for you. You'll be in and out. I transferred your things into the guest room so Harlan could have more space. Otherwise, all that roominess was going to waste. Doesn't that make sense?"

It made perfect sense, but it still wasn't acceptable. The reason was Harlan. If someone else were sleeping in her bed, she wouldn't have minded so much. The fact that it was *him* made her want to chew nails.

In that frame of mind, she said, "One might ask where Harlan planned to stay if he hadn't imposed upon your hospitality."

"In the first place, he didn't impose. I offered him the room. I saw no need for him to stay in that trailer alone."

"Trailer?"

"The Streamline I pull behind my pickup," he supplied, speaking for the first time.

"No offense, Harlan," Laurie said, laying her hand on his arm, "but it's seen better days. It's probably drafty," she told Sage. "I'm sure he's much more comfortable here."

"Oh, I'm sure he is, too." Sage gushed so sweetly it could have caused tooth decay. "I'm sure he's as contented as a pig in the sunshine. My room has always been very comfortable. At least I've always thought so. Ever since I was a little girl, I've thought it was comfortable."

Laurie frowned a silent but stern reprimand.

"Look," Harlan said, pushing himself away from the wall, "I don't want to be the cause of a ruckus. I'll move my things back to the trailer tonight, so you can have your room back."

"Don't do me any favors," she said tightly, her lips barely moving to form the words. "As Mother said, this house is only a stopover for me."

"Is that right?" His drawl suggested that he knew better.

"That's right," she retorted crisply. "Now, if you'll both excuse me, I'm going to shower and go to bed." She struck off down the hallway, clumsily toting her suitcases, which she felt were about to pull her arms from their sockets. She stopped midway to the guest bedroom and turned back. "I *do* still have bathroom privileges, don't I?"

"That's not funny, Sage," her mother said.

"You're damn right it isn't."

She disappeared into the guest bedroom and slammed the door behind her. Harlan whistled. "I sure as hell didn't mean to cause a family dispute. Sorry, Laurie."

"Don't worry about it tonight. I'll smooth things out with her tomorrow."

"If it would make things easier, I'm more than willing to move back into the trailer. Probably should have stayed there in the first place."

"That won't be necessary," she assured him, patting

his hand. "I'm delighted to have you here. You've given Chase and Lucky new hope for the business. In return, providing you with a room while you're here is the least I can do." She glanced down the hallway. "I apologize for Sage's rudeness. She's . . . well, she's rather high-strung."

"Yeah, I noticed that." His grin cancelled any hint of rancor.

"Good night, Harlan."

" 'Night."

Harlan went into the bedroom formerly belonging to Sage Tyler. He felt badly about this. She'd been fun to tease, but he hadn't wanted to really hurt her feelings. Not after what had happened to her earlier in the evening. Strange. She seemed more upset over the room situation than she had been over her breakup with Belcher.

"What a dumb sonofabitch," he said beneath his breath as he pulled off his cowboy boots, hopping on alternate feet while tugging them off.

Sage didn't know it yet, Harlan thought, but she was well rid of Belcher. It might take her a while to realize it, but one of these days she was going to wake up to the fact that she'd been rescued from the maws of unhappiness.

Sure, right now her pride was stung. Her self-esteem had taken a beating tonight. But deep down she was relieved. A smart woman like her had to know she'd been spared making a big mistake.

Life with a dreary wimp like Belcher would make her miserable, Harlan reasoned. She had more spirit, more spunk, more vibrancy in the pad of her little finger than Belcher had in his whole pale body. She shivered with vitality from the top of her head to the soles of her feet. That mama's boy couldn't have satisfied her or made her happy in ten million years.

Especially in bed.

If Belcher had been satisfying her, giving her all her healthy young body craved and then some, she would have protested the breakup more strenuously. She would have cried and kicked and carried on something terrible. She hadn't. Not really. He'd seen women shed more tears over a broken fingernail than Sage had over Belcher.

Getting cold feet might be something Belcher did routinely and she knew it would pass. She could think she had a surefire plan for winning him back . . . or perhaps in her heart she knew she wasn't missing much for having him out of her life.

If the last were the case—and Harlan hoped it was—her sex life with Hot Lips couldn't have been all that great. She had taken it too well for good, satisfying sex to be lying on the sacrificial altar.

Linking Sage Tyler and sex in Harlan's thoughts painted a provocative image in his mind, one which brought a smile to his lips. Damn. In bed, she would be as untamed as a lioness, all tawny and supple and savage.

He sobered instantly.

It wasn't right for him to be envisioning her sprawled across satin sheets as smooth as her skin, hair spread out behind her head, tangled and wild, like her nature.

What the hell do you know about her nature? he asked himself derisively.

A lot. Instinctively he knew that Sage's sensuality had never been tapped—a seductive thought he had no business entertaining. It was wrong. It was also down-right dangerous.

The Tylers had been good to him. They'd taken him under their collective wing. He had won their trust. But he knew they'd draw the line at him lusting after their sister. Hell, yes, they would. They wouldn't tolerate that. Nor should they.

He couldn't shake his thoughts though.

His heart had gone out to Sage when he watched her hugging the pillar and crying over that rich nerd. None of the photos of her that he'd seen around the house had prepared him for his first glimpse of her in the flesh. When she moved toward him, her long thighs encased in those leather pants, desire had slammed into his groin like a punch from a prize fighter. Ever since then, he'd been struggling to keep it under control.

Reminded of his discomfort, he unsnapped his jeans and unbuttoned the top button of the fly. He shrugged off his vest and hung it in the spacious closet, then peeled off his shirt, balled it up, and tossed it into the wicker hamper Laurie had provided him. His socks followed the shirt.

He flung back the covers of the bed and lay down, stacking his hands behind his head and staring at the ceiling. This was the position he usually assumed when he needed to think.

Tonight his thoughts centered on Chase and Lucky's kid sister. He wasn't surprised that she was attractive. The two men were attractive, each in his own way. Laurie Tyler didn't look anywhere near her age and could turn the heads of men much younger. She sure had turned the sheriff inside out, Harlan mused, smiling at the thought of the moony-eyed gazes they exchanged when they thought no one was looking.

So, he had it figured that Sage would be as good-looking as the rest of her family. What he hadn't expected was the impact she would have on him. Women were easy to come by. They were just as easy to leave behind when it came time to move on.

This one wouldn't be easy to say good-bye to. Sage would be a bottomless bag of surprises that would be hard to give up. Her roller-coaster range of emotions had captivated his attention as it had never been captivated before.

She had been so prissy when she caught him eavesdropping, he couldn't resist teasing her. She had been so sassy, he'd really had no choice except to kiss her smart mouth into silence. And the kiss had been so damn good, he'd wanted to carry her to bed and have her right then and there.

Recollections of their kiss made his lower body even more uncomfortable, so he unbuttoned another button of his fly. He wasn't proud of this desire. He was ashamed of it. The Tylers trusted him and he would never betray their trust.

On the other hand, they couldn't read his mind. And a man couldn't hang for what he was thinking. He'd been around Lucky and Chase long enough to know that each was madly in love and in lust with his wife. They were virile men who would understand desire.

Still, it wouldn't be too smart to—

His eyes sprang to the door when it suddenly flew open. Sage was silhouetted against the light in the hallway. It was difficult to take her militant expression seriously since she was wearing a bathrobe and her wet hair had been combed back from a recently scrubbed face.

"I want my blanket."

"Pardon?"

He could neither sit up nor stand. Currently it was a physical impossibility. The only activity his body was primed to do was out of the question—he gauged by her expression that Sage wasn't there seeking romance —so he lay as he was.

She marched into the room, not halting until she reached the foot of his bed. "My electric blanket," she said. "It's been mine since I can remember. I always sleep under it in the wintertime. I want it."

"Don't you ever knock before you come barging into a man's bedroom?"

"I was raised with two brothers. I'm used to seeing men in their skivvies."

"Lover-boy, too?" he couldn't stop himself from asking. For one thing, he was honestly curious about her sex life with Belcher. For another, he wanted to provoke her. "Somehow I can't quite picture him in his drawers. Bet he's got knobby knees."

She gave him a look that would have withered a dozen fresh roses in a matter of seconds. "Can I have my blanket, please?"

Harlan cast his eyes down the length of his body toward his bare feet. When his gaze moved back up to her, he said, "Anything you see that you want, help yourself right to it, Miss Sage."

She didn't like that. Not a bit. Her lips narrowed into a straight line of pique. She flung the bedspread to the floor and tugged on the electric blanket until it came free from its military fold between the mattresses. Turning on her bare heels, she stalked toward the open doorway, only to be brought up short when the electric cord ran out. She barely caught herself from falling backward and landing flat on the floor.

"Unless you've got a mighty long extension cord, I reckon you'd better unplug it," he drolly observed.

From where she stood, she yanked the cord from the wall socket. Gathering the blanket against her chest, she glared at him. "You might have buffaloed my whole family, but I'm not fooled. I'm onto you, mister. I don't trust you as far as I could throw you."

"Now that's an interesting thought."

Ignoring him, she continued. "It's amazing to me that my brothers, usually intelligent and intuitive men, have placed any confidence whatsoever in you, much less embraced you as one of the family.

"And don't be flattered by my mother's kindness. She'd feel sorry for a rabid dog, and I consider you much more dangerous. Mother loves everybody unless they proved to be totally wretched, which I fully expect you to prove yourself to be any day now.

"You're very good at your game. I'll hand you that. Even Pat's been fooled, and he can usually spot a con man a mile way. He's fallen for your act, too."

"Well not me," she said, thumping her chest with a small fist. "You might have hoodwinked everyone else, but I've seen you at your worst. I've see how you operate when you're not turning on the sickening, hokey, phony, good ol' boy charm.

"It's my moral obligation to expose you as a fake and a fraud to my gullible family, and that's exactly what I'm going to do the first chance I get."

"And get me out of your life at the same time," he said smoothly. "Won't that be convenient? Because I'm the only one who knows you're living a lie, right? That's the real reason you don't want me around. I make you nervous. You're afraid I'll let them in on our secret."

Quivering with rage, she headed for the door again, this time reaching it successfully. Windowpanes rattled when she slammed it behind her.

Harlan laughed. She had a hell of a temper when she got riled. Experience had taught him that when a woman's temper was hot, her other passions burned hot, too.

At the thought, he groaned with pleasure and pain. "Oh, to hell with it."

Rather than unbuttoning another button on his fly, he got up and pulled his jeans off altogether. While he was at it, he took off his underwear too. He straightened the bed linens, replaced the bedspread and climbed back in, assuming his original position, but pulling the covers up to his chest in case Miss Sage decided to make another unannounced entrance. Not that what he was sporting could be well hidden beneath the covers, he thought wryly, glancing toward his lap.

She was wrong, of course. She wasn't onto him. Nobody was. Nobody had been for the fourteen years he'd been on his own. A few people might understand his reasons for drifting and living the way he did, but he never gave anybody a chance to form an opinion. He didn't discuss his former life with anyone. Knowing his background might change an individual's opinion of him. At the very least, it would color an opinion.

He wanted to be accepted for what he was today. Now. He wanted to be appreciated for his sharp mind, and innovative ideas, and easygoing manner. He wanted to be judged on what stood in his size eleven boots and nothing more.

He was at peace with the decision he'd made fourteen years ago, but few women would be, not with their natural nesting instincts. Especially not a woman like Sage whose roots went deep and to whom family meant everything. She would never understand his need to roam. Of course, he would never have a reason to ask her to understand his lifestyle. Hell, no.

The sooner she was out of sight and out of mind, the better. Concentrating on the work at hand was going to be difficult, if not impossible, with her on the scene. Hopefully she wouldn't prolong her Christmas vacation. If luck were with him, she would leave as soon as the turkey leftovers ran out.

But until she did, he was going to have one hell of a time keeping his head on straight, his eyes off her, and the fly of his pants feeling comfortable.

Sage woke up to the tantalizing aroma of cooking pork. She grinned into her pillow, feeling warm, snugly, and content in the knowledge that her mother was downstairs preparing biscuits and sausage gravy.

Travis had called her favorite breakfast "country food" and made fun of it.

The thought of Travis brought with it all the unpleasant memories of the night before. They crowded against her contentment and dispelled it.

Her eyes came open. Hanging on the wall she was facing were familiar framed photographs—Sage as captain of the Milton Point High School cheerleading squad, Sage in cap and gown receiving her high school diploma, Sage in a similar photograph accepting her college degree from the dean of the business school at the University of Texas, Sage with her brothers and daddy in Yellowstone National Park, taken during the family vacation when she was seven. Beloved photographs.

Wrong wallpaper. Wrong room.

Then it really hadn't all been a bad dream. This wasn't her room. *He* was residing in her room, using her furniture, sleeping in her bed, wallowing in her sheets. That was the most disturbing thought of all.

She had been eagerly looking forward to Christmas, the burden of school finally having been lifted. Then Travis had started whining about having to divide their time between his family and hers, and she'd had to make concessions to spending the entire holiday at home. He had his nerve, breaking their engagement after getting her to compromise on the time she would be able to spend with her family.

He had his nerve, breaking their engagement, period.

For this, he was going to have to work for her forgiveness. He would find her stingy with it. When he came crawling back, she planned to let him know in no uncertain terms how churlish he'd been to pull this stunt during Christmas and ruin her holiday.

For the past year, they'd constantly talked marriage. They had made plans. They agreed that marriages should be well blueprinted and based on common goals rather than strictly romance. Sexual heat was a shaky foundation to build a life on.

Sage had decided long ago that she would never depend on a man for her happiness. Travis understood that. Likewise, he wanted his wife to be committed to the success of his medical practice. She loved Travis. Hadn't he admitted last night that he loved her? But they were more practical about love than some couples.

Travis could be driven to passion, just like any man. They'd had their steamy moments together. But it wasn't as though his center of gravity was in his loins. He didn't possess that raw, animal sexuality like her brothers. Not like—

Her mind snapped closed around the traitorous thought. She would not allow that man to spoil another minute of her holiday. She would put him out of her mind.

Unfortunately, her mind had a will of its own. Emblazoned upon it was the image of Harlan Boyd lying in the middle of her bed. It was almost too short for him. The crown of his blond head had been touching the headboard; his long legs had reached nearly to the foot of it.

He hadn't attempted to make himself more decent, but had just lain there, one knee bent and slightly raised. She'd seen layouts of naked men in *Playgirl* that didn't come close to being that sexy. It was sexier than being naked, lying there with the top snap and two buttons of his fly undone.

It disturbed her that she remembered it in such vivid detail, but she was absolutely certain that she was right. Two buttons had been undone. She had seen the elastic waistband of his shorts.

She had a clear mental image of his chest, wide and muscular and covered with fuzzy, brown hair. His stomach and belly were well muscled. She could have bounced a quarter off his abdomen, it was so tight. He hadn't even had the decency to take his hands from behind his head. Instead, he had exposed his underarms, which were lined with patches of soft hair.

He'd known all those nurses at the hospital were gawking at him. The jerk was well aware of his good looks. And he *was* good-looking, if the scoundrel type appealed to you. He was a conceited exhibitionist. When she went into the room, had he stammered apologies

SANDRA BROWN

for being caught without his shirt? No. Had he clambered to cover himself? No.

Instead, he had lain there with that insufferably complacent smile on his face, looking like he was either thinking about having sex, or had just had sex, or—she recalled the smoldering heat in his eyes—was waiting to have sex.

His thoughts might have been dirty, but at least he wasn't. The bedroom had been as neat as she had ever kept it, neater in fact. She'd noticed at the kitchen table, while she'd eaten her sandwich under his steady blue stare, that his nails were clean and trimmed. He didn't smell bad. In fact, in the cockpit of the airplane she'd caught a whiff of her favorite men's fragrance. His clothes certainly made no fashion statement, but they were right at home in Milton Point. He spoke with a Texas twang but sounded quite literate. He hadn't made any blatant grammatical errors.

However, his limited virtues hardly made up for his gross character flaws. How dare he kiss her like that? It had been a kiss straight out of an X-rated movie, which was probably the only kind of movie he went to see. She'd never been kissed like that. Not even Travis—

Judiciously she didn't carry the comparison of Harlan to Travis any farther. Loyally, she told herself the comparison wouldn't be fair to Travis, but she didn't delve into precisely why it wouldn't be.

All she knew was that Mr. Harlan Boyd was the most

annoying, aggravating, and arrogant individual she'd ever had the misfortune to meet, and he'd witnessed her most humiliating moment.

No way on earth could she live with that. It was untenable. Since he had bamboozled her family and made himself indispensable to Tyler Drilling, she could eliminate hopes of his disappearing any time soon.

Her only alternative was to get Travis back quickly. "Then we'll see who laughs last, Mr. Boyd."

Chapter FIVE

*S*ingle file, the Tylers paraded down the center aisle of the church for the midnight candlelight service. Attending was a Christmas Eve tradition that hadn't been broken for decades. Everyone in the family was expected to be there. This year, for obvious reasons, Chase and Marcie had been excused.

"But we have Harlan with us to take up the slack," Laurie had said happily as she slid her arms into the coat Pat had held for her.

Sage had patently ignored Harlan as the family gathered in the entry hall of the ranch house before leaving for town. He'd been away from the house all day, so she hadn't seen him since the night before.

That morning, she had visited Marcie in the hospital and taken another look at her nephew Jamie. The rest of the day she had been occupied with baking cookies and eleventh hour shopping. The prevailing Christmas spirit had lightened her dark thoughts of Travis.

Her holiday mood was squelched, however, when Harlan came loping down the stairs as they were preparing to leave for church. Failing to take the hint that she didn't want to acknowledge him, he sidled up to her as they were crossing the front porch.

"You don't mind if I go to church with y'all, do you, Miss Sage?"

"I do indeed. You're not family." She gave him a condescending onceover. He wasn't dressed up by any means, but he had on black slacks and a white shirt under a brown leather bomber jacket that looked battle-scarred. "But I suppose I should be glad that you won't disgrace us."

Grinning in the manner that made her grind her teeth, he lunged forward and opened the car door for her. Before he had a chance to get in beside her, she soundly closed it.

It was well known by the rest of the congregation that the third pew from the front was tacitly reserved for the Tylers. They had occupied it for as long as Sage could remember. Their processional down the aisle created quite a commotion. They were carrying the candles each of them had been issued at the church door, their programs, their coats, and baby Lauren and her paraphernalia.

Pat Bush stood aside and let Laurie precede him into

the pew. She had taken only a few steps when she backed into the aisle again and whispered, "I'd like to sit beside Sage. You go ahead." Pat went in first and moved to the end of the pew, followed by Laurie and Sage.

Glancing over her shoulder, she was relieved to see Devon moving in behind her. Lucky came next. Then Harlan. Thank heaven she had avoided having to sit beside him.

She looked toward the front of the church and let the ambiance seep into her. The altar and choir loft were decorated with bright red poinsettias. The organist and pianist were playing a Christmas medley. The atmosphere was hushed and reverent.

". . . but if she starts crying, we might need to slip out."

Sage was distracted by Devon's whispering.

"Good idea. We'll swap places with Harlan." Lucky didn't know how to whisper. His voice could be heard throughout the sanctuary. The pastor, sitting near the podium, frowned down at him, as he had been doing from the pulpit every Sunday of Lucky's life since graduating from the nursery.

Harlan stood up, Lucky scooted to the aisle seat, and Devon moved next to him, leaving a vacant space beside Sage. Harlan shuffled between the pews, trying to avoid feet and knees, and dropped into the space beside her.

Her back stiffened and she groaned audibly.

Leaning toward her, he whispered, "Did I step on your toes?"

"No."

"Did I bump your knee?"

"No."

"Were you groaning because I didn't?"

Her head whipped around in time to see him turn his attention to the podium and assume a righteous countenance. Steaming, Sage moved as close to her mother as she could get, so that even her clothes wouldn't be touching Harlan.

The yuletide medley ended on a crescendo. The pastor stood in the pulpit. The service always began promptly at eleven-thirty so that it could conclude at midnight.

"Hi, everybody."

Chase whispered to them from the outside aisle, leaning in over Pat's shoulder. His smile was for all of them seated along the pew.

"Oh, you got to come!" Laurie gladly exclaimed in a stage whisper.

"Marcie insisted that I not miss it on her account."

"How's Jamie?"

Chase grinned like only a new father can. "Wonderful." He cast an apologetic glance toward the pastor, who seemed to be waiting for the Tylers to get situated before starting the service. "I'll just sit up here," he whispered, and moved to take a seat in the row in front of them.

"You'll do no such thing. We can make room," Laurie said. "I want all of us to sit together. Scoot in, Pat."

They shifted again, barely making room for Chase and getting settled before the minister asked them to bow their heads for the opening prayer.

Sage's mood was hardly spiritual. She was crammed against Harlan's side. Her thigh was pressing his from hip to knee. Their shoulders battled over the forward position until Laurie nudged her and admonished her to be still. She had no choice but to relent and place her arm and shoulder behind his.

He stared forward, seemingly enraptured with the reading of the scriptures. Sage knew better. The soft lighting reflected the mirth in his blue eyes. He placed unnecessary pressure on her arm with the back of his. When he reached for the hymnal, she was sure the brush his arm gave her breast was no accident.

The thirty-minute service seemed to drag on interminably. At last the lights were turned off and ushers moved down the aisles with candles, lighting those of the people sitting on the aisles.

When Lucky's was lit, he turned to Devon and, after touching the flame of his to the wick of hers, kissed her softly. Devon, being careful of the baby, held her candle to Harlan's.

Sage held up her candle as he turned toward her. He didn't look at their touching wicks, but at her. Feigning indifference, she lifted her eyes to meet his gaze. Just as her wick ignited, something leaped inside her chest, as hot and spontaneous as the flame at the top of her candle. For a moment, she was held captive by his blue stare. Then quickly, shakily, she turned to light her mother's candle.

She refused to look at Harlan again during the candle lighting process. She sat with head bowed, staring at the burning candle held between her perspiring, unsteady hands. She tried to convey a picture of piety. Surely everyone would think that she was at prayer and not riotous with confused emotions.

Her insides churned. Her mouth was dry one minute and profusely salivating the next. It took all the self-discipline she possessed not to look at Harlan again. She was distinctly aware of every place her body was touching his. She felt lightheaded.

She had never felt this way before, and it was frightening. Maybe she was coming down with the flu. She felt uncomfortably warm and unaccountably flustered.

Her knees were weak and would barely support her when the pastor signaled for the congregation to stand. A cappella, they sang "Silent Night," before extinguishing the candles and filing out of the church while the chimes tolled midnight.

This had always been a reviving, uplifting moment for Sage. But tonight, as she moved toward the exit, the pounding of her heart had nothing to do with the spirituality of the moment. She had a guilty notion that it was carnal in nature.

"I'll have to skip the cider and cookies tonight, Mother," Chase told Laurie when they reached the parking lot. "This is our first Christmas together. I want to spend as much of it with Marcie as possible."

"I understand," Laurie said, hugging him. "We'll miss you. Give Marcie our love."

"See you tomorrow."

"Then you are coming for dinner?"

"I wouldn't miss that," he called back as he jogged toward his car.

Sage rode home with Pat and Laurie, while Harlan rode with Lucky's family. During the drive, they discussed the church service and Jamie and plans for Christmas Day, but Sage was uncharacteristically subdued.

It distressed her that Harlan Boyd had sparked such a drastic physical response in her. She had never been so sexually aware of a man in her life, not even the man she'd been planning to marry. Nor did she believe she could have been that tuned into him, to the point of being aware of each breath he took, if he hadn't been equally tuned into her.

Nonsense. It was the season. Christmas did crazy things to people's minds, made them believe in Santa Claus and such.

To be on the safe side, however, she avoided Harlan as she helped her mother set the table. Earlier they had prepared sandwiches and dips. A kettle of wassail was simmering on the stove. In deference to the occasion, they used the dining room, but Christmas Eve was always casual.

"Did you hear from Travis today?"

Sage choked on the cookie she'd been chewing when Laurie asked the unexpected question. "Uh, no, but he, uh, his family had plans for most of the day and tonight. I didn't expect to hear from him. Pat, another sandwich? You've only eaten two."

She teased the sheriff in an effort to divert attention away from herself. Only one person at the table wasn't fooled by her bluff. When she risked looking at Harlan, he winked at her.

Later, carrying a tray of dirty dishes into the kitchen, she met Harlan coming through the back door, his arms loaded with Christmas presents. She didn't even acknowledge him.

However, as he passed her, he leaned down and, placing his lips directly against her ear, whispered, "You lie real well, Miss Sage. They don't suspect a thing."

The shock of feeling his lips and breath on her ear nearly made her drop the tray. She slammed it down onto the counter. Dishes rattled. "I did not lie! I didn't expect Travis to call me today. And while I've got you alone, I want you to know that I didn't appreciate what you were doing to me in church."

"Probably not. But you *liked* it."

Before she could refute him, he slipped through the door.

* * *

Laurie, Devon, and Sage were in the kitchen by seven
o'clock the following morning, preparing Christmas dinner. Laurie fretted over the turkey, which she was afraid
would either be undercooked or overdone.

Sitting at the kitchen table, Harlan ate a light breakfast and then volunteered to carry in firewood and build
a fire in the living room fireplace. Laurie blessed him
with one of her special smiles. Sage pretended he was
vapor.

Lucky came in, saying to Devon, "Lauren's been fed,
bathed, and is down for her nap."

Sage dropped the celery stick she'd been chopping
and turned away from the counter, her jaw hanging
slack. "You're kidding!"

"What?" he grumbled as he poured himself a cup of
coffee and opened the Dallas newspaper.

"The former stud of Milton Point, ladies' man ex-
traordinaire, gives his baby daughter baths?"

"Yeah, and I'd better be the only man who ever
bathes her."

"Why, Lucky, what a strange thing for *you* to say,"
Devon cooed, batting her eyelashes in mock surprise.
He snarled at her, then buried his head in the newspaper,
coming up several minutes later to exclaim, "Hey, Devon,
this is your best article yet. No wonder you're syndicated statewide. Have you read it, Mother, Sage?"

They both answered that, yes, they had read her

Christmas editorial about the homeless in America and that it was both insightful and poignant.

Midmorning, Pat arrived bearing gifts. Lucky took them from him to place beneath the tree in the living room.

"When can we open our presents?" Sage asked.

"After dinner."

"Aw, Mother. *After* dinner?"

"Yes, after dinner."

Plans changed, however, with the unexpected arrival of Chase and his family. Laurie burst into tears when he laid her first grandson in her arms. She immediately forgot the turkey and retreated to the rocking chair in the living room with the newborn. Chase solicitously helped Marcie into an easy chair, though in Sage's opinion she seemed perfectly capable of moving under her own power.

"I hope you'll have enough room for us at the table," Marcie said, laughing. "I know you weren't counting on my being here, but when the doctor released me this morning, Chase and I decided we'd come out for a while."

"Just until she gets tired." He laid his arm across her shoulders. "Doesn't she look great?"

She did. Her red hair was falling loose and full on her shoulders. If anything, her gorgeous complexion had improved with pregnancy. Her figure was fuller, too.

"This really made my Christmas," Laurie said, nuzzling Jamie's sweet-smelling neck.

Everyone clustered around to admire the newborn. Sage suggested that since everyone was already there, they might just as well open their presents. She was indulged.

Pat played Santa Claus, removing the gifts from beneath the tree that was decorated, in Sage's opinion, as a Christmas tree should be. Among the candy canes and tinsel were ornaments that her brothers and she had made in school. Not even the most amateurish efforts had ever been destroyed, but were proudly displayed each year.

She was delighted with all her gifts, but especially with the new riding quirt from Chase and Marcie. "I know you'd never touch it to animal flesh," he said, affectionately tugging a lock of her hair, "but it looks good."

"Here's one more for you, Sage," Pat said, handing her a gift-wrapped box. "This is from . . ." Pat consulted the gift tag. "From Harlan."

"Harlan!" Her tone suggested that he was a descendent of Attila the Hun. Ameliorating it somewhat, she glanced at him and mumbled, "We only met night before last. You really shouldn't have."

"Oh, I wanted to."

His earnestness set her teeth on edge.

"What is it, Sage?" Laurie asked.

She unwrapped the package. "It's a bookmarker."

"There's a quotation on it," he said, making certain everybody's attention was called to it.

Sage scanned the swirling calligraphy, then scowled at him.

"What does it say, Sage?" Chase wanted to know.

"Read it to us."

"It's just a quote from H. L. Mencken," she told them all, hoping that would suffice. It didn't. They all looked at her expectantly. She was in the spotlight and on the spot, which was exactly where Harlan had wanted to place her. With absolutely no inflection, she read, " 'Conscience is the inner voice which warns us that someone may be looking.' "

Lucky laughed. "You should have given that to me."

"What have you done to have a guilty conscience about?" Devon asked, her eyes narrowing.

Everyone's attention moved to them. Sage, glaring at Harlan, stuffed the bookmarker back into the shallow box and stood. "I'll go check the turkey." Feeling his laughing eyes boring a hole into the center of her back, she retreated.

In spite of Harlan's presence at the table, Sage enjoyed Christmas dinner enormously. It was so good to be at home, surrounded by the people she loved. During the meal, she realized that she was more relaxed than she'd been in a long time, and it was because Travis wasn't there.

He had always annoyed her brothers, and their wisecracks had always annoyed him. Sage had been caught in the middle, trying to pacify all of them and to reassure Travis that teasing was a Tyler family tradition. Today, it was a relief not to have to pander to his supersensitivity.

As though her thoughts had conjured him up, the telephone rang just as they were clearing the table. Laurie went to answer. "Sage, it's for you. Travis."

As she left the dining room for the hall telephone, she shot Harlan a smug glance over her shoulder. Taking the receiver from her mother, she raised it to her ear and, loud enough for everyone in the adjoining room to hear, said, "Merry Christmas, darling."

"Uh, Merry Christmas." It was obvious he was taken aback. He hadn't expected her to sound so joyful. "I just called to make sure you'd gotten home all right."

"You shouldn't have worried about me. I made it fine."

"Well, uh, that's good. I'm relieved."

He didn't ask how she had made it. Didn't he care? Wasn't he curious? For all he knew she could have hitchhiked and been picked up by a sexual deviate . . . which, when she considered some of the things Harlan had said and the way he had kissed her, wasn't far from what had happened.

"Marcie's baby was a boy," she told Travis. "He's been nicknamed Jamie."

"Really? That's nice."

"Wait till you see him, Travis. He's so cute."

"Sage, I . . . What I mean to say is that nothing's

SANDRA BROWN

changed. The only reason I called was to see that you were safe. You weren't in a very stable frame of mind when you left. The maid found the bracelet I gave you lying on the end table in the guest bedroom."

"That's right."

"I wanted you to have it, Sage."

"Why?"

"Well, you know, I felt so rotten about having to tell you that we were off. It hit you hard. I could see that. Now that you've had time to adjust, how are you taking it? I don't want you to be too upset."

So, he wasn't calling with reconciliation in mind. He wasn't offering her apologies and an olive branch, only condolences and a gold bangle bracelet to salve his conscience.

By the tone of his voice, she realized that he never was going to come crawling back. Over the last couple of days, she had been deceiving herself into thinking that he might. This was for real. It was final. What she heard in his voice wasn't contrition and appeal, but pity.

How dare he be that conceited! Had he expected her to jump off a bridge? Or, having made it home, be prostrate in bed with cold compresses over her tear-bloated eyes? Apparently so.

Not bloody likely, she thought angrily. And she would rather have a shackle around her wrist than the bracelet he had given her as a consolation prize. She wished she had the opportunity to cram the thing down his throat.

Ever mindful of eavesdroppers, she said cheerfully, "Well I must run, Travis. Thanks for calling. Merry Christmas."

Replacing the receiver, she gripped it hard for several seconds, as though wanting to extract bravado from it. She still didn't intend to spoil everyone's holiday by announcing that Travis and she were no longer getting married. Until she could figure out a graceful way to break the news to her family and save face, she planned to brazen it out.

But she needed a moment to collect herself. Rather than returning to the dining room, she rushed upstairs. As she approached the door of the room she was now sleeping in, she heard voices coming from the other side.

Marcie was lying on the bed. Jamie was at her breast, sucking greedily. Chase was adoring both. "Oh, I'm sorry, Sage," Marcie said when she saw her standing in the doorway. "We'll go someplace else."

Masking her distress behind a smile, Sage breezed in. "Don't be silly. I just came in to repair my lipstick."

She moved to the vanity table and checked the mirror for signs of discomposure on her face. None were visible. She used a tube of lipstick, then crossed to the bed and sat down on the opposite side from Chase, who couldn't take his eyes off his wife and child.

The threesome embodied familial bliss. Tears threatened again, but they were easily explained. Everyone got emotional over babies. "Jamie is beautiful, you two," she said gruffly. "Truly beautiful."

"Thank you. We think so too." When Marcie and Chase's eyes met, they looked at each other with such naked love and devotion that Sage felt like an intruder. After a moment, Chase said, "I've barely had a chance to say hello, brat. We're damned proud of you for getting that master's degree."

"Thank you."

"It's a shame Travis couldn't be here to celebrate Christmas with us," Marcie said with commiseration. "I think Jamie and I ruined your plans."

"It doesn't matter. We—"

If she could tell anybody that her engagement was off, it would be Chase and Marcie. Marcie was extremely sensitive to other people's feelings. Chase had always been more serious than Lucky, who would either demand to know how dare the sonofabitch jilt his sister or tease her until she couldn't stand it.

But Sage couldn't bring herself to admit her failure yet. They would offer condolences, too. Their pity, like Travis's, would be intolerable. To spare them all an awkward scene, she perpetuated the myth that she was still engaged.

"We had changed plans so many times already, once more didn't matter."

"Hey, Chase." Lucky knocked on the door. "Can you tear yourself away from your wife and kid long enough to watch the Cowboys kick the Redskins' butts?"

TEXAS!
Sage

Chase looked at Marcie inquiringly. She laughed. "I couldn't possibly ask you to miss that."

"I could watch the game at home."

"No. Enjoy the day. I'm fine. After Jamie's finished here, I'll stay and rest for a while."

"Sure?"

"Sure."

He bent down and kissed her lips before leaving the room. Marcie's eyes followed him from the room, before they returned to Jamie. He had stopped sucking. She cupped her breast and moved it aside, her nipple popping from his mouth.

Sage extended her arms. "Do you mind if I hold him?"

"Not at all." Sage had learned how to handle an infant when Lauren was born, but she lifted the baby gingerly. Observing her, Marcie said, "You're getting a lot of practice before having one of your own, which shouldn't be too much longer."

Sage shook her head emphatically. "No, I don't think so."

"Haven't Travis and you talked about having children?"

"Oh, sure. But we planned to postpone it for five years at least."

"You've been that specific?" Sage nodded, and Marcie laughed softly as she settled against the pillows behind her. "Sometimes it doesn't work out that way."

"Chase said you got pregnant on your wedding night."

93

"That's right, even though we thought we were protected against it. Thank God we weren't," she said, gazing at her son lovingly.

Sage bent her head over the infant sleeping in her arms and rubbed her cheek against his soft, warm head. "Amen to that. He's an angel."

After a while, she returned the child to his mother. Marcie seemed content to lie there and watch him as he slept. She was perfectly serene, secure in the knowledge that she loved and was loved, where before she had been so career-driven.

"What about your business?" Sage asked.

"I'm taking a leave of absence, at least until Jamie is weaned and goes on a bottle. I have two agents selling for me now. Esme runs the office like a boot camp. Things are well in hand."

Sage felt a stab of envy for Marcie, just as she had for Devon earlier that day. She wasn't that much younger than either of them, yet she had accomplished so little. She didn't have a career. She wasn't diligently pursuing one. She didn't have a child who depended on her for its very existence. She didn't have a man who worshiped and adored her and wanted her forever as his partner in life.

Suddenly the walls of the room closed in on her, as suffocating as her own sense of worthlessness. "I think I'll try out my new riding quirt." With no more explanation than that, she virtually ran from the room.

She had dressed in her leather pants that morning, so she didn't have to change clothes. Within minutes of leaving the house via the back door, she was saddled and galloping across the open pasture.

It was a glorious day. The sky was so clear and blue, it hurt the eyes to look at it. The sun was warm on her face, but the wind was cold. As it tore through her hair, it brought tears to her eyes. At least that's how she explained them to herself.

What did her life amount to? Nothing. Where was she going? Nowhere.

Marrying Travis Belcher had seemed like the ideal thing to do when they began dating. Now she acknowledged that he had been right—she had only talked herself into believing she loved him. They had had a risk-free relationship. It had been safe because she didn't love him enough for him to hurt her. His *rejection* hurt, yes, but not because she was emotionally bonded with him.

There, she had admitted it. She hadn't been as much in love with Travis as she had been with the ideal that he represented. So losing Travis, the person, was no great loss, except that it left a gaping whole in her future where marriage to him had previously been scheduled. That was the loss that hurt. That's what she was crying over. What was she going to do with the rest of her life?

If she told her family what she really wanted, they

would be flabbergasted. They would pat her on the head and tell her that it was an amusing notion. None would take the "brat" seriously. They never had.

Her horse grew tired long before she had decided what action she should take next. All she had resolved was that she couldn't withstand another grievous disappointment right now. So, for the time being, her secret ambition would remain a secret.

She walked the gelding back to the stable, rubbed him down, and gave him a bucket of oats. Leaving his stall, she saw movement from the corner of her eye and turned to find Harlan lounging against one of the double doors.

"What do you want?" she asked crossly, hoping that her mascara hadn't left muddy tracks on her cheeks.

"Just getting some fresh air and stretching my legs."

"I thought you were watching the football game."

"It's halftime."

"Who's winning?"

"Redskins."

"Figures."

"You're not in a very festive mood. I thought Hot Lips's telephone call would cheer you up."

"It did."

"Did he beg for your hand back?"

"He made some overtures," she said coyly. "I told you he would come around." She lied brazenly. Her conscience didn't apply when it came to Harlan. "Every bridegroom gets premarital jitters and tries to back out at least once before the wedding."

"Not every bridegroom."

"Have you ever been one?" she demanded, planting her hands on her hips.

"Can't say that I have."

"Then how in hell do you know what they do or don't do?"

He whistled. "Cussing, too. We really ought to do something about this blue funk you're in."

"I lost the Christmas spirit the moment I opened that stupid present you gave me."

He grinned unrepentantly. "You didn't like it? When I saw it, it cried out, 'Buy me for Sage.' "

"You should have saved your money."

"Well, now I really feel responsible for your lack of holiday merriment." He glanced above his head. "Maybe that would help."

She looked up. A fresh sprig of mistletoe was hanging from the doorjamb. "Who put that there? It wasn't there earlier." She leveled a gaze on him. "Oh, that's cute."

"Call it charity. I figured you'd be missing Travis. Since he's not here to give you a Christmas kiss . . ." He raised his arms at his sides as though offering himself to her service.

"Are you serious?" she exclaimed.

"Never more so."

"You expect me to kiss you?"

Sliding his hands into the back pockets of his jeans, he tilted his head to one side. "Why not? It won't be the first time."

"I didn't kiss you before."

"That's not how I remember it."

"You forced it on me by rubbing our mouths together."

"Fun, wasn't it?"

"Hardly."

He laughed as he sauntered toward her. "Come on, what do you say?"

"No."

"How come?" He had moved so close they were almost touching. His eyes were heavy lidded, impelling. "Scared you might like it again, even more than you did the first time?"

His challenge was as brassy as a trumpet. No Tyler, particularly Sage, had ever backed down from a dare. She had picked up every gauntlet her brothers had ever tossed down. If she hadn't, she would have been called a chicken and a crybaby. Harlan had probably guessed that and was using it to goad her. Even so, Sage couldn't back down from such a flagrant challenge.

"Oh, what the hell? One kiss under the mistletoe. What's the big deal?"

Chapter
SIX

The big deal was that he knew how to kiss.

The big deal was that if a panel of expert kissers were ever asked to appear on "Donahue," Harlan Boyd would serve as chairman.

The big deal was that she felt the kiss straight through her body to her toes.

She had planned to call his bluff but keep the kiss short and chaste, to show him that she wasn't intimidated by his dare. Even when he cupped her head between his hands and tilted it back like he meant business, she hadn't panicked. She could handle this. He was only a man. This was just a kiss.

But before she realized quite how he had accomplished it, her lips had been seduced to separate and she was receiving his tongue. Receiving was the appropriate word. He hadn't forced his way inside her mouth with brutal thrusts. He didn't make hit or miss stabs at the seam of her lips like some of her less talented boyfriends had done in their vain attempts to thaw her.

His tongue entered nonaggressively, stroked lazily, explored leisurely, tasted thoroughly. The only thing abrupt and shocking was her response. His lips were firm, not loose and floppy. He applied just the right amount of pressure and a delightful degree of suction. His mastery was startling, but too marvelous to stop. It would be like cutting off the hands of a gifted magician.

Harlan spun his own kind of spell. Her stomach fluttered weightlessly, yet her limbs felt heavy. She was lightheaded, but her earlobes throbbed with an infusion of pressure. Her breasts tingled, especially her nipples. Between her thighs she experienced a dull, feverish ache.

Without releasing her mouth, he moved his hands from her head to her shoulders. They slid down her back, then over her derriere. He pulled her against the front of his body.

Feeling his hardness, Sage whimpered. Her knees went weak, much as they had the night before in church. Her bones seemed to have liquified, so she leaned into him for support. Her mouth clung to his. She laid her hands on his shirt, her fingers involuntarily curling into his sturdy chest.

"Damn, Sage," he muttered, momentarily lifting his lips off hers and gazing down at her.

Her eyelids were afflicted with the same lassitude as the rest of her body. She could barely lift them. Later, she knew she would bitterly regret this, but right now, she thought she would die if he didn't go on kissing her.

Apparently he was of the same mind because he walked her backward into the barn, out of the doorway where they could be spotted by anyone inside the house who might glance out a window. He didn't stop until her back came up against the slats of the first stall.

Barn smells filled her nostrils. Animal flesh and fresh hay and old leather . . . and Harlan. His smell was a mix of man and cologne and outdoors and sunshine. Healthy. Sexy. Masculine.

As his head lowered to hers again, she reached for his lips with her own. When his tongue slid into her sweetly receptive mouth, he made a low, wanting sound and angled his body against hers, pressing into her softness. She reached up and sank her fingers in his hair.

By the time they broke apart for breath, they were panting. Their faces were flushed, their bodies on fire with yearning, their loins pounding with lust.

"Damn," he murmured again, burying his face in her neck.

He kissed it hungrily, with an open mouth, drawing her skin against his teeth. She had threatened to murder the last man who had left a mark on her. Now, she ran her hands up and down the rippling muscles of Harlan's back, dropping her head back and giving him access to her throat.

At first he only nudged aside her collar with his nose. Then he undid the first button of her blouse and kissed the hollow of her throat. She moaned, arching her back and sliding her middle across his. He undid the second button of her blouse, then the third. As they came undone, he tracked the fragrant opening with hungry lips.

Finally he raised his head so he could see her breasts. They were rising and falling rapidly, nearly tumbling out of the sheer, lacy cups of her low-cut brassiere. Her nipples, raised and pointed, strained against the weblike lace.

"Damn, Sage," Harlan hissed through his teeth. He laid a hand over each breast.

Her eyelids closed and she released a long, staggering sigh. "Yes."

He ground the stiff centers of her breasts with his palms.

"Hmm, yes." She moaned, swaying slightly.

Suddenly, not only were his hands withdrawn, but his warmth as well. Sage struggled to open her eyes and pull him into focus. He was standing several feet away from her. The hands that had been gently caressing her, were now planted firmly in the hip pockets of his pants, as though he didn't trust them. His eyes were trained on her breasts. He was gnawing his lips and cursing beneath his breath.

Sage came to her senses, as though she'd been snapped out of an hypnotic trance. If she had discovered herself prancing naked in front of a sideshow audience, she couldn't have been more furious with her hypnotist. She closed the distance between them in two short strides and slapped Harlan across the face as hard as she could.

To her consternation, she privately acknowledged that she wasn't slapping him for what he'd done, but because he had stopped doing it.

Rubbing his cheek, he said, "Well, it almost worked."

"It didn't even come close." Her voice was low, vibrating with outrage. "You've got nothing to pat yourself on the back for." Clumsily she began rebuttoning her blouse, then gave up on that tricky endeavor and pulled her jacket together over her exposed chest. "I didn't feel a thing."

"I wasn't referring to my efforts," Harlan calmly remarked. "I was referring to yours."

He wasn't making sense. Either that or she was too angry to piece the words together to form a cohesive thought. She shoved back her mussed hair. "What are you talking about? Not that I really care."

"I'm talking about your unsuccessful attempt to get rid of me." Sage stared at him, blinking stupidly. Her incomprehension seemed to annoy him. He pulled his lower lip through his teeth several times. "It's obvious what you were up to, Sage."

"I wasn't up to anything."

He snorted scoffingly. "I wasn't born yesterday, you know." Then, moving in closer and leaning down to her, he added, "A woman doesn't go from icicle to sexpot in that short a time, unless she's got a real good motive."

"Icicle? Sexpot! Motive?" She was uncertain which offensive word to take issue with first.

"With good reason, you want me out of your life. So you figured you'd get me to try something with you, then run screaming to your brothers, didn't you?"

"What?" she gasped.

"That's right. You thought that if I messed with you, they'd kick my butt right outta here. You're probably right. Only it didn't work." He glanced down at her breasts. "It came close, but I regained my head in the nick of time." Having said that, he turned and sauntered toward the door.

For the space of several seconds Sage stared at his back. Then she launched herself at him, grabbed his sleeve, and whipped him around. "In all my life, I've never been accused of anything so low, so demeaning, so— What kind of woman do you think I am?"

"You're a liar."

"I am not!"

"Could've fooled me. You haven't told your family that Casanova dumped you."

"No one's asked."

"So he *has* dumped you. When he called a while ago, it wasn't to kiss and make up."

Sage stood accused guilty as charged. Harlan laughed. "Okay, so I lied to you," she shouted. "I haven't lied to my family."

"But you haven't volunteered the information anytime Travis's name comes up."

"What business is that of yours?"

"None, I guess. I'd like to keep it that way. Don't make it my business by trying to manipulate me the way you do everybody else."

"I didn't try any such thing."

One of his eyebrows rose sharply. "Is that right?"

"Yes," she said defiantly. "That's right."

"Then why'd you kiss me like that?"

She opened her mouth to make a sharp retort, but suddenly realized she didn't have one. She closed her mouth quickly and looked away.

"Say," he said slowly, advancing on her until she had to back up a few steps, "you didn't by chance really lose your head over our kisses, did you? I thought you were faking all that moaning and groaning, that grasping and clawing. Are you saying it was for real? Was that begging and pleading, that 'yes, yes' genuine?"

"Shut up. You're disgusting."

"Disgusting huh?" He laughed, repeating the word several times as though he found it more amusing each time he said it. "Yeah, that's probably why you took to my tongue the way a baby does a pacifier."

His self-assurance was unbearable. She had had a momentary lapse in common sense, that's all. Mark it up to her recent rejection, or the pervasive love and good will of the season, or an inexplicable hormonal imbalance. For whatever reason, she had experienced temporary insanity.

Not only had she allowed him to take liberties, she had convinced herself that she was enjoying them, even craving them. If he ever realized that, he would utilize it to make her life miserable. Better to let him think she was a heartless schemer.

She tossed back her hair and looked down her nose at him. "Well, it was worth a try, wasn't it? If you'd gone any further, I'd have exposed you to my brothers for the lowlife you are. I still might."

"They'd probably believe you too," he said, scanning her from head to foot. "You look like you've just been well smooched. Lips all red and pouty. Hair a mess. Eyes dilated. Yeah, looking as sexy as you do, if you told them I'd tumbled you, they'd no doubt come after me with a loaded shotgun."

He grinned cockily and closed one eye. "But you aren't going to tell them, are you? 'Cause then I'd have to tell them that you kissed me back and moved against me like we were lying down. And because they're fair men who understand lust, they'd ask how you could lead one man on like that while being engaged to another. Then that whole business about Hot Lips's rejection would have to come out in the open and . . ."

Smacking his lips and shaking his head, he looked at her regretfully. "That'd ruin Christmas Day for everybody, wouldn't it? They'd miss the last quarter of the football game. Laurie would probably start crying because she couldn't believe her little girl would toy with a man like that. Marcie might get so upset her milk would go bad, and then baby Jamie would get sick and—"

"You're scum." She drew the word out, straining it through her teeth, saying it like she meant it with her whole heart and soul. Seething, she pushed past him and headed for the wide doors.

"Hey, Sage?"

She spun around. "What?"

"Did you ever kiss Mama's Boy like that?"

"Ha!" Striking a defiant pose, she declared, "Much better than that."

"Then he's no more than a damn fool you're well rid of, is he?"

"What's the matter, Marcie, can't you sleep?"

Chase reached for the lamp on the nightstand and switched it on. His wife was lying beside him on her back, gazing at the ceiling. She was rubbing her hand back and forth across her abdomen. Chase was instantly alarmed.

"Is there something wrong?"

"No," she said, smiling over his concern.

"You did too much today. We should have come straight home from the hospital. I shouldn't have let the doctor convince me that you were ready to leave. He probably wanted to take Christmas Day off."

"Will you relax? I'm fine. I'm just not used to having a flat tummy again. It feels good. I'm glad he's where he is now instead of where he was." She glanced toward the bassinet across the room where their son lay sleeping.

"Your flat tummy isn't what's keeping you awake." Chase propped himself up on his elbow and looked down at her.

"It's almost time for Jamie to nurse again. Mothers have this sixth sense, you see."

"Ah." He studied her teasing grin for a moment. "Something else is on your mind. What is it?" Taking her hand, he raised it to his lips and kissed the backs of her fingers. "What?"

"Sage."

He stared at her with perplexity. "Sage? What about her?"

"I don't know. That's why she's on my mind. Something wasn't right with her today, but I couldn't put my finger on what it was."

"She was piqued because Travis wasn't spending Christmas with her."

"Maybe," Marcie mused.

"You don't think so? You think it was something more than that?"

"I got the feeling that she's going through a difficult time. She was restless."

"She's always restless."

"Unusually so today. She didn't light for more than a few minutes at a time."

He thought for a moment. "She's probably still keyed up from her exams."

"That could be it, but somehow I don't think it's so simple. It goes deeper."

"Any theories?"

"Hmm. I remember how I felt when I left college. I suddenly realized that I was officially a grownup. It was scary, like being on a cliff about to take a plunge into life."

He chuckled. "You can hardly compare Sage with you. You're a brain. She's an airhead."

"Is she?" she asked tartly, snatching her hand from his. "Have you ever really talked to her, paid any attention to what she was saying, considered her opinion as something worth listening to?"

"Hey, Marcie, I—"

"No you haven't," she said, answering her own questions. "Lucky and you treat her like she's still your kid sister. Well, she's not. She's a woman. A well-educated woman."

"I hope so. Her education cost enough."

"And that's another thing," Marcie said, sitting up. "Every time her education is mentioned, it's in the context of how much it cost you. Have you told her how proud you are of her?"

"Well sure," he said. "Today, in fact. You were sitting right there."

"It sounded obligatory to me. Your education and Lucky's cost just as much as Sage's. Are you afraid that because she's a woman you won't get a return on your investment?"

"Possibly, especially if she marries that wimp Belcher."

"So you don't think she's even capable of choosing her own mate."

"I didn't say that."

"That's what you intimated. What's worse, you've let her know how you feel about him. Don't you rather imagine that hurts her feelings?"

"Sage never gets her feelings hurt."

"Of course she does!"

Chase plowed his fingers through his hair and blew out a gust of air. "I can't believe that we're lying here in the middle of the night having an argument about my kid—my *younger* sister."

"We're not arguing. I'm just pointing out a few things that have previously escaped your notice." She paused, and he indicated with a nod of his head that she should proceed. "First of all, she's no longer a child. She's an adult, equal to Lucky and you in every way."

"I'm not a caveman, Marcie. I believe in the equality of the sexes."

Ignoring him, she continued. "She's highly intelligent. She's sensitive." He raised his brows skeptically. "She is, Chase. She just doesn't show it because she's afraid her two brothers would mock her. Which you would."

"Okay, so we tease her. But we acknowledged a long time ago that she had grown up."

"But you still exclude her, the same way you did when she was little and wanted to tag along with you." He grudgingly admitted that her point was well taken. "I think she feels left out. Lucky, Devon, and Lauren are a unit, the same way you, Jamie, and I are. Laurie's wrapped up in Pat and her grandbabies. Can you see how Sage might feel alienated?"

"I guess so."

She reached across the pillows and laid her hand against his cheek, a gesture of forgiveness. "Treat her with a little more understanding and respect."

He nodded. "I promise to be more aware of it."

"Thank you, honey. I'm sure Sage will appreciate a shift in your attitude."

"Speaking of Mother and Pat, when do you think they're going to stop their silly game?"

Chase had told Marcie about seeing Pat kissing his mother the day Lauren was born. He knew their secret would be safe with her.

"I don't know, but I wish they would hurry and do something about it." Marcie looped her arms around his neck. "I want everyone in the world to be deliriously in love, so they'll understand how happy I am every time I look at you."

He closed his arms around her and drew her close, kissing her with passion and love. "How long before—"

"Eight weeks. At least," she breathed against his lips.

"It's going to be a long, tortuous two months."

Reaching beneath the covers, Marcie caressed him. "It doesn't have to be. Not for you anyway."

At the touch of her hand, he groaned with pleasure. "If every new mother was as sexy as you, men all over the world would be impregnating their wives."

Jamie chose that moment to wake up. Rather than resenting the interruption, Chase got out of bed and pulled on a robe. He changed the diaper, then lifted his son out of the bassinet and carried him back to Marcie, who had already lowered her nightgown, preparing to feed him.

Chase laid the crying infant in her arms and watched with wonder and love as Jamie found and latched onto Marcie's nipple. "Greedy little cuss," he said, chuckling.

"He takes after his father." Marcie looked up at her husband through her lashes and smiled.

"He takes after me if he loves you." His throat grew thick with emotion as he watched his son nursing. "I never would have thought it was possible to love you—or anyone—the way I love you, Marcie. Only you could have made it possible for me to love again after Tanya died."

Her own eyes misted. "Lie beside me," she whispered. He dropped his robe and slid between the covers again. Marcie curved her hand around his head and drew it to her other breast.

Each year, Sage was stricken with postholiday blues. This year they were so dark they were almost black. For the first few days after Christmas, she managed to stay busy by helping Laurie take down the decorations, repack them, and store them in the attic until next year.

They prepared meals for Chase and Marcie, making numerous trips back and forth to their house on Woodbine Lane. Sage even offered to sleep there and help out with Jamie, but Marcie's parents came up from Houston to spend several days, so her offer was graciously declined.

She made the rounds of her friends who still lived in Milton Point, but that was depressing to her. Most were either involved in their careers or with husbands and young families. She had little in common with them anymore.

Although she avoided Harlan whenever possible, he

was at the dinner table each evening. To her vast relief, he paid no more attention to her than she did to him, but spent most of his time discussing business with Lucky. Laurie passed along his offer to vacate her room. She refused. The damage had been done. The beloved room was tainted now, and she never wanted to occupy it again. The subject was dropped.

She adroitly dodged talking about Travis with either members of her family or close friends who inquired about her wedding plans. One evening when Pat dropped by, Sage overheard Laurie speculating to him that Travis and she must have had a lovers' spat.

"To the best of my knowledge, he hasn't called her since Christmas Day, and then their conversation was short," Laurie had said. "They must have had a quarrel. What do you make of it?"

Sage could envision Pat rolling a matchstick from one side of his mouth to the other while he ruminated. "Damned if I know. Boys are sometimes hard to figure out, but girls are impossible."

Because she didn't discuss any immediate plans with them, their curiosity increased a little each day. No one asked questions, but she could sense their concern.

Her time was running out. She had to tell them the marriage to Travis was off. But how could she do that and save face? For the time being, she could only bide her time until something happened that would take care of the problem for her.

Something did happen, but it wasn't quite what she expected.

Early one morning, while she was dressing, someone tapped lightly on her bedroom door. Grabbing a robe and holding it against her like a shield, she padded across the floor and opened the door a crack.

"What do you want?"

Harlan wasn't put off by her rudeness. Instead he held up a newspaper clipping. "This was in this morning's society section of the Houston paper. I cut it out before anyone else got to it."

Puzzled, she scanned the society page headline.

New Year's Eve Gala To Be Held in Honor of Engagement.

There was a subheadline that read, "Childhood sweethearts announce plans to marry."

Beneath that was a picture of Dr. and Mrs. Belcher, Travis, and his new fiancée.

Chapter SEVEN

"... and when I walked into the room to check on him, he was holding his head up and looking around at all the ducks and stuff on his blanket."

Lucky glanced at Harlan, his skepticism plain. Harlan gave a noncommittal shrug.

Chase intercepted the exchange. "I'm not lying. I swear. He was holding his head up. And that's nothing. Listen to this—"

"How long is it going to take?" Lucky asked. He had the desk chair tilted back as far as it would go. His boots were propped on the corner of the desk.

"Why?"

"Because you've been going on about Jamie for the last fifteen minutes. He's a cute kid, but give us a break, will ya?"

"Do you remember when Lauren was born? I had to

sit and listen to you carry on about every little accomplishment. Well, it got boring after a while."

Lucky sprang erect. "You took the words right out of my mouth."

Chase signaled his brother back into his chair. "But I listened anyway."

"Jeez." Groaning, Lucky once again sought help from Harlan.

He had a straight chair angled back and precariously propped against the wall. The atmosphere in the office of Tyler Drilling Company was always casual. He liked it that way. He also enjoyed the affectionate bantering between the two brothers who, he knew without any qualification, would die for each other.

Trying to remain impartial, he said, "He's plumb dotty over that baby, Lucky."

Encouraged, Chase leaned forward in his chair. "Jamie's hung, too. I mean h-u-n-g."

"He's just a baby!" Lucky cried incredulously.

"I know, but you can tell he's going to make the ladies mighty happy when he's grown up." Chase grinned smugly. "He takes after his old man."

"You mean his uncle Lucky." The younger brother looked over at Harlan and winked. Harlan chuckled.

"Go to hell," Chase told his brother. "Anyway, he's smart as a whip. Did I tell you about—"

"Yes!" Lucky cried.

Chase glowered at him with exasperation, but before

he could say anything more, Sage walked in. Silently, Harlan caught his breath and held it. His gut always drew up tightly whenever he saw her, and that was the least of his physical responses.

That's why he'd been keeping his distance the last couple of days. He had had a close call with trouble in the barn on Christmas Day. From now on he intended to stay out of harm's way.

This morning, of course, he'd had to break his own resolution. When she had opened her bedroom door to his knock, her shoulders had been bare except for the satin straps of her bra. She had bunched a robe against her front; he couldn't see anything but his imagination had gone into overdrive.

Only half of her makeup had been applied and her hair was still damp, but she had looked fantastic. She looked even better now. There was tension around her smile, but considering the news he had brought her earlier, he had to give her credit for pulling herself together so well. He shouldn't be surprised. He had already seen her bounce back after receiving a felling blow. That kind of gumption he had to admire.

They made eye contact, but it didn't last as long as a blink before she looked away. He couldn't blame her. She was embarrassed about what he knew, although she shouldn't be. Travis Belcher was the fool, not her.

"Hey, Sage," Chase said, "did I tell you about Jamie—"

"Yes," she said quickly. "Twice."

"You don't even know what I was going to say."

"Whatever it was, I've heard it. Can't you say hello first?"

"Sure. Hi. Want some coffee?"

"No thanks. I just finished breakfast."

"What brings you out, brat?" Lucky asked. His question was obviously rhetorical. Before giving her time to answer it, he picked up the morning newspaper and opened it.

Sage moved to the desk and snatched it from his hands. Smart girl, Harlan thought. She'd got to him before Lucky had a chance to see the society section. Not that he was likely to read that anyway. It had been pure chance that Harlan had run across that article about Belcher.

"I want to talk to you."

"To me?" Lucky asked.

"To both of you."

She included Chase, then turned and looked pointedly at Harlan. Behind her imperious expression, he detected nervousness, near desperation.

The front legs of his chair hit the floor as he rolled off his spine to stand up. "I've got some work to do over in the garage. See y'all later."

He put on his vest and cowboy hat, pulling it low on his brows. Meeting Sage's eyes again, he touched the brim with the tips of two fingers before opening the door and stepping outside. As he pulled the door closed behind him, he wondered what she wanted to talk to her brothers about. Whatever it was, he sensed that she was dreading it.

Thankfully Harlan left the office without giving away, either by word or sign, that they had seen each other earlier that morning. After handing her the newspaper clipping, he had tactfully withdrawn, closing her bedroom door as he went.

The last thing she wanted from him was pity. She almost preferred his teasing and taunting to sympathetic silence. He was behaving as though someone—or something inside her—had died. However, she now had more to worry about than Harlan Boyd and his opinion of her.

She had spent a tumultuous hour in her room, pacing, brainstorming, trying to make up her mind what to do. Should she return to Austin and look for work there? Should she stay in Milton Point and twiddle her thumbs while waiting for inspiration? Or should she do the courageous thing and seize control of a bad situation and try and make it better?

Once she had decided her next course of action, she wasted no time, but dressed quickly and left the house. When Travis's engagement to another woman became a well-known fact, no one would find Sage Tyler huddled in a dark corner licking her wounds. She would already have alternate plans in place.

As soon as the office door closed behind Harlan, Lucky asked, "What's up?"

Since time was of the essence, Sage saw no point in beating around the bush. "I want a career."

The two stunned men looked at her for a moment, then at each other, then at her again. "A career?" Chase repeated.

"I didn't stutter."

"You've got a career," Lucky said. "You'll soon be getting married."

"Marriage isn't a career!"

"Being married to Travis Belcher will be the most demanding job anybody could ask for."

"Lucky." Chase sighed retiringly.

Sage gripped the back of the nearest chair in an effort to control her temper. It would serve no purpose now to spar with Lucky. She had to plead her case convincingly. Flying off the handle would accomplish nothing except make her look immature and unprofessional.

"I'm not sure when I'll be getting married," she said, evading a bald lie yet skirting the truth. "In the meantime, I need a job, something challenging to keep me occupied and interested. I want to earn my own living."

"Well, hey, I'm sure there are lots of jobs to be had in Houston," Lucky said, breaking into the charming grin that had earned him a reputation with women. "Or do you plan to stay in Austin until you and Travis tie the knot?"

"I . . . I thought I'd stay in Milton Point for a while. That is, if it won't be too much of an imposition on you and Devon for me to live at home."

"Hell, no. That's your house, too, Sage. It belongs to all of us. What the hell do you mean about being an imposition?"

"Lucky," Chase said, intervening again, "let's hear her out first, okay? Then open it up for discussion."

"Wasn't that what I was doing?"

Chase, ignoring his brother, turned his intense gray eyes onto Sage. "Are you asking us to run interference for you, Sage? Grease the skids? Put in a good word with a prospective employer? Write you a letter of recommendation? We'd be glad to, wouldn't we, Lucky? Give us a name, we'll do what we can. Where would you like to work?"

They still didn't get it. To them she was their kid sister, useless except as an object to play practical jokes on. It crushed her to know that what she wanted to do would never have even occurred to them.

She couldn't afford the time to indulge her disappointment, however. So much more than hurt feelings was at stake. Squaring her shoulders and holding her head up proudly, she stated, "Here. I want to work for Tyler Drilling."

Again, they stared back at her with stupefaction. Chase managed to speak first. "Here? Well, hey, Sage, that's, uh, that's terrific."

"What the hell are you—" Lucky clamped his jaws shut when Chase shot him a warning glance. "Uh, yeah, Sage, that's great."

She released a deep breath. The band of tension around her ribcage relaxed. A soft laugh erupted from her mouth. "Really? You mean it?"

"Sure," Lucky drawled expansively. "Why not? There's always something to do around here. We're always behind on our filing. Even in these hard times, book-keeping is a bitch that Chase and I both hate dealing with. Neither one of us is very good at it. And, as you can see, we're not very good housekeepers either."

Sage, seeing red, turned on her heels and marched toward the door. Chase went after her and caught her wrist. "Let me go." She struggled to be released.

"No, and if you bite me the way you did when you were a kid, I'll slug you. Now, be still." He rounded on Lucky. "The next time you're tempted to shoot off your big, dumb mouth, do the world a favor and keep it shut."

Lucky spread his arms wide in a gesture of total confusion. "What'd I do? What'd I say?"

Sage managed to wrest her arm free. Rather than leaving, however, she forgot about her resolve to control her temper and confronted them with the ferocity of a brave, young lioness, fangs bared, claws extended. She was, after all, fighting for her life.

"I wasn't looking for work as a file clerk, or a gofer,

or a maid, Lucky," she shouted. "When it comes right down to it, I'm as qualified as either of you to operate a business. Maybe not in practical, hands-on experience, but I've got more education.

"I was weaned on discussions about the oil industry, every single aspect of it. By osmosis, I've absorbed a lot of knowledge. This business is currently failing. I'm not blaming that on either of you, but it sure as hell can't hurt to bring another person into the company. A member of the family, that is," she added, thinking of Harlan.

"No one has thought to ask, but I just might have some fresh ideas. Besides, even if I don't, I've got as much right to be here as the two of you. The only difference between us is that I've got ovaries instead of balls. If I had been born male, you would have expected me to join the company straight out of college.

"And before you go labeling me an aggressive feminist, let me set you straight on that. I love being a woman. I wouldn't want to be anything else. But I want to be treated fairly and equally when it comes to a career, the way both your wives are treated in their professional fields. I don't think either of you doubts their femininity.

"I want you to start thinking of me as an intelligent adult and not the child in pigtails you used to torment for recreation. I'm not merely precocious, I'm intelligent. I've been grown up for a long time, though obviously you haven't noticed.

"Well, it's time you did. I refuse to be patted on the head and then pushed aside and overlooked as though I were invisible. I won't be shut out any longer."

A long silence followed her speech. Her breasts heaved with indignation and her golden brown eyes flashed with remnant anger.

Finally Lucky said, "Whew! That was some lecture, br . . . uh, Sage."

"Thanks."

"Did Devon coach you?"

"I did it all myself."

Chase spoke for the first time. "We didn't intentionally exclude you from the family business, Sage. But since you've been grown, you've been away at school. We assumed that you wouldn't be working at all after you got married, certainly not here in Milton Point." He frowned. "I assume you've discussed this with Travis. What does he think about it?"

"It doesn't matter. I never have been, nor will I ever be, his chattel." Never had she been more truthful. "Until I get married I want to be productive."

"What did you have in mind doing for the company?"

She looked at them uneasily, then cast her eyes downward. This was a weak link in her argument. "I'm not sure. I know that for several years you've been trying to think of ways to diversify. Maybe I could help there by providing a fresh perspective.

"Or maybe I could try to cultivate new clients, since

most of our old ones are currently out of business. I think if I had access to the figures, I could put together deals that would be profitable, but provide good incentive to potential clients."

"We couldn't pay you much," Lucky said grimly.

"You don't have to pay me at all." They looked surprised. She hastened to add, "I could work on commission. You wouldn't have to pay me anything until I generated some business, and then I'd take an agreed-on percentage of the net."

"What'll you live on?"

"I didn't use all the money you gave me for that last semester of school. It's still in savings. Besides, if I'm living at home, I won't need much beyond gasoline money. I'm accustomed to making do with what clothes I've got and stretching my wardrobe."

Chase looked chagrined. "I'm sorry about that, Sage. We haven't been able to lavish material things on you the last several years. You've been damned understanding about it."

"You never asked for much either, and we appreciate that," Lucky added.

Her heart melted and she moved toward them, wrapping an arm around each. "We're all in this crisis together, aren't we? From now on, I want to do my part to get us out. Is it settled?"

"Fine with me," Lucky said.

Chase looked down at her. "Okay, you're in. But

don't thank us too soon. It might only mean that you sink right along with us."

Hearing only his consent, she threw herself against him and hugged him hard before turning to Lucky and hugging him with equal exuberance. "You won't be disappointed in me. I swear. Thank you for giving me this chance."

"You don't have to prove yourself to us, Sage," Chase said.

"Maybe not. But I have to prove myself to me."

"You know, Chase," Lucky said, "she might be able to sell Harlan's idea to somebody better than we could."

"Harlan," she muttered. Her burst of elation dissipated at the mention of his name. In her excitement, she had almost forgotten him. "Exactly what *is* Harlan's idea?"

Taking her arm, Chase steered her toward the door. "Come on, we'll show you."

Situated a short distance from the office, the garage was a large, cavernous building. Several years earlier, it had burned to the ground. Lucky had been accused of setting the fire, but Devon Haines, with whom he had spent that night, had provided him with an alibi. Alvin Cagney and Jack Ed Patterson, local no-accounts, were still in prison serving time for the crime.

The building had been reconstructed on its original

site and all the equipment destroyed in the fire had been replaced. For all that, the garage wasn't what it had been in its heyday. Sage remembered it from her childhood as a dirty place, smelling of oil and mud and hardworking men, a place ringing with the racket of machinery and the salty language of the roughnecks.

It hadn't been a proper environment for a young lady, and for that reason it had been generally off-limits to her when she was growing up. She had envied her brothers their freedom to come and go at will, to mix with the men who worked for their father. Many times, she had wanted to visit the drilling sites and take part in the celebration when a well came in.

She was sad to note, when Chase drove his pickup through the wide double doors, that the garage had changed. It was too clean. The equipment stood silent and dusty. There were no roughnecks milling around wiping their dirty faces with grimy bandannas while cursing bad weather, rotten luck, and dry holes. The laughter and tall tales of the good ol' days in the East Texas oilfields had disappeared.

There was only one man in the garage now and he was bent over a drafting table, studying a mechanical drawing. At the sound of the pickup pulling in, he stood upright and shoved a yellow school pencil into the thick blond hair behind his ear. He looked at Sage inquiringly as she approached him with her brothers walking on each side of her.

"Any progress, Harlan?"

He shook his head. "Not much. I just don't see a way to make it any cheaper."

"Make what?" Sage asked.

Harlan stepped aside and waved his hand over the drawing. She studied it for a moment but couldn't make heads or tails out of it. She hated to show her ignorance, but had no choice.

"It's not a surrealistic still life of a bowl of fruit is it?"

The men chuckled. "You explain it to her, Harlan," Chase suggested. "It's your idea."

"Well, it's like this," he began. "I figured that with some adaptations, an oil well pump could be converted into a pump for something else, namely water."

"Sometimes water is pumped into an oil well."

"Very good," Lucky said, patting her on the head. Then, as though remembering her earlier words, drew his hand back. "Meaning no offense."

"None taken," she said automatically. Harlan was holding her attention with his dynamic blue eyes, which weren't only insolent and mocking when he wanted them to be, but clearly the windows into a clever mind as well. "What application did you have in mind?"

He hesitated. Chase said, "Sage is part of the company now. You can tell her what we've been working on."

"Oh, I'm sure she can keep a secret," he remarked with just a trace of laughter behind his words. "The

application would be irrigation, Sage. With a little ingenuity, and some working capital," he added, giving
Chase and Lucky a grim smile, "we could adapt the
drilling equipment into an irrigation system."

She digested that a moment. "For whom?"

"That's where you might enter in, Sage," Lucky told
her. "Once we get a prototype, we'll need to do some
marketing."

"Farmers," she said.

"That would be a good start."

"And the citrus growers down in the valley." The
wheels of her mind began turning, but before she carried her ideas too far, she saw the immediate and
pressing problem. "You said you needed working capital."

Chase sighed. "Harlan's almost finished with the prototype, but we had to stop him because we haven't got
any cash to invest."

"But you can't let that stop you!" she cried. "Before
you can do anything, you've got to have a prototype."

"Tell us about it," Lucky muttered.

"Surely you could borrow—"

"Forget it. There isn't a bank in Texas that's loaning
any money to anyone in the oil business."

"Outside the state," she suggested.

"Once they hear your Texas twang, they all but hang
up on you. Being from the Lone Star State is the kiss of
death if you're looking for financing," Lucky said.

"We're dead in the water," Chase told her.

"No pun intended," Harlan said.

"We've got literally miles of pipe stacked up behind this building ready to be put to use," Chase said. "But for right now, we have to leave it there."

"What do you need?" she asked Harlan.

"Minicomputer," he told her.

"What for?"

"Automatic timing."

"I see. It wouldn't work without one?"

"It would, but it wouldn't be state of the art."

"And we need it to be high tech."

"Right."

For a moment they silently considered their frustrating situation, then Lucky glanced at his wristwatch. "I need to get back to the office, Chase. Even though this is the week between the holidays, some people are still doing business, and I've got some calls out. I should be there if they call back."

"Sage, why don't you stay here with Harlan till suppertime," Chase suggested. "He can bring you home. Let him explain how this thing is going to work. If you're going to be selling it, you've got to know all the answers."

"A-all right," she faltered.

She would rather be strung up by her thumbs than pass the rest of the afternoon in Harlan's company, but she couldn't very well refuse her first official assignment as an employee of Tyler Drilling Company.

Chapter EIGHT

After her brothers had departed, she glanced around the silent building, folding her arms across her chest against the chill.

"Cold?" Harlan asked.

"A little."

"Scoot over here closer to the heater."

There was a small, electric space-heater on the floor near his feet. She moved toward its directional heat rays and extended her hands to capitalize on the warmth. The fisherman's sweater she was wearing over her slacks had been sufficient outside, but the building seemed colder.

"I guess I owe you my thanks for not telling them about Travis's engagement."

Their eyes connected and held for a moment. He looked vaguely disappointed in her. "You don't owe me anything. Hand me that ruler, please."

She reached behind her into the tray of drafting tools he indicated. He took the narrow metal ruler from her and used it to add a line to his drawing.

She leaned forward for a closer inspection, but the schematic still looked to her like nothing more than an odd arrangement of lines and arcs. "Are you sure you know what you're doing?"

"I've got an engineering degree from Texas A&M that says I do."

"*You* have a college degree?"

Her incredulity didn't insult him, as it might have. Instead, he grinned and turned his head toward her. "If he pays his tuition and completes the required courses, they'll give a degree to just about anybody."

"I'm sorry I sounded . . . well, I'm surprised, that's all. Where'd you graduate from high school?"

"I didn't." He made an erasure and readjusted the length of a line, measuring it precisely. "I got my high school diploma by correspondence."

"Why, for heaven's sake?"

"I was working in a refinery. That was the only way I could get an education and earn a living at the same time."

"You were working full time while you were in high school?"

"That's right."

"Supporting yourself?"

"Hmm. No football games, no homecoming pep rallies, no proms. I worked the graveyard shift and studied during the day when I wasn't sleeping."

Sage felt incredibly sad for him and had to stop herself from laying a consoling hand on his shoulder. "What about your parents?"

He dropped his pencil and faced her again. "You sure ask a lot of questions, you know that?"

"If we're going to be working together, we should know something about each other."

"I don't think that's necessary."

"I do."

He studied the stubborn angle of her jaw and apparently saw the advisability of humoring her. "What do you want to know?"

"What about your family? Why were you working in a refinery to support yourself when you should have been enjoying high school?"

"I left home when I was fifteen."

"Why?"

"I just split, okay? I've been on my own ever since. As soon as I got my high school diploma, I enrolled at A&M and went through in three years. By the time I was twenty, I was educated and accountable to no one except myself." He tapped her chin with his fingertip. "That includes you."

"I can't imagine being so adrift."

He shrugged laconically. "You get used to it. Wanna see this thing or not?"

Whether she liked it or not, he had brought the discussion to a close. She regretted not having learned more about him. What little he had told her had left her more intrigued than pacified. For the time being, it seemed, he would remain an enigma.

He ushered her toward a large tarpaulin and pulled it back, uncovering a piece of machinery that looked to her like any other oil well pump. "This is as far as we've got," he said. "It still needs—"

"Were you a runaway?"

He dropped his head forward and studied the concrete floor for several moments. Finally he looked up and said resignedly, "I guess you could call me that, yeah."

"Fifteen," she murmured. At fifteen the biggest crisis in her life had been if she woke up with a new zit. During her adolescence, her brothers had teased her incessantly about her budding figure and any yokel who became smitten with her. Home life hadn't always been grand, but she couldn't imagine leaving her family at that age, walking away from everything familiar and dear. She told Harlan so.

"Well, Sage, consider yourself lucky. Not every kid had it as good as you."

"Was your home life and childhood that terrible?"

"I thought you wanted to know about the irrigation system."

"You're not going to tell me about your past, are you?"

"No."

Now it was Sage's turn to sigh with resignation. She had met her match in being obstinate. She could tell by the determination in his expression that he had divulged all he was going to.

Turning away, she critically examined the pump. "A machine is a machine. They all look alike to me."

"If you're going to sell folks on this idea, you'll have to know what it's capable of doing."

"I only want to know what's absolutely necessary. Keep the explanations simple and in layman's terms. I don't understand the mechanics behind a hair dryer."

A smile spread across his features. "You've got moxie, I'll say that." She tilted her head inquiringly, so he expounded. "Without any prior experience, you convinced your brothers to let you work for them."

"*With* them," she corrected.

"That took guts. Or desperation." He eyed her keenly. "Do you think that working for Tyler Drilling will get you over Lover-boy?"

"I'm already over Lover-boy."

"Just like that?" he asked skeptically.

"What you fail to understand," she said loftily, "is that my involvement with Travis wasn't based on passion. We weren't like Chase and Marcie or Lucky and Devon. Those are love affairs of the heart, mind, body, and soul. One would be devastated if anything happened to the other because they depend so much on each other. That kind of marriage rarely works."

"Theirs seem to be rock solid."

"They are, but they're the exception. I would never have thought that Lucky could remain faithful to one woman or that Chase could love again after losing his first wife. Logically, neither of their marriages should have worked. From the outset of our relationship, Travis and I took a more pragmatic approach to matrimony."

"And look where that landed you."

She swiftly gave him her back and stalked away. Reaching far, he grabbed her by the seat of her pants. "Hold on. Hold on. I was just kidding."

"You're not funny," she said slapping his hand off her fanny.

"Sometimes life isn't either."

"Your point?"

"Well, life's full of unpleasantness," he said. "Backed-up plumbing, crabgrass in the lawn, sick kids, bills you can't pay. If you're going to share all those hassles with somebody, it seems to me that the passion you're downplaying could go a long way to make the bad stuff more bearable." Eyes crinkling at the corners, he added, "And it's damn good fun."

She kept a straight face. "Your point is moot because I'm not marrying Travis."

"Did you tell Chase and Lucky?"

"No. I didn't want them hiring me out of pity. I told them that I wasn't sure when I would be getting married, which is the truth. I even used the singular pronoun and not we, as in Travis and I. I told them that, in the interim, I wanted to be productive and work in the family business. By the time they learn my engagement is off, they'll think that the breakup was gradual and mutual, that Travis and I merely grew apart. Mother already suspects that we're embroiled in a lovers' quarrel. No one will be surprised."

"I see you've got it all figured out."

"I do."

He shook his head with misgiving. "You know what they say about well-laid plans. They usually backfire. I'll bet you ten to one that before it's all over, they'll find out that Hot Lips dumped you."

Her temper snapped. "Why is it that every time—"

Laughing, he grasped her by the upper arms and lifted her off the ground, dangling her body so close to his, she could feel each hard muscle in stark detail. Her face was level with his. She feared, and half hoped, that he was going to stop her angry outburst with another bone-melting kiss.

"They'll probably quiz you on all you learned today," he said. "You have a bad habit of talking too much. If you want to impress them, sit down, keep your mouth shut, your eyes open, and listen."

He pivoted on the heels of his boots and deposited

her on a high stool. Then, shoving up the sleeves of his faded denim jacket, he began to explain the workings of his invention.

"So it could be programmed to irrigate certain areas at certain times on certain days, very much like an ordinary home sprinkler system."

Harlan grinned at Sage's basic understanding. "Except it could cover acres. It could be pumped from a reservoir or through a normal water source."

"That would require a lot of pipe."

"Laying the pipe will be a piece of cake. This is what counts," he said, patting the piece of machinery. "The whole system would be controlled from this computerized pump."

"Only you need a computer before you can even lay some pipe and try it out."

"Yeah, at least some kind of timing device. And the company till is empty."

After two hours of intense indoctrination, Sage believed that she had a decent grasp on his idea. She had listened carefully to every word Harlan had said—and not to just what he said, but how he said it.

His vocabulary was extensive. He was articulate. She began to believe that maybe he did have a college degree. Certainly there was more to him than what one saw on the surface. He camouflaged his intelligence with his good ol' boy demeanor. Why? As a defense mechanism?

Possibly. She could understand that. Hadn't she sometimes assumed a bratty posture as a defense mechanism to cover feelings of insecurity and inferiority?

What did Harlan have to be defensive about?

He glanced toward the wide doors. There was a cloudy sky, and it would be growing dark soon. "We'd better close up shop for the day. You've got a lot to absorb. Your mama'll get worried about you if you're not home by dark."

"Did your mama worry about you when you split?"

His eyes cut to hers sharply. "No. She didn't."

That's all he said before clamming up. Sage waited for him inside his pickup truck while he closed the garage, checking everything meticulously before padlocking the door. Her brothers had entrusted him with securing their building, a responsibility he took seriously.

"Mind if I stop at my trailer for a minute?" he asked as the truck chugged down the narrow road that led to the main highway.

Instantly suspicious, she asked, "What for?"

"I'm gonna ravish you." He laughed when she jumped reflexively and turned her head so quickly her neck popped. "Don't get your hopes up, Sage. I need to pick up a book."

"You have a warped sense of humor, Mr. Boyd."

"It may be warped, but at least I have one."

He was justified in putting her down. Even to her own ears, she sounded prissy and prim. Why couldn't she just laugh off his jokes? He continued teasing her only because her reactions were always so violent. Hadn't her mother advised her to ignore her brothers when they became their most obnoxious? It was a lesson she had never learned and, therefore, couldn't exercise now.

"My sense of humor is one of the many things you don't like about me," he said. Looking at her across the ramshackle interior of the pickup, he added, "One of these days, I'm going to get you to admit all the things you do like." His voice was soft, the words spoken like a warning. Sage was the first to look away.

His trailer was parked in a vacant, uncultivated field not too far from the Tyler Drilling Company office. They reached it within a few minutes of leaving the garage. Sage wasn't surprised that the Streamline looked like it was barely holding together at the seams. A coughing generator provided it with electricity.

"You can stay put or get out. Suit yourself." He got out and jogged up two concrete blocks serving as steps. The doors weren't even locked. He opened them and disappeared inside. Through the curtains hanging over the narrow windows, Sage saw a light come on.

Her curiosity got the best of her. She left the truck and moved up the steps. The screen door squeaked when she pulled it open. She winced, but pushed on the metal door and stepped inside.

She expected it to be a disaster, littered with girlie magazines and empty beer cans. Instead it was rather cozy and very neat. The furnishings were tacky and cheap, but everything was clean. He did have some reading matter, quite a lot in fact, but it ran more toward news periodicals and current fiction paperbacks, bestsellers mostly. There was one respectable copy of *Playboy*.

Without being obvious, she nosed around, looking for family photographs, mail with return addresses, anything that might give her clues about his background. There was nothing. She had no inkling of what he'd been doing before he came to Milton Point.

She sensed his presence before she heard him and turned to face him. She didn't think before she spoke, but asked the question at the forefront of her mind. "Have you always lived alone?"

"Yes."

"Have you ever been married?"

"You asked me that already."

"I asked if you'd ever been a bridegroom."

"That's splitting hairs, isn't it?" Seeing her ill-concealed annoyance, he said, "I've never been married."

"Children?"

His lips twitched with the effort of suppressing a smile. "No."

"How old are you?"

"Twenty-nine. Going on thirty soon."

He looked older, as old as Lucky who was in his early thirties. "Where's your family?"

"I don't have a family."

"You have a mother. You said she hadn't worried about you when you left, so you must have had one."

He laid aside the book he'd brought from the back room and took a step closer. By doing so he seemed to reduce the size of the trailer by half. "Why are you so curious, Sage?"

"I don't know. I just am."

"Besides my family, what else are you curious about?"

"Where you came from. What you did before you met Chase in Houston. Why you don't bother locking your doors. Why, since you're college educated and intelligent, you choose to live like this."

He gave the dim surroundings an assessing glance. "What's wrong with the way I live?"

She floundered, not wanting to state the obvious at the risk of sounding unkind.

"I like the way I live, Sage. Very much. I don't lock my doors because I don't own anything anybody would want. When you don't possess anything, you can't be possessed by things either. You don't have to worry about somebody taking something valuable from you. I like being free from all that."

He took another step, closing the distance between them. The toes of his boots grazed the toes of her shoes before he widened his stance and placed his feet on

either side of hers, a stance that tilted his hips slightly
forward.

His nearness in the quiet, still trailer overwhelmed
her. Because he was looking down at her so intently
with those laser-beam blue eyes, she was a little afraid
of him. Or was she afraid of the marshy feeling she got
in the pit of her stomach every time he stood this close
to her?

"Ask me something else, Sage."

"You answered all my questions," she said breathlessly. "There's nothing else I need or want to know."

"Yes, there is."

"What?"

"You want to know when I'm going to kiss you
again."

"I want to know no such thing! What gave you that
idea?"

He wasn't the least bit fazed by her hasty rebuttal.
"You're like a cat, aren't you, Sage? Always scratching
and clawing and hissing in self-defense. Every time
anybody gets close to the real Sage, you arch your
back." His eyes moved down to her mouth. "If you gave
yourself half a chance, you'd purr."

She swallowed with difficulty, wanting to move away,
but unable to, wanting to look away, but incapable of it.
"You'll never know. I'll never let you kiss me again."

"Yes you will. You liked it too much."

"I didn't like it at all."

His hands came up and framed her face. His thumbs took turns sweeping across her lips. "We both know you're a liar, Sage. A lousy one at that."

Then his mouth settled on hers. It was warm, soft, undemanding, fluid. She allowed the contact for several seconds, but when the tip of his tongue touched the tip of hers, she recoiled and turned her head away.

"Harlan—"

"That's it. Say my name."

His lips captured hers again. Her whimper of protest was feeble and thoroughly disregarded. When he introduced his tongue this time, she obliged him, greeting it with a stroke of her own.

He slipped his arms around her waist and drew her up against him as he angled his head to one side and deepened the kiss. Sage's ears rang with a cacophony of sound, and she realized it was the pounding of her own heart and the rushing-wind sound of consuming lust. She had never heard it before, yet she recognized it immediately. A tide of heat rivered through her body, pooling between her thighs.

He tasted her again and again, sending his tongue deep into her mouth for samples. When they had to either breathe or die, he buried his face in her neck, kissing it madly. He worked his way to her ear. Sage felt the warm, damp stroke of his tongue and gave a soft cry. Her knees buckled and she stumbled backward onto the sofa.

He followed her down, partially covering her body with his. She plowed her fingers into his hair and pulled his head down to her. She needed this. She needed a man's weight crushing her, his desire hot and hard for her, his mouth stealing her breath.

She kissed Harlan as though she were starving for his love. She bent one knee up and pressed the inside of her thigh against his hip. It felt so right, so good. His erection was firm against her cleft. She moved her hips, rubbing against it, wanting more.

Harlan slid his hand inside her sweater to caress her breast. "Sage, do you want me to touch you like this?"

She raggedly sighed an affirmative answer while randomly kissing the features of his face, which, she now admitted, had mightily appealed to her from the first time she'd laid eyes on him.

His hand scooped her breast from the cup of her bra. He caressed the raised nipple with his fingertips. Sage moaned and arched her back, begging for more.

"Honey, baby, Sage." Sighing miserably, he withdrew his hand and tried to stave off her ardently seeking lips.

At last she realized that he was no longer fondling her and wanted her attention. Her thrashing head came to rest between his palms as she gazed up at him through wide, golden eyes cloudy with passion. "What's wrong?"

"Not a damn thing," he replied thickly. "You're perfect. You look perfect. You feel perfect. You taste perfect."

"Then why'd you stop?" she asked, her voice husky.

"I like your brothers, Sage. They like and trust me. I don't want to do anything to betray their trust."

Still restless, she shifted slightly, lodging him more comfortably between her thighs. He closed his eyes and groaned softly. When he opened his eyes again, they were exceptionally bright. The lines on either side of his mouth were tense. His breath was short and shallow.

"I never should have kissed you again. I didn't think it would go . . . I didn't think you would be so . . . Aw, hell." He grimaced as though in pain. "Believe me, Sage, I'd love nothing better than to have my mouth all over you right now. You know where I want to be. Inside you. Deep inside you." Again, he shut his eyes briefly and sucked in an uneven breath.

"But before we go any farther, I've got to know that you know what you're doing and want it as much as I do. I don't want to be used to salve a spoiled little girl's ego."

She wouldn't have believed that any emotion could override the desire pumping through her. However, when his words registered, she discovered that outrage could conquer anything. With a growl of pure fury, she pushed him off her, almost dumping him onto the speckled linoleum floor of the trailer.

She scrambled off the sofa and shoved her disheveled hair out of her eyes. "You won't have to worry about any retribution from my brothers," she shouted. "One day I'm going to kill you myself."

Having issued the threat, she threw open the door, jumped over the steps and marched off into the darkness. She'd gone about a quarter of a mile on foot when he pulled the pickup along side her.

"Get in," he said through the open window.

"Take a flying leap straight into hell."

"What are we going to do, swap invectives? Stop acting like a brat and get in. It's starting to sprinkle."

She came to an abrupt halt and confronted him. "I'll walk. I'd walk a hundred miles through a torrent to keep from riding with you."

"What'll you tell your family when you show up hours late for supper?" She paused to consider that. Harlan pressed his advantage. "Are you prepared to tell them what held us up?"

She glared at him through the gloomy dusk. He looked away from her, toward the horizon. His regret was evident. When he looked at her again, all traces of his characteristic arrogance were absent.

"I take full responsibility for starting something today that shouldn't have got started, Sage. I apologize for ever laying a hand on you. After what happened in the barn on Christmas Day, I should have known better than to touch you again. But," he continued softly, "you've got to accept part of the blame for where it went from that first kiss, and where it would have gone if I hadn't stopped it."

Sage, remembering how wantonly she had writhed against him, privately acknowledged that he was right, though she would rather have her tongue cut out than admit it. Her present behavior only demonstrated to him how upset she was that he had called off their lovemaking. That was untenable. Besides, Chase had asked him to bring her home. If he didn't, her family would want to know why.

Walking stiffly, she rounded the hood of the truck, opened the passenger door, then climbed inside the cab. The window hadn't been replaced, the opening was still patched with cardboard. Since that didn't offer a view, she stared stonily out the front windshield.

Feeling the sting of tears in her eyes, she blinked them away, unwilling to let him see them. She would rather have him think that she was a spoiled little girl than a woman whose raging desire for him had been thwarted.

And she did desire him.

If she hadn't been totally honest with everyone else the last several days, she should at least be honest with herself now. As aggravating as he was, she desired him.

Whatever brand of magic he weaved, it was none she had encountered before. With his loose cowboy's gait, lean body, piercing blue eyes, shaggy blond hair, aura of mystery, and insufferable arrogance, he had made her want him in a way she had never wanted another man.

She was acting like an ingenue in the throes of puppy

TEXAS!
Sage

love. Her girlfriends used to go positively ga-ga over her brothers, and she had scoffed at such silliness. It was beneath her dignity to respond to a man that way, to get all warm and dewy and feverish every time he looked at her.

But Harlan wasn't like other men. He possessed secret powers. He hadn't merely kissed her—he'd made love to her mouth. Travis's kisses had certainly never weakened her to the point of losing her balance. She had never lost her head in his embrace.

Harlan also coaxed more than physical responses from her. He tapped into her emotions. Apparently he'd been deprived as a child. His telling of missing high school had touched a cord in her, made her somehow want to make up for his deprivations.

She had wanted him to make up for hers too. She had wanted his touch, his fervent kisses. What he'd said about having his mouth all over her had been outrageous, yet the very thought of his lips on her skin made her body tremble even now.

She sneaked a glimpse of his profile from the corner of her eye. He would die without knowing how he had affected her. He would never know how much his rejection had wounded her, no matter how honorable his motives had been. He had rebuffed her when she was feeling more vulnerable than she had in her entire life.

Travis had raked her self-esteem over the coals. Now,

while it was still seared and blistered, Harlan had drawn her back into the fire.

What bothered her most, however, was that this man had the capability of hurting her so badly. She couldn't figure out why.

Chase and Lucky were sitting together on the porch, sipping beer, when Harlan parked his truck in the driveway. What would they think of her if they learned that, on her first day on the job, she had made out with the hired help?

She glanced uneasily at Harlan. "What happened in the trailer was strictly between us."

"Right."

"So don't make any heartfelt confessions."

"Right."

"Forget it happened."

"Wrong."

She swung her gaze up to his. It had such impact, she had difficulty recovering her breath as she alighted and shakily made her way toward the house. "Hi."

"Where've you been?" Chase wanted to know.

"What difference does it make?"

"We've been waiting for you," Lucky said. "Chase didn't want to leave for home until you got here."

"Well, I'm here," she said testily.

"There's no call to get your dander up," her older brother said. "We had a brainstorm and wanted to discuss it with you."

"What kind of brainstorm?"

She moved beneath the porch covering to get out of the cold, gray drizzle. In her peripheral vision, she noticed that Harlan propped himself against one of the support posts, just as he'd been leaning against the corner of the Belchers' ivy-covered wall the first time she saw him.

"How'd she do, Harlan?" Lucky asked.

He cleared his throat. "She, uh, she did fine. Just fine. She's got a real feel for it."

Sage felt her cheeks growing warm. She didn't dare look at him, but tried to put him and his sexy kisses out of her mind and concentrate on what her brothers were saying.

Lucky was speaking excitedly. "The final say-so is up to you, of course."

"Say-so about what?"

"We wouldn't want you to approach him if you didn't feel absolutely comfortable about it," Chase said.

"Approach whom?"

"And he might say no," Lucky said.

"In which case," Chase butted in, "there would be no hard feelings."

"But he's got an inside track. He knows people with money who might be willing to invest in our new enterprise."

"All you have to do, Sage, is sell him on the idea."

Sage had been dividing her puzzled gaze between them. Now, holding up both hands in a gesture of surrender, she laughed. "*Who?*" she cried. "Would one of you please tell me what and who you're talking about?"

"Dr. Belcher," Chase replied with a grin. "Travis's dad. Your future father-in-law."

Chapter NINE

"Hi, Lucky. I'm sorry I'm calling so late."

"Harlan? What time is it?"

Harlan checked his wristwatch. "Just after two. Jeez, I'm sorry. I lost track of time."

"It's all right. I asked you to call me. Well?"

Harlan heard the sleepiness fading from Lucky's voice. He hated like hell waking him up from a dead sleep to tell him bad news. "Now I know why the school board was willing to sell me that computer so cheaply."

For days he had been scavenging the town for a secondhand computer and had finally heard of one the public school system was willing to part with for a nominal price.

"It doesn't work," was Lucky's dismal guess.

"Not so far."

"Damn."

"Ditto."

The silence between the two telephone terminals was rife with disappointment. "Well, come on home," Lucky told him. "You shouldn't have stayed with it this long."

"No, I'm going to try one more thing before calling it a night. Should I telephone Chase?"

"Naw. I know he asked you to, but why wake him up if the news is bad?"

"My thoughts exactly."

"Damn," Lucky repeated, "I wish Sage would call and report in, so we'd know where we stood with Belcher."

Harlan concentrated on a hangnail as he picked at it. Trying to sound casual, he asked, "Nothing yet?"

"Not a word. I guess she didn't want to talk business over New Year's Eve. She and Travis probably had plans."

Though he knew better, Harlan went along with Lucky's theory. "Yeah, probably."

"I'm sure the Belchers were either entertaining or being entertained on New Year's Day, so I guess in light of the holiday, Sage hasn't had a chance to talk to Dr. Belcher. Still, you'd think she could call and tell us that much."

"I'm sure she has her reasons," Harlan said lamely.

"Who the hell knows what goes on in a woman's mind? Ouch, Devon, that hurt!" he exclaimed. Harlan heard him speak softly, "I thought you were asleep." After a pause, he spoke into the receiver again. "Come on home to bed, Harlan."

"I won't be much longer."

"See you in the morning."

Harlan hung up, feeling bereft and jealous of his friend for having a bed partner he could curl up with and go back to sleep. Harlan not only didn't have a partner, he really didn't have a bed, unless one counted the lumpy, narrow bed in the trailer.

The bed he was sleeping in was borrowed. When he was in it at night, he couldn't sleep for thinking about the woman who had slept in it prior to him.

"What's she doing tonight?" he wondered out loud as he picked up a small screwdriver and began tinkering again.

He had worked on the prototype almost around the clock. He never minded hard work, but he was especially glad he had this challenging project to occupy his mind and keep it off Sage.

She had guts, that lady. She had showed the stuff she was made of when Chase and Lucky suggested that she contact Travis's father as a potential source of financing. Placed in that kind of compromising position, any other woman might have fainted. Or burst into tears. Or begun stammering explanations.

Sage had foundered for only a heartbeat or two before smiling brightly and saying, "That's a great idea!"

Harlan had watched and listened with disbelief. She was indefatigable. At the risk of letting her brothers down, she perpetuated her original lie.

One had to admire her tenacity and unselfishness. Because she wasn't lying now to save her own skin. In fact, just the opposite. No matter how much pride she had to swallow, she would go see Dr. Belcher for her brothers' sake.

She had maintained the pretense all through dinner, babbling on about how much influence Belcher wielded and how certain she was that he would be the solution to their problem.

"I know he's invested in other ventures and has been very successful," she had told them over homemade enchiladas. By the time they'd got to the orange sherbet and Oreos, she was saying, "I'll leave first thing in the morning."

That's when she had looked him straight in the eye, something she had avoided doing up to that point. Her eyes dared him to expose her. He wouldn't, of course. This was her gig. She had to play her part as she saw fit without any direction from him.

"Excuse me now," she had said, leaving the table. "I'll go upstairs and pack." Her voice was high and light, her eyes unnaturally bright, but he seemed to be the only one who noticed.

He'd sat there mute, dipping his spoon into melting orange sherbet, and watched her climb the stairs, knowing that going to Houston and having to face the father of the man who had jilted her would be the hardest thing she'd ever have to do. He doubted he would have the courage to do something like that.

Sage did. She was the damnedest woman he'd ever met.

By the time he came downstairs the following morning, Laurie informed him that Sage was already on her way. "I hate for her to be driving on a holiday weekend, but I couldn't talk her into postponing her trip. She's so headstrong."

That was an understatement. Sage Tyler was about the stubbornest individual he'd ever come across, inordinately obstinate and proud and courageous. She was also the most desirable woman he'd ever had any contact with, and there had been no small number of them.

From that mane of blond hair to the tips of her toes, Sage Tyler was sixty-some-odd inches of fascinating female. He liked the way she tossed her head with impertinence and the way she tapped her foot with impatience. He liked her sauciness. He admired her spunk. And he positively loved the way she kissed.

She was a compact package of vibrant femininity.

The sad thing was, he didn't think Sage knew just how feminine and desirable she was. She had been so busy proving that she was as important to the family as her brothers, that she hadn't realized no one except her doubted it. She saw her femininity as a weakness, not a strength.

It wasn't going to be easy to convince her of the contrary either. Anything Laurie said, Sage dismissed as the words of a loving mother, blinded by bias. She thought she was merely tolerated and patronized by her brothers.

What she needed to convince her of her value was the right man.

"And you ain't him," he said, jabbing the screwdriver to emphasize each grammatically incorrect word. "So put that thought right out of your head."

When he kissed her, he could tell instinctively that the power of her passion was unknown to her. Once she made up her mind to kiss, she poured her all into it. Her mouth became the soft core of her world. If that were true of a kiss, Lord only knew what it would be like to—

He snapped his wandering thoughts away from treacherous territory.

The strength of her sensuality had probably scared off a lot of men because it posed a threat to their masculinity. Belcher, no doubt, was among them. But some lucky man would eventually acknowledge it, welcome it, and seize it. He would be a charmed sonofabitch. He would spend the rest of his life satisfying the hungry lioness he had unleashed.

In the course of the last few minutes, Harlan's jeans had grown uncomfortably tight. Just thinking about Sage prompted a physical response. That had to stop. Twice he'd come close to showing her what she was capable of, and where had it got him? She hated him.

He couldn't afford that. Not if she was going to be

working with him at Tyler Drilling. He knew the Tylers. They liked him and believed in his ideas, but if it came down to a choice between Sage and him, he would be out in no time flat.

Of course, leaving at some point in the future was inevitable. He never stayed anywhere long. But he always liked to finish what he'd started before moving on. He had never walked out on a project, except one time when he'd discovered the man he was working for was a gangster.

Sage Tyler, with her fiery temper, tempting body and cream-center mouth, posed a far more serious danger than that temporary alliance with the mob. He'd do well to stay the hell away from her.

But as he tinkered with the insides of the machine, his thoughts kept drifting back to her. He wondered where she was, what she was doing, and if she felt as lonely as he.

"This was a hell of an idea," Pat grumbled as he nudged Laurie forward. They were standing in the breakfast line at Milton Point's new McDonald's restaurant, waiting to place their order. "I feel like a damn fool, Laurie."

"Why should you?"

"Because I've never eaten a breakfast wrapped in paper with a goofus clown printed all over it."

"I explained the reason I wanted to meet here," she

whispered over her shoulder. "You've been out to the house for breakfast every morning this week."

"So?"

"Two Egg McMuffins, two orange juices, two coffees," she told the smiling hostess. Then to Pat she said, "I'm afraid the children are going to think you're sneaking in to spend the night with me."

"Which isn't a bad idea."

She shot him a withering glance over her shoulder, then moved aside so he could get their tray. They found a vacant table near the windows. Highway traffic sped past. Pat squeezed himself between the bright orange banquette and the small table. Muttering swear words beneath his breath, he removed his Stetson and placed it on the padded seat beside him.

"You're acting like a big baby."

"Babies don't get horny," he mumbled around the first bite of his sandwich.

Laurie blushed and tried to look annoyed. "Watch your language in front of me, Pat Bush. I swear, I don't know what to make of you lately. You've been so ornery."

"I'm tired of all this. I'm tired of having to beg. New Year's is over. What's your next deadline, Easter? Memorial Day?"

Into his argument, he leaned across the table. "Listen, Laurie, it's not like we don't know each other. It's not like you doubt I love you. I've loved you for almost forty years. If Bud had lived, I'd have gone on loving you in my own silent way.

"Even after he died, I bided my time. I didn't want to offend you or have you thinking I was trying to take advantage of your loneliness. The day Lucky's baby was born and I kissed you in the hospital corridor, well, that was about the happiest day of my life.

"But stealing a few kisses now and then isn't enough. Sitting beside you in church, having meals at your house, and escorting you to this and that doesn't cut it anymore. Neither one of us is getting any younger." She opened her mouth to speak, but he shook his head sternly and continued.

"I don't want to waste any more time. I want us to live together. I want to see you naked. I want to make love to you."

"Shh, Pat! People will hear you."

"Let 'em. I don't give a damn. I want you, Laurie. All of you. All the time. Through my entire adult life, I've had to share you with my best friend, and your children, and everybody else you take under your wing. Well, dammit, I'm feeling real selfish all of a sudden. I want to be the center of your attention, or I don't want your attention a'tall."

After a moment of combative staring, she said, "That was some speech."

He gnawed off a bite of his cold and nearly forgotten sandwich. "That's how I feel."

"So now I know."

"So now you know."

She pinched a crumb off her biscuit and rolled it between her fingers. "Pat?"

"What?" he asked crossly.

"I was just wondering."

"What?"

She looked up at him through her lashes. "Is your bed large enough for the two of us?"

Sage hummed in tune with the radio as she approached the Milton Point city limits. It was a cold morning. A raw north wind was blowing, but the skies were clear.

Her mood was just as sunny.

She passed the town's new McDonald's restaurant and considered stopping for breakfast, but decided against it. She was so eager to tell her brothers her good news, she would go straight to the office. After hearing what she had to report, they would probably want to take her out for an elaborate, celebration lunch.

Long before dawn she had checked out of the budget motel where she'd been staying the last few days—including New Year's Eve and New Year's Day—and headed north. Luckily she had beaten Houston's rush hour traffic and had made good time. Devon's car, which she had borrowed since hers was still in Austin, was newer than hers and much sleeker. The miles had ticked by.

Or maybe time had only seemed to fly because her spirits were soaring. Her meeting with Dr. Belcher couldn't have gone better. He'd been surprised, no *shocked*, to hear from her when she finally worked up enough nerve to phone his office. She had asked to speak to him personally about a nonmedical matter. He had expressed reservations, but had finally agreed to an appointment yesterday afternoon.

It had gone splendidly.

Still on the outskirts of town, she exited the major highway and jounced along the rough road that led to Tyler Drilling. Both Lucky and Chase's vehicles were parked in front of the building, signaling that they were already there. She checked her hair and makeup in the visor mirror before hopping out of the car and heading for the door.

The mood inside the office was sepulchral. Lucky was desultorily tossing a baseball toward the ceiling and catching it. Chase was contemplating the contents of his coffee cup. They raised grim faces to her when she came bouncing in, smiling and rosy-cheeked.

"Hello, Sage."

"Hi, Sage."

"Hi! Why so glum? I've got great news."

"We heard it already."

"You heard about Belcher?"

Lucky's lips drew thin with dislike. "Yeah."

"I don't get it." Their lack of enthusiasm rubbed the

gilt off her brilliant smile. "Didn't he tell you that he agreed to finance the prototype?"

"That's what he said," Chase remarked.

"Then—"

Lucky interrupted her, but not before sending the baseball crashing into the farthest wall. "We told the pompous sonofabitch to shove his money where the sun don't shine."

She fell back a step and wheezed, "What?" All her anxiety, the hard sell, the pride she'd had to swallow! For nothing? "*Why?*"

"You don't have to pretend with us any longer, Sage. We know about Travis and you. We heard about the way he just dumped you and announced his engagement to another girl at the big New Year's Eve bash."

"You . . . you . . ." She couldn't form a coherent thought, much less vocalize it.

"If our sister isn't good enough for that slimy, wimpy bastard, then we don't want any part of his ol' man's damn money!" Lucky stood up so fast, he knocked over the chair he'd been slouching in. "To think of him leading you on all this time and then jilting you right before Christmas." He slammed his fist into his other palm. "I'd like to get my hands around his scrawny neck. Harlan said—"

"Harlan?" *Harlan!* "Where is he?"

"He's sleeping late this morning in his trailer," Chase told her. "He called a while ago and said he'd been up all night and that—Hey, Sage, where are you going?"

She bolted out the door and clambered down the steps to the car. She jammed the key into the ignition, shoved the transmission into gear, and floored the accelerator. The chuckholes went unnoticed as she sped toward the trailer. Her rear wheels skidded on the loose soil and sent up a shower of pebbles when she braked in front of the Streamline.

As before, the doors were unlocked. She didn't bother to knock, but stamped inside and turned left, storming through the tiny galley into the narrow hallway that led to the sleeping area.

He was lying diagonally across the bed on his stomach, all four limbs extended. The covers were twisted around him. Sage picked up the extra pillow and hit him on the head with it.

"You bastard! You scum! You lowlife creep!"

Harlan rolled to his side and brought up one arm to protect his head from the raining blows. "What the—"

"I'm going to kill you!" She raised and lowered the pillow in rapid succession. "How could you do this to me? You ruin everything. You've ruined my life. Ever since I met you—"

The breath whooshed from her body when Harlan grabbed one of her arms and yanked her down onto the bed. He wrestled the pillow away from her and tossed it aside. It fell against a red lava lamp on the nightstand and sent it crashing to the floor.

"What the hell's the matter with you?"

"Let me up!"

She began to buck and kick and flail her arms. He anchored her legs to the bed by throwing one of his across her thighs. She tried to knee him in the groin. He managed to avoid emasculation, but barely.

"Stop that! Dammit, Sage, calm down. What the hell brought this on?"

"You told them. How long did you wait after I left town to go blabbing everything? The minute my back was turned you betrayed my confidence."

"I don't know what the hell—Ouch!"

Astonished, he gazed down at the four thin lines of blood oozing from his chest. Cussing elaborately, he manacled her wrists together and pulled them over her head, stapling them to the mattress with his own hard fingers.

"If you scratch me again, I swear, I'll cut off every one of your fingernails at the quick."

"I don't care. I don't care if you shave my head. I don't care what you do to me. You couldn't humiliate me any more than you already have."

"Just what did I do that was so horrible? Huh? I haven't even seen you for almost a week." He secured her by lying across her.

She squirmed beneath him, trying to get away. Eyes narrowed with loathing, she said, "You waited until I got out of town, then, like a sneaky coward, you told them."

"Told who what?"

"You let me go through the humiliation of begging that old buzzard for an appointment. I had to sit there and listen to his patronizing explanation for Travis's seemingly sudden engagement. 'She's been his friend and companion since they were children, Sage. I'm sure you understand these things, Sage. Travis honestly didn't want to hurt you, Sage. It has always been more or less understood that he and this other young lady would marry one day, Sage.' On and on he went until I wanted to throw up all over his desk.

"But for the sake of Tyler Drilling's future, I sat there with my eyes lowered and my mouth zipped and took every condescending word he uttered. I wanted to tell him how glad I was to be away from his weak-willed son and his overdressed, overbearing, overweight wife. Instead, I acted demure and properly heartbroken."

She glared up at Harlan, whose face was bent low over hers. "But it was worth eating humble pie because I came away with his promise to finance the prototype. I got what I wanted out of the old codger.

"Then you ruined everything by telling Chase and Lucky about Travis. Didn't you realize how they would react? Didn't you know that their family pride wouldn't tolerate his rejection of me? Are you sure you didn't forget any titillating details? Did you tell them every heartrending word he said when he jilted me?"

"I didn't tell them."

His firm but quiet denial only made her more furious. She renewed her efforts to get away from him. "You did! I know you did. You're the only one who knew."

"Belcher knew."

She ceased struggling and gaped at him. "What?"

"Belcher knew. If someone told your brothers, it was Dr. Belcher. Not me. I swear it, Sage."

He didn't look like a lying man. His blue eyes were still puffy from lack of sleep, but they were steady as they probed hers. She moistened her upper lip with her tongue and was surprised to taste perspiration there. Or had that saltiness come from tears?

"But Lucky said that you said . . . something." She hadn't waited to hear the quotation. Was it possible he was telling her the truth?

"The only thing I've said about Travis in Lucky's presence was that my opinion of the guy coincided with his. He asked me if I'd met him when I went to Houston to get you. I told him that, no, I hadn't had the pleasure. I said I had only seen Travis from a distance, but that to me he looked like a guy who was more interested in a woman's position on the social register than her favorite position in bed.

"After a few off-color remarks, which I doubt you'd enjoy hearing repeated, I told him that when I arrived, Travis and you were having a serious discussion. He asked me if I knew what the discussion had been about. I hate lying, Sage, but for your sake, I told him no.

"That conversation took place on Christmas Day, long before you even thought about returning to Houston and asking Belcher for money. So if Lucky and Chase know about your broken engagement, the news came from somebody else."

She pulled her lower lip through her teeth and tried unsuccessfully to stem the flow of tears. They fell anyway, rolling down her temples into her hair.

"I've made a fool of myself in front of you again. I hate you," she whispered earnestly.

"Right now, the only one you hate is yourself." He shook his head sadly, as though he deeply regretted the agony her stubborn pride continually put her through. "Don't be so hard on yourself. Everybody makes mistakes."

One of his hands still had her wrists pinned to the mattress. The fingers of the other sank into her hair and settled against her scalp. "Shave your head, huh?" Laughing softly, he dipped his head and caught one of her tears on the tip of his tongue, then brushed his lips across her damp cheekbone.

"Stop that. What are you doing?"

"Giving you what you've been asking for all along."

"I don't know what you mean. You always talk to me in riddles. You—"

"Sage, be still and shut up."

"I said to, uh, stop. Harlan . . . Harlan, don't. I mean it now. Hmm . . ."

His mouth settled firmly on hers, and when he parted her lips with his agile tongue and delved into her mouth, she was all too willing to keep quiet. Only small sighs of gratification escaped her throat. Her anger dissipated like morning fog after sunrise.

She purred.

He released her hands but she didn't even realize it until he slid both his beneath her sweater and, after unfastening her brassiere, laid them on her breasts. He tenderly squeezed her, reshaping her flesh to fit his strong, yet gentle, hands.

With her hands free, she could have pushed him away or scratched him again. Instead she laid one arm across his bare back and cupped his head with her other hand. Her mouth became his to explore and penetrate. She did some exploring of her own, slipping her tongue into the sweet heat of his mouth, tasting him, and sipping at his lips when they had to pause for breath.

His caresses grew bolder and more impatient. She moved restlessly beneath him. Tacitly they agreed that she had on too many clothes. When he angled her up to peel off her sweater, she obliged him.

That's when she noticed that he was naked. She sucked in a quick breath of surprise. He shrugged. "Never sleep in anything."

The muscles of his long arms were well defined, as was each strong vein. His chest was wide and hairy. The swirling pattern of hair tapered at his narrow waist, then flared again, dark and abundant, around his full sex. He was quite beautifully made.

A small, airless exclamation of excitement escaped her before she could stop it.

The sheets felt cool against the skin of her back when she lay down. They smelled like Harlan. She wanted to wallow in them but wasn't given the opportunity.

He lowered his rumpled, blond head over her breasts and flicked her nipples with his tongue, catching them briefly between his lips, bringing an ache of longing to her lower body and a sense of euphoria to her soul.

When he drew one raised crest into his mouth, her back arched off the bed and she moaned with shameless need. He laid his fingertips against her lips; she kissed them while his mouth tugged on her with exquisite finesse. Mindlessly, she clutched him, raking her nails through the pelt of golden hair on his chest.

"Before you draw blood again, we'd better get you out of these clothes." He spoke jokingly, but his eyes were concentrated points of vivid light. Much as hers must look, she thought.

When she lay beside him naked, he gazed at her, cursing softly beneath his breath. "Lord, but you're something to look at, Miss Sage."

His lips drew hers into another entrancing kiss. Only the introduction of his fingers into her soft, vulnerable flesh could have jolted her out of the golden haze spinning around her.

"Harlan, don't hurt me," she whispered breathlessly.

He raised his head and looked down at her inquisitively. "Hurt you? What do you take me for? I wouldn't dream of hurting you." Smiling at her gently, he bent down to kiss her again as he positioned himself between her thighs.

She felt the velvety smooth tip of his penis separate, enter, stretch, penetrate her.

She gave a soft cry.

Harlan went rigid. His head snapped up. Bridging her with stiff arms, he pushed himself up and looked searchingly into her face. In the space of seconds, a thousand questions were telegraphed from the depths of his eyes. Then he pinched them shut, bared his clenched teeth, and swore lavishly.

He didn't move, didn't say anything for so long, that Sage became anxious. She raised her hands to his armpits and slid them down his corrugated sides.

His breath hissed through his teeth. "Don't. Please don't move." His eyes came open. "See, baby, you're just so . . . tight," he grated. "So . . . ah . . . so small." He ducked his head, his eyes fastening on her breasts beneath his chest. "So beautiful," he added huskily.

He palmed her breast and stroked the dainty pink nipple with his thumb. When he did, her body reacted by closing around him reflexively.

"Aw, Sage," he groaned, lowering himself on top of her again. One arm curved around her waist and lifted her lower body up against his. He buried his face in her neck and closed his teeth over a bite of her flesh.

Sage felt his spasms deep inside her. It was a thrilling sensation, but she wasn't sure what he expected of her. Her recent mistakes had made her self-conscious and unsure. The feelings rioting inside her were so new and transporting, she didn't want to spoil them by doing something foolish, so she tried to lie still.

Her body, however, countered the commands of her brain. Her hips lifted and ground against his in a circular pattern. She clasped his taut buttocks between her thighs. Grasping hands kneaded the supple muscles of his back.

For several moments after his climax, Harlan didn't move. Gradually, he unsnarled his fingers from her hair and disengaged their bodies. He rolled away from her to sit on the edge of the bed, elbows propped on his knees, his head held between his hands. Staring at the floor, he muttered self-deprecations.

Now that it was over, the enormity of what she had done hit Sage. She hastily gathered her clothes and slipped into the closet-sized bathroom.

Chapter
TEN

here wasn't much she could do about the whisker burns around her mouth or on her neck. The ones on her breasts wouldn't show. She rinsed her face with cold water. She washed all over with a washcloth, redressed, and raked her hands through her hair, trying to restore it to some semblance of order. In her enraged haste, she had left her purse in the car. With the resources that were available, she'd done as well as she could.

She gripped the doorknob for several moments, garnering all the courage possible before returning to the bedroom. There was no more than twelve inches of space on either side of the bed, so she instantly came face-to-face with Harlan.

Or rather belly to face, as he was still sitting on the edge of the bed. He had, however, pulled on a pair of jeans. Sage thought she must be the most wanton woman in the history of the species because—with his touseled hair, whisker bristle, bare chest and feet—Harlan looked mouth-watering. Her tummy fluttered, and, though she hadn't even begun to chastise herself for what had just happened, she wanted it to happen again.

"Sage," he began, raising his hands in a gesture of helplessness, "I don't know what to say."

"Good. Because I don't want to talk about it. I've got to go. G'bye."

She slipped through the narrow door and hastened down the passageway. He caught up with her in the galley and turned her to face him.

"We've got to talk about it."

She stubbornly shook her head no.

"Why didn't you tell me that you were . . . that you hadn't . . . that I was the first?"

"It wasn't any of your business."

"Maybe not until ten minutes ago. Then it became my business."

"That's where it ended, too."

"Like hell it did. Did I hurt you?" He reached up and touched the corner of her whisker-burned lips. "Christ, Sage, I could have hurt you."

"Well, you didn't, so stop acting guilty."

"Are you . . ." He paused to swallow hard. "Bleeding?"

Embarrassed and exasperated, she lowered her eyes. "You're the one who's bleeding." There were still four distinct red lines on his chest. "I'm sorry I did that to you."

He made a negligent motion with his hand, dismissing the scratches. "I've got to know if you're all right."

"Yes!" she cried, her voice cracking. Rather than show him how emotional she felt, she resorted to anger. "I thought you'd be crowing. Now I've really given you something to gloat about, haven't I?"

She freed her arm from his grasp and left the trailer. She was tempted to run but didn't, wanting to maintain a shred of dignity. On the other hand, she didn't dawdle. From the open doorway, Harlan watched her leave, the expression on his unshaven face grave. She avoided meeting his eyes as she backed the car away before turning into the road. She hadn't gone far when she met Chase driving toward her in one of the company trucks.

"Sage," he called from the open window. Extending his arm, he flagged her down. "What's going on? Why'd you hightail it out of the office like that?"

Her choices were limited to two. She could either burst into tears and confess to her older brother that she was afraid she had fallen in love with the wrong man. Or she could brazen it out.

Since the former was unacceptable, even to herself, she forced a smile. "I lost my temper."

"Over Belcher?"

"Indirectly. See, I thought Harlan was the one who'd told you about Travis and me."

"Why would you think that?"

"He overheard my conversation with Travis the night

he came to Houston for me." Nervously, she wet her lips and tasted Harlan. Was his taste visible, like a milk mustache? "I confronted Harlan about it. He . . . he claimed he hadn't said anything."

"No, we didn't hear it from Harlan. Dr. Belcher called this morning to say how glad he was that we could work together on a business venture despite what had recently happened between you and Travis. I was in the dark as to what he meant. When I asked him for an explanation, it all came out."

"I'm sure he painted me as the wounded loser in a love triangle."

"Something like that."

"Well, he's wrong."

Chase hesitated a moment, studying her, as though gauging the veracity of her statement. "Then why didn't you tell us, Sage? Why put on an act this last couple of weeks?"

"Because I didn't want to involve the rest of the family with my problem. It would have put a pall over Jamie's arrival. The holiday would have been spoiled. What purpose would it have served except to make everyone uncomfortable and uptight?"

"You still should have confided in us, Sage," he said gently. "That's what this family is about. If one of us is suffering, we all take it to heart. You know that." He grinned. "Ever since Belcher's call, Lucky has been threatening to go to Houston and pound Travis to mush."

She rolled her eyes. "And wouldn't that be dandy?"

"Say the word and we'll both go."

Heart swelling with love, smiling her gratitude, she shook her head no. "But thanks for the thought."

"Mother's gonna have a conniption fit."

"Oh, Lord, you're right, Chase. I dread having to tell her. She'll want to ply me with hot tea and extra food."

"Humor her. It'll make her feel better to fuss over you." He reached across the space that separated his truck from her car. She extended her hand and took his through the open window. "Sure you're okay?"

"Don't worry about me. I wasn't as brokenhearted as everyone might presume."

"I'm glad to hear you say that, Sage. Travis is no big loss."

"True. The other loss is much greater—Dr. Belcher's contacts in the business community."

He shook his head with a stubbornness she recognized. "No way. We'll survive without the Belchers' help, thank you."

It was gratifying to know that her brothers felt that strongly about it, although it wasn't the wisest stand for them to take. It demonstrated their loyalty and formed a family bond that included her.

She squeezed Chase's hand before releasing it. "I was on my way home. I left Houston awfully early. I'm ready for a nap."

"You do look a little ragged around the edges. Marcie's

a good listener if you'd like to talk to another woman about the breakup."

"I don't want to dwell on it. I'd rather mark it up as a bad experience in my past and go forward from here."

His expression was still full of misgiving. He sensed that something was bothering her, but couldn't isolate it. "Go home and get some sleep."

"I intend to. Bye."

She raised her car window, waved at him, and drove away. Arriving home, she was glad to see that no one was there. Laurie and Devon were probably out running errands. She climbed the stairs, one hand trailing wearily along the polished bannister as she lugged her suitcase with the other. Instinctively, she headed for her former room before remembering that someone else now occupied it. Retracing her steps, she went into the guest room.

After her bath, she examined her body in the long mirror mounted on the back of the bathroom door. She looked remarkably the same. It didn't seem possible. She felt so drastically different, it was a mystery to her why the changes were invisible.

More mysterious than that, however, was why she had allowed "it" to happen with Harlan Boyd. Countless young men had tried to woo her in a variety of ways ranging from the ridiculous to the romantic. She flung herself on to her bed.

Harlan. Expending very little effort, he had accomplished what so many had tried to do and failed.

It had never seemed right or natural before. Travis had asked, of course. At one time, he had even suggested that they get an apartment together. He wanted to elevate the intimacy of their relationship, he had said. Her reasons for not wanting to were vague, even to herself, so for months she had hedged. Finally, he'd stopped pressing her.

Then this blue-eyed, slim-hipped drifter had come along, and she melted when he looked at her. It made no sense. Harlan represented everything she did *not* want in a mate. She wanted at least a promise of future prosperity. He had no visible means of support. She wanted big-city slick. He was country scruffy.

In the last thirty-six hours, she had groveled to Dr. Belcher, failed in her first endeavor for Tyler Drilling, and had had sex with the hired hand.

"You're doing great, Sage," she muttered sarcastically into her pillow.

Maybe Harlan was right about her being too hard on herself. To err was human. Perhaps she was just more human than most. There was a positive side to everything negative.

Even though she had swallowed a great deal of pride in order to go to Dr. Belcher, he had been impressed with her courage to face him so soon after Travis's rejection. She must have convinced him that their irrigation system was marketable. Her sales presentation had sold him on the idea. He had enthusiastically pledged to invest in it. The reason for the deal falling through had been circumstantial, not poor salesmanship.

Only Harlan and she would know what had happened between them this morning. He wasn't going to tell because he didn't want to sacrifice his job or his friendship with her brothers.

She'd just have to grit her teeth and bear his smugness, which shouldn't be too difficult to do because, if things went well, she would be traveling for the company. They wouldn't be spending that much time together.

She snuggled deeper into the covers, nursing the kernel of optimism that was germinating. Now that everyone knew about her broken engagement—her brothers were certain to tell her mother and their wives—she could relax. The deception would no longer be a dark cloud hanging over her head.

As she had told Chase, she wanted to leave the past behind her and move forward. She now had specific career goals, which would not only serve her self-esteem, but also benefit the family business.

During the years spent at the university, she had missed living at home, surrounded by her family. Now she had a niece and a nephew to spoil. Her mother would be delighted to have her back. They could spend much more time together. It would be like old times. Her mother loved to baby and indulge her.

Comforted by the thought, she drifted off to sleep.

*   *   *

She woke up to the delicious aroma of roasting meat. Her stomach growled, reminding her that she hadn't eaten in almost twenty-four hours. As she dressed, she noted that the sun was setting. She had slept nearly the entire day. Feeling fresh and rested, despite the incident that morning, she opened the door to the bedroom and skipped downstairs.

She met Harlan coming up. Sage froze. He stopped. Their gazes locked. Sage might have stayed petrified beneath the power of his gaze had he not lowered it to encompass the rest of her body. When he did, a surging fever took the path of his eyes, engulfing her.

She forced herself to move. With both of them living under one roof, this was likely to happen often. She wouldn't let his presence intimidate her into being a prisoner of her bedroom. Whose house was this anyway, his or hers?

Her intention was to brush past him with a mumbled word of greeting. Nothing more. She didn't quite succeed. When she reached the step immediately above him, he raised his hands and bracketed her hips, stopping her in midflight. The heels of his hands settled on the knobs of her pelvic bones. His fingers followed the curve of her hips toward her back.

"Sage?" He looked up at her entreatingly. "You okay, baby?"

His voice was so soft and compelling, it alone was

almost capable of stopping her in her tracks without the use of his hands. She was extremely conscious of their position on her body because it was reminiscent of that morning. She might have moved into his arms and begged him to hold her if she hadn't seen the one emotion in his eyes which was anathema to her—pity.

"Excuse me," she said coldly. She pushed away his hands and went around him, jogging down the remainder of the stairs without looking back. "Mother?"

"In here," Laurie called from the kitchen.

Her cheeks were flushed from the heat of the stove. An old apron covered her flannel slacks and sweater, but she'd never looked prettier to Sage.

"I'm so glad you're back, dear."

She held out her arms, and Sage moved into her maternal hug. "It's good to be back, Mother."

They prolonged the embrace, each sensing that the other needed to. Sage inhaled Laurie's familiar fragrance and felt like a child again, in search of comfort and getting it where it could always be found.

When at last they pulled apart, she said, "I know that by now Chase and Lucky have told you about Travis."

"Yes."

"I want to assure you that I'm fine. I was mildly disappointed at first, but that didn't last long."

"I'll bet you were more mad than disappointed. You didn't mind the breakup so much as the fact that he was the one who did it."

"You know me too well, Mother."

"I am very pleased by the outcome," Laurie said staunchly, stabbing a boiling potato to test its tenderness. She replaced the lid on the pot and turned back to Sage. "It'll take a stronger man than Travis Belcher to satisfy you."

Sage's insides took a free-fall. She had a clear recollection of how strong Harlan was, yet how tender. How greedy, yet giving. Every time she thought about him stretching and pulsing inside her, she grew weak. She had entertained a foolish notion earlier today that what she had felt for him was love, when, in fact, he was just particularly gifted at sexual stimulation.

She turned away before her mother could notice that her own cheeks were turning rosy. She couldn't use cooking as an excuse. "What's all this food for?" she asked.

"I invited Chase and Marcie over for dinner."

Sage groaned. "We aren't going to have a wake for my dead romance, are we?"

"Nothing of the sort."

"I really don't want anyone's condolences, Mother."

"Chase made that clear to everybody. Now stop fussing about it and help me set the table."

By the time they were finished, Devon had brought Lauren downstairs and set her in her high chair to watch while they dished up the food. Lucky returned home from work, kissed his wife and daughter, then excused himself to go wash up. On his way through the kitchen door, he paused.

"Are you surviving, brat?" Sage stuck out her tongue at him. He grinned broadly. "She seems perfectly normal."

Pat arrived at the same time Chase's family did. In the ensuing confusion, Sage didn't notice precisely the minute Harlan came down from upstairs. But she knew the instant she backed into a solid body that it was his. Her bottom bumped against his middle.

With a grunt of pleasure and surprise, he raised his hands to rest lightly on her ribcage. "Careful there."

"Sorry."

"No problem."

Her hands were occupied with the heavy platter of food she was carrying. Quickly, she moved away from him and scurried into the dining room. His touch had left her jumpy. She could still feel the hot impressions of his fingers through her clothing. The low, confidential tone of his voice reminded her of everything he'd said while their bodies had been joined.

They all gathered around the dining table. To her consternation, Sage was relegated to a place next to Harlan. Amidst the aromas of of roast beef, steamy, buttery vegetables, and Laurie's homemade yeast rolls, she picked up whiffs of his cologne.

Keeping up with the mealtime conversation was difficult. Harlan's nearness proved to be a constant distraction. They bumped knees numerous times. When they reached for the salt shaker at the same time, their fingers collided.

She covertly watched him handle his silverware. Those were the same hands that had elicited chills and heat waves from her skin. When he blotted his lips with his napkin, she recalled those lips repeatedly kissing her nipples until they were raised and aching, then sucking them into the damp heat of his mouth.

Everyone behaved normally, but Sage sensed that her family was closely observing her, as though her indifference to being jilted might be a facade and that at any moment she was going to succumb to emotional collapse.

She might, but not for the reason they believed. Little did they know that the reason for her strained expression, insincere smile, and uncharacteristic nervousness wasn't Travis, but the man sitting right beside her.

With a gusto she didn't feel, she ate food she couldn't taste with an appetite that was counterfeit. What she felt was arousal. All she wanted to taste was Harlan. The only thing she had an appetite for was the weight of his naked body upon hers.

While they were demolishing a chocolate layer cake and drinking coffee, Pat surprised them by rising from his chair and clinking his fork against his water glass. Everyone fell silent and looked toward him curiously.

"Uh, Laurie figured that I ought to be the one to, uh, tell y'all."

"Jeez, Pat," Lucky remarked, "the last time you looked

this sickly, you were telling us that I was being formally charged with arson."

Laughter went around the table. Pat didn't laugh. In fact he looked ready to throw up. He ran his finger round the inside of his collar. "No, it's nothing like that this time. It's . . . well, you see . . . we, Laurie and me that is, uh . . ."

Laurie left her chair and moved to stand beside him. She slid her arm around his waist. "What Pat is trying to tell you, and doing a poor job of it, is that he's asked me to marry him and I have accepted."

"If y'all don't mind," Pat interjected.

"Mind?" Lucky was the first one out of his seat. "I'm relieved. I was afraid she'd get a reputation as a loose lady before you got around to marrying her."

"James Lawrence!"

He silenced his mother's admonitions with a bear hug. He was moved aside by Chase who also enveloped her in a hug. Devon and Marcie were kissing Pat's ruddy cheeks and dabbing happy tears from their eyes. Harlan added his hearty congratulations by pumping Pat's hand and unself-consciously hugging Laurie.

Sage stood up slowly and moved toward the middle-aged couple, who were smiling as giddily as children. No one could doubt or begrudge the love between them.

Sage hugged Pat first. "I'm so happy you're finally becoming an official member of this family. We're all slightly nutty. Are you sure you know what you're getting into?"

"Damn sure," he said, affectionately tugging on a lock of her hair.

When Sage turned to Laurie, the older woman gazed anxiously into her daughter's face. "I know this isn't the best time to spring this on you, Sage."

"It's the best time for you and Pat. That makes it the right time. He's waited years for you."

"You knew?"

"How could I not?" she exclaimed. "You didn't raise any dimwitted children. Except for Lucky."

"I heard that," he shouted over Lauren's crying.

Sage gave her mother a sustained hug, squeezing her eyes tightly shut, holding in the stinging tears. Not for anything in the world would she have them know that another rug had been yanked out from under her. She wondered how many were stacked beneath her. Which one would be the last one, the one that sent her plunging into a black abyss of despair?

*C*hapter
ELEVEN

*T*he wedding took place two Saturdays later, although the sisters-in-law complained that such short notice barely gave them time to prepare.

"Give the guy a break," Chase had said in response to their protests.

Lucky had agreed. "From the looks of him, poor Pat's about to burst."

Despite the joke he had cracked directly following Pat's announcement, Lucky and the rest of them knew that their mother would never sleep with a man, even one she loved as much as she loved Pat, until she was married to him.

"Laurie, Pat, you've asked your family and friends to gather here today to witness your exchange of wedding vows and to celebrate your love for each other."

The officiating pastor had known the bride and groom

for years. He seemed as happy about the marriage as the other guests who filled the first several rows of the church.

Sage, serving as her mother's attendant, tried to concentrate on every word coming from the pastor's lips, but her eyes strayed beyond Pat's shoulder to the man seated in the second pew.

Harlan wasn't attentive to the ceremony either. He was watching Sage. Every time she turned around, she fell victim to his eyes, which seemed to follow her everywhere, even into her dreams.

They no longer gloated or provoked her with their know-it-all smugness. The intensity that had replaced it, however, was even more disturbing. She was afraid he would see too much, perceive things she didn't want him to know.

For the last two weeks, she had avoided him whenever she could. Along with her sisters-in-law, she'd been terribly busy making arrangements for the wedding.

Harlan spent most of his time at the garage working on the prototype, which even the prenuptial chaos hadn't deterred. He began to look thin and drawn. At first Sage thought it was her imagination, then she heard Laurie nagging him about his lack of rest, overwork, and poor appetite.

There were lines making deep parentheses around his mouth today, but he looked extremely handsome. His hair was combed, somewhat. He had dressed up, somewhat. He was wearing boots, but they were shined. His dark slacks were pressed, and, though he had on his bomber jacket instead of a suit coat, he had compromised by wearing a necktie. His shirt was starched and showed up starkly white against his tanned face.

During the brief ceremony, against her will, Sage's gaze was drawn again and again to his electric-blue stare. The magnetic power of it made her angora sweater-dress feel uncomfortably warm and snug. The padded, beaded shoulders felt like football pads weighing her down. The butterscotch color was one of her most flattering.

She knew she looked good. But the last thing she wanted to do was look good to Harlan. She would rather die than have him think she was trying to attract him. According to the single-minded way he was staring at her, however, he liked not only what he saw on the outside, but what was underneath too.

"You may now kiss your bride, Pat."

Tears collected in Sage's eyes as she watched the big, burly sheriff, his own eyes glistening suspiciously, draw Laurie into his arms and kiss her. Sage remembered how much her mother had suffered through her father's lengthy illness and eventual death. She deserved this happiness. Apparently she was flourishing in Pat's love. Looking incandescent, she turned and faced the congregation.

Sage had hostess duties to attend to at the house, so

she and Devon left the church as quickly as possible. They had decorated the house with flowers, greenery, and candles and had prepared all the food with the exception of the tiered wedding cake.

The guests complimented them effusively. The rooms of the house rang with laughter and echoed genial conversations. It was a joyous day.

The party passed in a blur for Sage, who welcomed the tasks that occupied her. They kept her away from Harlan and gave her something else to think about.

Before she realized how much time had elapsed, everyone gathered on the front porch to see off the newlyweds. Laurie went to each of her children individually and hugged them, then she drew Chase, Lucky, and Sage into one giant hug. Pools of tears collected in her eyes as she said her final good-byes.

"I love you all so much. Thank you for being such wonderful children. Thank you for being happy for me."

"Better get her away from here, Pat," Chase quipped. "She's beginning to leak."

Amidst laughter and a barrage of good wishes, Pat escorted his bride to her car—they couldn't very well take his squad car on their honeymoon—and drove off beneath a shower of rice.

The guests began to disperse until only the family was left. While both babies were asleep upstairs, the men pitched in to help with the unpleasant chore of cleaning up.

When everything was done, they convened around the kitchen table for sandwiches. "Wedding cake and canapés just doesn't do it," Chase said, stacking sliced ham and Swiss cheese onto a piece of rye bread.

"Maybe we should have packed Laurie and Pat a lunch to take with them," Devon said. "They ate less than anyone and have a long drive ahead of them."

Their plans were to drive to the New Mexico mountains, where there was snow in the higher elevations. Neither had any desire to ski, merely to enjoy each other and the scenery from their cozy suite at a ritzy lodge.

"Are you kidding?" Lucky chortled. "They've probably already stopped for the night not ten miles from here. I'll bet Pat made it no farther than one of those motels on the interstate."

"I understand they can be very romantic," Marcie said, glancing teasingly at Devon and Lucky.

Lucky reached over and squeezed his wife's shoulder. "Damned if you're not right, Marcie."

Devon was known to give as good as she got. With no compunction whatsoever, she hooked her hand around Lucky's neck and kissed him long and hard on the mouth. When she finally released him, he gasped for breath. "I love weddings. They make the womenfolk horny as hell."

Sage cast a nervous glance toward Harlan. He was observing her with the motionless concentration of a jungle cat. She left her chair and carried her empty glass to the refrigerator to get a refill of her drink. A moving target was harder to hit, she thought, feeling like prey caught in the fine cross-hairs.

Chase groaned. "Little good it does me for Marcie to be horny."

"That's the only bad thing about having a baby. How much longer?" Lucky asked sympathetically.

"Two more weeks and counting," Marcie replied, laying a consoling arm across her husband's shoulders. He lowered his head and laid it on her chest.

"The thing about weddings and women," he said dreamily, "is the organ music. It reminds them of the sounds they make when they make love."

Sage dropped her glass. It crashed to the floor and shattered. Milk splashed up on her shoes and stockings.

Marcie shoved Chase's head away. "You should be ashamed of yourself! You embarrassed your sister, and I don't blame her one bit."

Lucky was laughing so hard, he was clutching his waist. "That was a good one, big brother. Wish I'd've thought of it myself."

Devon was trying as hard as Marcie to stifle her own laughter.

Sage didn't dare look toward Harlan. This conversation was for happily married couples who were comfortable with jests about sex. It was torture for two people who had a guilty secret to hide.

She mopped up the spilled milk with a dishtowel, and, in the process, cut her hand on a piece of broken glass. As she was bent over the sticky mess, a familiar pair of boots moved into her field of vision.

Harlan squatted down beside her and began picking up the larger chunks of glass. "Let me help with this."

"No thanks."

He caught her hand. "You're bleeding."

"It's nothing," she said, pulling her hand from his grasp. "I'm going upstairs to change."

She darted upstairs, shimmied out of her dress, kicked off her suede shoes and peeled off her hosiery. She replaced the finery with her oldest pair of jeans, riding boots, and a heavy jacket. In the bathroom medicine cabinet, she located a Band-Aid and placed it over the cut before working her hands into tight leather gloves. Within minutes, she was on her way down the stairs, carrying the new quirt she'd been given for Christmas.

"I'm going riding," she announced as she sailed through the kitchen without even slowing down.

"Now?" Chase glanced through the kitchen window. "It's almost dark."

"I won't be gone long."

Before they could stop her, she bolted through the back door and ran toward the barn. She saddled her favorite horse in record time. As soon as they cleared the yard, she nudged the gelding into a gallop.

The wind tore at her hair. It felt icy on her cheeks

when it connected with the wet patches her tears had left. She had ridden quite a distance before it no longer felt as though her chest was going to crack from internal pressure.

She sucked in the cold air. It hurt her lungs and brought new tears to her eyes, but at least it was a new pain. For two weeks, ever since learning of her mother's intention to marry, she'd been coping with her sense of loss.

It was selfish of her, she knew. She wouldn't begrudge either her mother or Pat their happiness together. But their marriage only compounded her feelings of alienation.

What was she going to do? Where was she going to live? With whom did she belong?

Laurie had told them of their plans to live in Pat's small house. Lucky had objected.

"This is your house, Mother."

"It's *our* house," she had corrected. "It belongs to all of us. But Devon and you are using it to raise your family in, and I couldn't be happier about that. I love this house. I loved the man who built it. But now I love another man. I want to live in his house, with him, as a newlywed."

Sage knew she would always be welcome in the ranch house. It was her home, too. As Laurie had said, it belonged to all of them. Devon and Lucky wouldn't boot her out.

Even so, she would feel like an intruder now. The house should be home to a nuclear family. She wasn't part of that anymore. She didn't belong there any longer. She didn't belong with Laurie and Pat. She didn't belong . . . period.

There were hundreds of thousands of career women who lived alone. That wasn't what bothered her. It was that she felt so cut off from everything familiar and dear. Laurie's first priority would be Pat now. That was as it should be. Chase and Lucky had their families.

What did she have? Nothing. No real home. No real career. No one.

She reined in her horse and dismounted. Laying her cheek against his muzzle, she admitted to him that she was indulging in a bad case of self-pity. Sympathetically, he nudged her shoulder.

"I'm no use to anybody. What am I going to do with the rest of my life?"

The gelding, his short supply of sympathy expended, dipped his head and began to graze.

Sage's swift departure left a vacuum in the kitchen. Lucky was the first to speak. "What got into her?"

Harlan reached for his jacket on the wall rack and pulled open the door. "I'll go after her." He left almost as hastily as Sage had.

"I haven't wanted to bring it up, but Sage has been acting peculiarly," Marcie said.

"How can you tell?" They all shot Lucky a dirty look. "Well, she's always been a little off the wall, hasn't she?" he said defensively.

Chase said to Marcie, "You've mentioned this before. I've gone out of my way to be nice to her. You don't think it's helped?"

Marcie shrugged. "Something's still bothering her."

"I've noticed it too," Devon said. "She hasn't confided anything to me though."

"Me either," Marcie said.

"Could it be Belcher?"

Devon's brows puckered. "I really don't believe so, Lucky. I never was convinced she was madly in love with him. I think I would recognize the signs." She exchanged a tender look with her husband.

"I agree, Devon," Marcie said. "All I know is that she hasn't been herself since she came home for Christmas."

"You don't think she could be jealous of Pat, do you?" Chase suggested. "Taking her mommy away, his becoming more important to her than Sage is."

They silently pondered that for a moment, then Marcie said, "Their marriage might have contributed to the problem, but I don't think that's at the base of it. Sage is too emotionally well-grounded for the marriage to throw her for such a loop."

Worriedly, she glanced toward the door. "I feel badly

saying this, but, I'm not sure Harlan is the right one to go after her."

"You think Sage's weirdness might have something to do with Harlan?" Lucky asked.

"I don't know," Marcie hedged. "There seems to be a lot of latent hostility between them." Almost as soon as the words were out, she negated them with a wave of her hand. "I'm probably imagining it."

"You're not," Devon remarked. "The other day I saw them meet on the stairs. He tried to engage her in conversation. She moved right past him with barely a civil word. I didn't think too much of it then, but, now that you mention it, on more than one occasion I've seen her snub him."

"Well, I'll be damned," Lucky muttered. "He's such a likable guy." He looked across the table at Chase. "What do you make of it?"

"Hell if I know. Maybe she's sore because we brought him into the company. It's always been strictly family before. In any event, I'd better find her before he does."

"I'll come too."

Minutes later, the brothers were in Chase's pickup, following the dirt path across the pasture.

At the sound of approaching hooves, Sage raised her head from her horse's neck. The twilight had turned so deep that at first the rider appeared only as a dark, moving shadow. He slowed his mount to a walk and clip-clopped toward her.

Recognizing the shape of his hat and breadth of his shoulders, she warred over being irritated or overjoyed that he had followed her. Harlan threw his leg over the saddle and dropped to the ground.

"What are you doing here?"

He hitched his head in the direction from which he had come. "They were worried about you. The way you tore out, we were scared you'd break your neck. Or the gelding's."

"I appreciate your concern, but, as you can see, the horse and I are fine and don't need any assistance. Especially yours."

"I'm just relieved we won't have to shoot either him or you."

Sage, her expression thunderous, moved to the animal's side and placed her boot in the stirrup. Before she could boost herself up, Harlan caught her arm and pulled her around.

"How long did you figure on avoiding me?"

"Forever."

"After what happened between us?"

"I told you I didn't want to talk about it."

"Well, I do," he said, raising his voice to a near shout. "I've got plenty to say on the subject. And since I risked my own neck galloping out across this prairie after dark, you're damned well going to stand there and listen until I'm finished."

With the grip he was keeping on her arm, she couldn't very well leave. Not that she wouldn't fight for her freedom if she really wanted it. In spite of herself, she wanted to hear everything that was obviously pressing on his mind.

"Okay. You've got me," she said tersely. "What's so important that I've just got to hear it?"

"You were a virgin, Sage."

"I know that better than you."

"So now I've got to wonder whether or not you were taking birth control pills."

She inhaled a short, little breath. When she opened her mouth to speak, she discovered she was temporarily mute. She shook her head no.

He removed his hat and slapped it against his thigh. "Christ."

"Well, don't worry about it, Mr. Boyd," she said acidly. "If there's a *problem*, I'll take care of it. I absolve you of any and all responsibility."

"Guess again, Miss Sage," he said, pushing the words through clenched teeth. "I didn't ask to be absolved. I just wanted to know everything we're up against. What the hell were you thinking about to go to bed with a man who didn't protect himself and didn't protect you? You ought to be horsewhipped for such criminal disregard for yourself. For all you know I could be carrying a disease."

She swayed and placed her hand upon the gelding's flank for support.

"I'm not." His voice gentled a bit. "I've always taken the proper precautions before. As you'll recall, I didn't have any pockets on me when you came barging into my bedroom."

The memory of his beautiful nakedness left her cheeks warm. "Is that all you have to say?" she asked huskily.

"No. Hell no." He released her arm and slid both hands into his back pockets. He stared into the dark distance for a moment, before looking at her again. When he spoke, his breath vaporized in the cold air, creating a cloud between them.

"I didn't want anything bad to happen to you, Sage. You've got to believe that. It blew my mind when I realized you were a virgin. By the time I did, it was too late. I was in solid." Their eyes collided. Sage's fell away quickly. His voice had dropped an octave when he continued. "I planned to just, uh, you know, pull out."

She swallowed hard and stared fixedly at the point of his shirt collar.

"But, you were . . . It was . . . Hell, I don't have to tell you how it was." He blew out a gust of air and muttered a swear word. "You moved a little, baby, and I was lost."

His breathy words brought back all the sensations that had assailed her as it happened. His voice and the intensity with which he spoke made it real again. Feeling dizzy, she instinctively reached for support.

He captured her shoulders and drew her against him,

then tightly wrapped his arms around her. His lips moved through her hair.

"Tell me you're all right. Reassure me, Sage."

"I'm all right. I promise. I'm fine."

"I didn't hurt you?"

"No."

"Swear?"

"Swear."

"I couldn't have lived with myself if I had hurt you, but, damn, you felt good, Sage. Did you, uh, get any pleasure at all out of it?"

She nodded against his chest.

"A little?"

"Some," she murmured shyly.

"You mean more than a little?"

Again she nodded.

Sighing "Ah, Sage," he used a fistful of her hair to pull her head back. His parted lips sought hers. The cold night only made his mouth feel hotter, wetter, softer. They kissed hungrily until he pulled away and pressed her face into his open collar, where she could smell his clean skin, feel his strong heartbeat in his neck.

"Listen, I know you haven't had time to know if there's a baby or not. With the wedding and all that's been going on, you might not have even thought about it."

She hadn't. The act itself had so overwhelmed her

that she hadn't had room in her brain to consider anything else, even the consequences.

"What I'm saying," he went on, "is that if you skip a period, I want to know about it right away. I'd want to do the right thing, Sage. I'd marry you."

The warmth of his body, the security of his embrace, the low tone of his voice had lulled her into a false sense of tranquility. The edges of cold reality had been blunted by his caresses, his deep kiss, and the feel of his breath in her hair.

But when the meaning of his words finally penetrated this lovely haze, it dispelled it completely and instantly. Immediately replacing the rosy fog of romanticism was a red mist of rage.

Sage shoved him away from her at the same time the toe of her boot connected with his shin. "You bastard!" She doubled her fists and aimed blows at his head, most of which he succeeded in dodging. "I don't need your charity. I can take care of myself. Who would want your help? I wouldn't marry you—"

"Sage, calm down. I didn't say it right. What I meant—"

"I know what you meant." She flew into him again.

"Stop that. Dammit! Stop. I don't want to have to hurt you."

"Hurt me!" she shrieked. "All you've done since I met you is hurt me in one way or another," she said, belying her previous assurances.

He managed to grab both her wrists, which infuriated

her. She struggled and kicked and curled her fingers into claws that, if ever freed, would scratch his eyes out.

It startled them when a pair of headlights cut a swathe through the darkness and landed on them like a spotlight. Seconds later, Chase and Lucky stood silhouetted against the bright lights.

"What the hell is going on here?" Chase demanded.

"You'd better have a damn good reason for holding her like that, Harlan," Lucky barked.

"I do. If I let her go, she's liable to kill me."

"I will!" Sage threw her shoulder into his ribs. He grunted and bent at the waist.

Wheezing, he said, "She . . . she might be—"

"No!" She froze, ceasing all her struggles, and gazed up at Harlan imploringly.

"I've got to tell them, Sage." He gave her a look full of regret, then faced her brothers again. "She might be pregnant with my baby."

For a moment the atmosphere crackled with expectation, like the suspension of time between a close lightning flash and the clap of thunder.

"You sneaky sonofabitch!"

Lucky launched himself at Harlan. Harlan pushed Sage out of the way just in time. Lucky's fist caught him in the gut. He doubled over only to be brought upright by a crunching uppercut to his chin.

"Lucky, I don't want to fight you. I want to—"

Whatever appeal Harlan was about to make was cut

short by another punch that glanced his shoulder. Dodging it caused him to lose his balance. He landed on his bottom in the dirt.

He flung his head up and glared at her brother. Sage recoiled from the fury in his eyes. "Dammit, I said I didn't want to fight you, but you give me no choice." Then he pulled himself to his feet, ducked his head, and charged Lucky.

"Chase," she shouted, "do something!"

Chase wasn't as short-tempered as his younger brother, but he was as powerful, strong, and quick. He had never backed down from a fight, especially one where the family's honor was at stake.

But, although Sage had threatened to kill Harlan herself moments earlier, she was relieved to see that it wasn't going to be a two-against-one fight. Rather than joining in, Chase tried to break it up.

Lucky and Harlan were having none of it, however. They were slugging it out ferociously. Both men fought off Chase's peacemaking overtures. He got a bloody nose for his efforts. Sage wasn't sure whose fist had landed the blow.

For a while Lucky had the upper hand. Harlan was on the defensive. Then the tables turned. Harlan became the aggressor. He pummeled Lucky's middle, paused, and then sent one vicious fist into his chin. It was a solid punch. Lucky's head snapped back. He stumbled backward, turned, and careened into the grill of the pickup.

Even from where Sage was standing, she heard the bone in his forearm snap. He seemed to hang in suspension for an agonizing eternity before sliding to the ground. Cradling his right arm against his stomach, he collapsed into the dirt.

*C*hapter
TWELVE

*S*age had thought she understood the definition of misery.

As thorough as *Webster's* was, however, the definition fell far short of comprehensive explanation. Until tonight Sage hadn't realized misery's total dimensions, its height and breadth. Misery went bone-deep. Like a severe chill, it could cause one to huddle beneath layers of blankets without any hope of ever getting warm. Misery caused one's teeth to chatter. It cramped muscles until they ached.

She stared wide-eyed into the darkness beyond her bed, reviewing the bizarre events that had taken place in the last several hours.

If she closed her eyes, she could still see Harlan and Lucky fighting in the unworldly glare of the pickup's headlights, raising clouds of dust that swirled dizzily in the twin beams. She heard again the sickening sounds of splitting skin and snapping bone. She vividly recalled seeing her brother's face, grimacing in agony, his lips white with pain.

Chase had hustled her and Lucky into the cab of the truck and then driven like a bat out of hell to the ranch house. It had been a rough ride. Lucky had cursed elaborately with every jolting motion of the truck.

Their arrival had created panic and pandemonium throughout the house. All their clothes were blood-stained, though exactly whose blood it was remained uncertain. In addition to his broken arm, Lucky's jaw was bruised, one of his eyes was swelling shut, and there was a nasty cut on his lip. Within minutes he was on his way to the hospital accompanied by Devon and Chase. Marcie and Sage stayed with the children, who were already down for the night.

It was a while before Sage remembered the horses that had been deserted in the pasture. She ran to the stable. The horses had been returned to their stalls, unsaddled, and rubbed down. Obviously Harlan had done it, but he was no longer around and his truck was gone.

Near midnight, Chase and Devon returned home without Lucky. The break in his arm had been clean and would heal without complications, but the doctor advised that he spend the night in the hospital for observation.

"He didn't want to," Devon had told them. "But I

insisted. Could I prevail on you to spend the night here? If I was needed at the hospital or something . . ." she finished lamely.

Chase and Marcie agreed to spend the night. Sage showered and got ready for bed, executing each task routinely. Her body and mind were numb. No one had pointed a finger and specifically blamed her for what had happened, but the silent consensus must be that it was her fault.

Chase knocked on her door just as she was turning out the light. "Is there any possibility of truth to what Harlan said about you being pregnant with his child?"

"A possibility, Chase," she answered meekly, unable to look at him directly, "but very little likelihood."

"Did he rape you, Sage? Because if he did, I'm not going to bother calling the police. I'm going after the sonofabitch myself."

"No! Don't do anything, Chase." She couldn't bear the thought of causing her family more grief, worry, and difficulty. "He didn't force me. It wasn't like that at all."

"Did he coerce you in any way?"

"No. It was . . . mutual."

He stood on her threshold for several moments more. She could almost feel his eyes boring into the crown of her bowed head in search of the truth. "All right," he said at last. "Good night."

"Good night. Oh, Chase," she said, calling him back.

"You're not going to try and notify Mother and Pat, are you?"

"We discussed it on the way to the hospital and decided not to ruin their honeymoon."

Vastly relieved, she said, "That was my thinking, too. Good night."

That conversation had taken place hours ago, and she still couldn't sleep. Lucky was in the hospital on account of her. Chase was threatening to hunt down Harlan and inflict bodily harm or worse. Her sisters-in-law had been told the reason for the fight. They kept their eyes lowered when speaking to her, either out of pity or scorn. She couldn't be sure.

Her whole family was in an uproar, and it was her fault. How had things become such a jumble? The week before Christmas she had thought she had her life under control. When it began to topple, it had come crashing down and now lay around her feet in shambles.

She had made some bad decisions which had affected not only her, but everyone around her and the family business. Thinking of that, she groaned and buried her head in her pillow.

Chase and Lucky were so optimistic about this irrigation system. They saw it as a means of getting them in the black again. What possible future did it have now? As things stood, their working with Harlan again wasn't even within the realm of possibility. The business would sink until it hit bottom. The blame would rest on her shoulders.

The chill in her bones suddenly vanished. She grew uncomfortably warm and kicked off her electric blanket. Leaving the bed, she began to aimlessly prowl around the room.

She couldn't allow the family business to fail. If it did as a result of her poor judgment, she would never recover her self-respect. Her Grandpa Tyler had started that business. Damned if it was going to be said that it had collapsed because his only granddaughter had had hormones that made her succumb to the allure of sexy blue eyes and a well-fitting pair of old Levi's.

"I'll be damned first," she vowed into the darkness.

She had to do something, anything, to prevent that from happening. But what? She was almost afraid to do anything except stand still. Recently, every step she'd taken had been a wrong one. If she wanted to prove herself worthy of the Tyler name, she couldn't afford any more errors.

But, no pain, no gain.

No guts, no glory.

The T-shirt philosophies echoed through her head. Some of them began to carry weight and make sense. That was probably dangerous thinking, because the idea that was jiggling the lock on the back door of her mind was risky to say the very least. Should she invite it in to take a look around?

All she knew for certain was that she couldn't return to bed and pull the covers over her head. She had to make a move now, before the light of day and the dawn of reason stopped her to reconsider.

Before she could talk herself out of it, she hurried to the closet, took out her suitcase, and began to pack.

"Hellfire and damnation!"

Harlan stuck his injured thumb into his mouth and sucked on it hard. While trying to attach the trailer to his pickup, he'd mashed his thumb between two immovable objects of metal. The trailer hitch was being uncooperative. He could hardly expect anything to go smoothly after the evening he had spent.

"Just goes to show what being honest and open with folks can get you," he said to the trailer hitch, which finally connected.

He heard the approaching car before he saw the headlights slicing through the trunks of the surrounding pine trees. He eased himself into an upright position, although standing perfectly straight caused some parts of his battered body to ache and throb. Of course, a few cuts and bruises wouldn't matter if the Tyler boys were toting shotguns this time.

Resigned to having another fight, he braced himself for it, mentally and physically. He didn't relax one iota when he saw Sage, not her brothers, alight from the car. If anything, he tensed up tighter.

"Before you say anything, hear me out," she stated for openers.

"You'd better get out of here, Sage, before they catch you with me. Or did they send you in as bait to see if I'd bite?"

"I told you to hear me out," she snapped. "I'm alone. Chase is at home asleep and Lucky is in the hospital."

"Jesus." He dragged his hand over his face. He hadn't intended to hit him that hard. The sound of the breaking bone had turned his stomach. He had wanted to go with them and help out, but knew his help wouldn't be welcome.

"Don't look so stricken," Sage said. "It could have easily been you instead. The doctor's only keeping him there overnight for observation." She pulled her coat tighter around her. "It's cold out here. Can we talk inside?"

"No way. Besides, in case you haven't noticed, I'm clearing out. Five minutes more and you would have missed me."

"Then you'd have missed a golden opportunity."

"To do what? Get beaten to a pulp by one of your irate brothers? No thanks. I'll pass. Right now the only option open to me is to leave."

He pointed his finger at her. "But I swear to God, Sage, I'm coming back. When I do, if you're carrying my baby, I'm laying claim to it if I have to hogtie you and carry you off. I'll keep you and my baby, and I don't care if your brothers come after me with all the bloodhounds of hell."

"There won't be a baby," she said with annoyance. "I'm going inside."

She sashayed past him and stepped into the trailer. Knowing it was a bad idea that he would surely regret, Harlan followed her. The door slapped shut behind them. It wasn't much warmer inside the trailer. He'd already disconnected the generator and turned off the heat.

Sage was rubbing her hands up and down her arms, but he sensed the action was more from restlessness than cold. She was keyed up, moving around like a high-strung filly at the starting gate of her first race.

"Say what you've come to say and then scram," he said. "You're a peck of bad news."

"I have a proposition to make you."

"Isn't that usually left up to the man?"

"Not that kind of proposition."

His eyes narrowed suspiciously. "Then what kind?"

"Answer a question first."

"Conditions already, and I haven't even heard the proposition."

She frowned, but didn't address his sarcasm. "How far are you from finishing the prototype?"

He folded his arms across his chest and leaned against the door. "Why?"

"I want to sell it."

"That's no surprise. That's been the goal all along, hasn't it?"

"No, I mean sell it now. You and I. Together. We start making calls and sell clients on the idea. If they want to see the prototype, will we have something to show them? Before we get to that point, I need a guarantee from you that the damn thing will work."

Several thoughts sprang immediately to his mind, but uppermost was that this was the damnedest woman he'd ever met. Knock her down, she bounced back for more. Fighting or making love, she was fascinating. Her ideas, however, were a little harebrained.

"You want to just strike out and start selling irrigation systems door-to-door?"

"Don't make fun of me, Harlan. I'm serious. I'm committed to this."

"Yeah, well I think you ought to be committed, all right. To the state hospital."

"Damn you, I'm fighting for my future and for the future of my family's business. Stop cracking stupid jokes and answer my simple question. Can you get it to work?"

"It does work."

"It does?" Her mouth hung open for several seconds. Her eyes were wide with disbelief. "It really does?"

"Yep. While everybody else has been in a tailspin doing wedding stuff, I managed to acquire a used computer."

"Acquire?"

"Don't ask."

"Okay, I won't. Go on."

"It didn't fit inside the casing I'd built, but I hooked it up. I tried out the system day before yesterday. If it had been attached to a pipeline, this whole field would be well-watered by now."

Her voice was high and shrill with excitement. "Why didn't you tell anybody? Why keep it to yourself?"

"I was waiting for all the excitement over the wedding to die down. Besides, I wanted to make some adjustments and try it several more times before I broadcast it."

"But there's no doubt in your mind?"

He grinned, unable to contain his own excitement over his success. "No doubt. It'll work."

Sage clasped her hands beneath her chin. "Oh, Harlan, that's great news! That's wonderful!" Galvanized, she shoved him away from the door and reached for the latch. "Let's not waste any more time. We'll take your truck as far as Austin and pick up my car there."

"Whoa! Hold it. Stop right there." He barred her exit. She turned to face him, her expression quizzical. "Correct me if I'm wrong, Miss Sage, but I don't think you discussed this idea of yours with anybody. You sneaked off in the middle of the night with this wild notion and figured to surprise them later, right?"

"Of course I didn't discuss it with anybody. After tonight, they wouldn't let me go away with you."

"Um-huh. So what makes you think I'm going to take you anywhere with me? I'd have to be crazy to take you out for coffee, much less leave the city limits for parts unknown. I don't want every law officer in this state out looking for me with an arrest warrant in one hand and a loaded pistol in the other."

"Don't worry about it."

"Well, I do worry about it. When it comes to my hide, I'm funny like that."

She sighed with exasperation. "I left them a note. I told them that I was with you by choice and asked them not to come after me. I promised to call periodically and let them know that I was safe."

"But you don't intend to tell them what you're up to."

She adamantly shook her head. "Not until I can bring them a contract. I won't come back without one."

"You're forgetting something, Sage." He bent in closer. "You've got nothing to sell."

"That's where you come in. I want you to bring all your blueprints and drawings of the machinery. First we'll sell potential customers on Tyler Drilling's excellent reputation, which they should already know is the best in the oil business. Then we'll show them your designs for adapting drilling pumps to an irrigation system and give the impression that the machinery is already in production and that they'd better get in line if they want one any time soon."

"Which constitutes fraud."

"I wouldn't commit a crime!" She seemed incensed at the very thought. "As soon as we get a contract, we'll rush the machinery into production. In the meantime, you can be working on a solution to the computer problem."

He stared at the floor between his boots, shaking his head and chuckling. "Damnedest, craziest plan I ever heard of."

"It'll work."

"That's what's really scary."

"Harlan," she said, moving forward and laying her hand on his arm. "I know you don't want to disappoint my brothers any more than I do. You told me that you didn't want to betray their trust. What happened between us," she said, her voice thickening, "was as much my fault as yours. I'm not blaming you, but Chase and Lucky, with their outdated code of chivalry, might.

"Doing this provides each of us a way to win back their respect and confidence." She pulled her lower lip through her teeth and looked at him imploringly. "Anyway, I think it's worth a try, don't you?"

"What about this thing that happened between us, Sage?"

"It was an isolated incident, nothing more."

"You think so?" he asked softly. She didn't answer, but he could tell that her own affirmation hadn't convinced her. "We'll be traveling together, in each other's company day . . . and night."

"We're adults," she said hoarsely. "From now on, we're strictly business partners. Agreed, Harlan? Please?"

He studied the face that had already gotten him into trouble with two men he respected more than any men he'd met in a long time. Before it was all over, he'd probably dig himself in deeper, but damned if he seemed to be able to help himself.

She had a way of worming her way beneath his skin, burrowing down into his gut, and curling around his heart. He doubted he could deny her anything when she looked up at him like that, entreating him with eyes the color of smooth whiskey. He'd gotten drunk and done foolish things on whiskey a whole lot less intoxicating than those eyes.

What the hell? He didn't have any particular destination in mind when he left here. He hadn't figured on leaving this soon, so he hadn't made plans. Besides, he hated leaving a job unfinished. He always tidied up after himself before moving on. That had always been important to him. He had never left anyone disappointed in his association with Harlan Boyd.

"Okay, Miss Sage," he conceded on a sigh. "Haul your buns into the cab of my truck. *But*, one derogatory word about it, and you walk."

Lucky hobbled into the kitchen under his own muscle power, but Chase hovered nearby in case his brother needed additional support. Lucky had been discharged from the hospital early that morning and had called asking Chase to come drive him home. As soon as they cleared the back door, Devon raised a hand to her mouth to cover her gasp.

"It's worse than last night," she murmured sympathetically. Hugging him gently, she kissed an undamaged spot on his forehead and led him toward a chair at the kitchen table.

"Yeah, but you ought to see the other guy," he joked through swollen lips.

He had earned a reputation as a hotheaded fighter during his youth and had maintained it up until he met Devon. It had been several years since he'd had a split lip and swollen eye. Wincing, he lowered himself into the chair.

"Does your arm hurt?" Devon asked solicitously.

"I'll live."

"Can you eat?"

"Just coffee, please, for now." He removed something from his jacket. "They gave me this at the hospital." He held up an elbow-shaped straw. "It sucks."

His joke didn't spark much laughter. What little there was sounded forced. The mood around the kitchen table was somber. Marcie glanced warily at Chase as she rocked Jamie. Lauren was taking her morning nap upstairs. Devon kept herself busy pouring coffee for everyone.

While they drank it, Chase told the women the doctor's report. "Lucky'll have to wear that splint for six to eight weeks. He'll look like hell for several days—"

"Thanks," Lucky threw in.

"But then he'll be his usual handsome self."

"Hopefully before your mother and Pat get back," Marcie commented.

Devon reached up to ruffle Lucky's hair, which the hospital pillow had flattened to his head. "I doubt they would be too shocked. From what I understand, he used to look like this frequently."

"Not since I met you." He reached for her hand and squeezed it, then took a sip of his coffee through the straw. "Is Sage up yet? I'd like to talk to her."

For several moments, no one said anything. The other three avoided making eye contact with Lucky. At last Chase cleared his throat and said, "She's gone."

"Gone? Gone where?"

"We're not sure. Just gone."

Lucky's eyes darted around the circle of averted faces. "You're leaving something out, and whatever it is, it's already eating a hole in my gut."

"She left with Harlan."

Lucky swore and banged his bruised fist against the edge of the table, then cursed because it hurt. "And you let her go?"

"I didn't *let* her go." Angrily Chase left his chair and began to pace the width of the kitchen. "She didn't exactly ask my permission, Lucky. She packed her suitcase and sneaked out, leaving a note saying not to worry and that she would call in occasionally and for us not even to think about coming after her.

"I checked, and Harlan's trailer is gone. So are all his schematics of the prototype. By the way, did you know he had a computer attached to it?" he asked out of context.

Lucky plowed his fingers through his hair. "I can't believe you let her waltz out of here with that womanizing bum. Are they eloping or what?"

"Damned if I know. Maybe they took the drawings so he could peddle the idea to some other company."

"I don't believe what I'm hearing!" Marcie exclaimed, surging to her feet.

"Neither do I," Devon said. "Listen to yourselves." She included her brother-in-law and husband in her critical glare. "All we've heard for months is how smart and wonderful Harlan Boyd is. 'He's got terrific ideas.' 'This idea of his is great.' 'If it works, we'll have all our people back on the payroll soon.' 'This is going to save us.' "

"Devon's right," Marcie said. "That's exactly what we've heard. Chase, just a few nights ago you were telling me how you planned to take over the manufacturing while Lucky handled installation."

"You said the same thing," Devon reminded her husband. "You were so excited about the prospect of working hard again. You took Harlan's idea and ran with it. I haven't seen you so optimistic and full of energy about your business since I met you."

Marcie again picked up the argument. "And all because Harlan figured out a way to adapt your equipment and know-how to do another job. Now, all of a sudden, he's persona non grata. Yesterday, he was a hero. He could work miracles."

"A hero who, behind our back," Lucky mumbled through his swollen lips, "seduced our baby sister."

"So what?"

"*So what?*" he incredulously repeated.

"Yes, so what?" Marcie said. "She's *not* your baby sister. She's a grown woman. If she wanted to sleep with Harlan and vice versa, it was none of your business. Or yours," she said, making a jabbing motion toward Chase's chest.

"By jumping to conclusions, you're doing Sage, as well as Harlan, a grave disservice," Devon said. "I'm appalled by your lack of confidence in them, particularly your own sister. On top of all that, you're making yourselves look like a couple of fools."

"How's that?" Chase asked.

"I see exactly what she means," Marcie said. "Don't you trust your own judgment of people? You had every confidence in this man twenty-four hours ago."

"Twenty-four hours ago I didn't know he'd taken advantage of Sage."

"You still don't," Marcie shouted at her husband. "Maybe Sage took advantage of him. Did you ever think of that?"

"You, Lucky Tyler," Devon said angrily, "are a fine one to be accusing any man of taking advantage of a woman!"

"Aw, come on, Devon." He spoke hastily in self-defense and winced when the cut on his lip reopened. Nursing it, he muttered, "You can't compare them with what happened between you and me the night we met."

"All I know," Chase shouted over everyone else, "is that Sage is vulnerable right now on account of the breakup with Travis. She's probably feeling bereft over Mother's marriage too. Otherwise, she would never fall for a guy like Harlan."

"Why not? Harlan's gorgeous and sexy."

Lucky's discolored jaw fell open. He was stunned by his wife's comment. "Well now, that's a fine way for a married lady with a baby to be talking about a man."

"I'm married, not blind," she snapped. "And he *is* gorgeous and sexy. Even Laurie thinks so."

"My mother?" Lucky shrieked.

"Yes, your mother. She told me so."

"What makes you an expert on the kind of man Sage would fall for?" Marcie demanded of Chase. Lucky and Devon, occupied with shooting each other fulminating glances, subsided and gave the other couple the floor. They squared off chin-to-chin.

"I know her," Chase said. "I've known her a hell of a lot longer than you have. Harlan, with his lack of polish and breeding, is the last man Sage would go to bed with if her head were on straight."

"Well, love does that sort of thing to people," Marcie said loftily. "It spins their heads around."

"Love? Who said anything about love? At best, we're talking lust here."

"Whatever it is, it has a powerful effect on people. It makes them do crazy, out-of-the-ordinary things."

"Crazy things like running off in the middle of the night with no explanation?"

"Crazy things like making Chase Tyler marry Goosey Johns," she shouted. "What do you figure were the odds against that?" Reining in her redhead's temper, she eyed her husband coolly. "Before you and Lucky get up a posse to go rescue Sage, you'd be wise to consider that she might not want to be rescued." She sniffed sanctimoniously. "You'd better come upstairs with me, Devon. I think I hear Lauren crying."

Carrying Jamie with her, Marcie swept from the room. Devon was right behind her.

Lucky raised his one good eye to his brother and said dejectedly, "I warned you that if they ever teamed up against us we'd be sunk."

"Well," Chase said, then sighed, dropping into the nearest chair, "we're sunk."

*C*hapter
THIRTEEN

*H*arlan's pickup didn't even make it as far as Austin.

About thirty miles north of the capital city, the engine began to wheeze. After another ten miles, white smoke started curling from beneath the battered hood.

Sage opened her mouth to speak, but, remembering his threat to make her walk, closed it again. She glanced at him. He was wearing a smug grin.

"I see you're taking my warning to heart," he said, sounding pleased.

Testily, she asked, "Are you going to let it blow up and take us with it?"

"I'm looking for a convenient place to stop."

A quarter of a mile farther, he took an exit to a roadside park. The choking, coughing truck was a laughingstock to the other motorists using the facility. Sage wanted to crouch down in the seat and cover her head.

Harlan, however, didn't appear to be the least bit self-conscious as he got out and ambled toward the front of the pickup. The rusty metal hood screeched in protest when he raised it. A cloud of white smoke billowed out.

He waited, waving most of it away, before ducking his head and bending over the motor. After a few minutes, he came around to the passenger side. Since Sage had no window to roll down, she put her shoulder to the door and shoved it open.

"What's the diagnosis?"

"Busted water hose," he reported. "The radiator has boiled dry."

"Is that bad?"

He propped one elbow on the corner of the door and looked at her with amusement. "It is unless you want to burn up your engine."

That sounded like an attractive way of dispensing with the detestable vehicle. "I don't suppose this heap is insured."

He shook his head. "Don't believe in it."

"Triple A?" she asked hopefully.

"Nope."

"Then what do you suggest?"

He began unbuttoning his flannel shirt. When the buttons were undone, he tugged the shirttail from the waistband of his jeans and peeled it off. "Hold this."

She took the shirt he thrust at her and watched

speechlessly as he crossed his arms over his chest and pulled up the hem of his plain, white T-shirt. He took it off over his head, leaving his torso bare.

It bore bruises from last night's fist fight. Morning sunlight glistened on his chest hair. The chilly wind shrank his nipples.

Sage's tummy did a flip-flop.

With both hands, he ripped his T-shirt down the middle, then tore off the sleeves. He moved to the front of the pickup again, giving Sage a good view of his shirtless back, which was almost as tantalizing as the front. His pale blond hair curled down over his nape. His skin was stretched smooth over supple muscles.

Curious, she leaned out the door so she could see what he was doing beneath the raised hood. Dry-mouthed and fascinated, she watched the muscles of his lean arms flex and relax as he wrapped the strips of cotton around the leak in the hose. His veins stood out. His hands looked strong and capable as they tied a hard knot in the cloth. From a nearby hydrant, he replaced the water that had leaked out.

He slammed the hood cover and headed for the square brick structure that housed the public toilets. "Be right back," he said over his shoulder. "Got to wash my hands."

Sage hastily turned the rearview mirror toward her. The image it reflected came as an unpleasant shock. Not only did she feel like she had been up all night, she looked it. Since getting eight hours of sleep was currently out of the question, she did the best she could with the cosmetics in her handbag.

As Harlan had improvised to repair the pickup, she improvised to repair her face, working quickly so he wouldn't think her vanity had anything to do with him. Just as he rounded the corner of the building, she crammed her hairbrush back into her purse and tried to appear impatient and bored over the delay.

Moments after he climbed into the cab, he sniffed the air. "Do I smell perfume?"

"I wanted to freshen up a little. Is that all right with you?"

"Sure, it's fine with me. You looked like hell before." Miffed, she pushed his shirt toward him. He caught it and began to laugh. "You can't take a joke, can you?"

Resting his forearms on the unfashionably large steering wheel, he turned his head and gazed at her. "If it makes your ego feel any better, Sage, I've had a hard time keeping both hands on the wheel."

The stare they exchanged became uncomfortably long. During it, Sage reminded herself that theirs was a business-only relationship. That had been her rule. She had decreed it, so she couldn't be the first one to break it. Besides, she couldn't let anything distract her from her ultimate goal. Harlan didn't even have to try very hard to be a distraction. In fact, he didn't have to try at all.

She finally pulled her eyes away from his stare and nodded toward the hood. "Is it, uh, working now?"

"Oh, it's working all right," he replied huskily.

"Do you think it will explode?"

He swallowed hard. "It might. I've just got to make sure it doesn't get too hot."

Having the distinct impression that they were talking about two different engines, she nervously moistened her lips. "Aren't you going to put your shirt back on?"

"Why? Does looking at my bare chest bother you?"

"Not at all."

He grinned in that knowing way that made her feel transparent. As he connected the two bare wires that started the motor, he added, "Miss Sage, you're no better at lying than you are at taking a joke."

"This is really fun. I feel a sense of freedom, don't you?"

"I've been free since I was fifteen, remember?"

They were speeding down the six-lane divided highway that bisected the Texas map from the Red River, south to the Mexican border.

"Well, being completely unencumbered might be nothing new to you, but it is to me," Sage said. "I feel as carefree as a gypsy."

From Austin she had insisted that they travel in her car, which had been left parked at her apartment since the day Travis had picked her up and driven her to Houston for the holidays.

Over the last several months of her college career, she had gradually been moving things from the apartment which had been home for three years. Her two roommates were pleased to purchase her share of the furniture and household items since they planned to continue living there. What few personal items that remained, they promised to store in a spare closet until a convenient time for her to take them.

At the bank, she emptied her savings and checking accounts. It wasn't a sizable sum, but she wouldn't soon starve. While she had been settling her affairs, Harlan had gone off alone and returned to the apartment on foot.

Within a matter of hours, they were heading south from Austin, traveling lean. She had asked him to drive because she was too excited and nervous to concentrate. Now that old ties were severed, her mission well defined in her mind, her plan in full swing, she was bursting with energy and enthusiasm.

They had gone several miles before she thought to ask him about his Streamline trailer. It had been necessary for them to leave it behind since her car didn't have a trailer hitch.

"I left it with a friend," he told her. "He owns a filling station. Said I could park it behind his building."

"Are you sure it'll be there when you come back for it?"

He frowned at her. "I said he's a friend. We worked on the same offshore rig for a time. That's like going through a war together."

"What about your truck? Did you just desert it on the side of the road?"

"That would've been a waste, wouldn't it? I sold it for two hundred dollars."

"Two hundred dollars! What idiot gave you two hundred dollars for that piece of junk?"

"A junk dealer."

"Oh." They smiled at each other. His eyes returned to the road. Sage asked, "Have you always worked in oil-related industries?"

"Mostly."

She waited for him to elaborate. He didn't. His reticence aggravated her, so she probed. "If you had to fill out a form of some sort, what would you write down as your occupation?"

"I never fill out forms," he said.

"But if you had to."

"I don't."

"Harlan!" she cried in frustration. "Just suppose you did."

He heaved a sigh. "Okay. I guess I'd say I was a professional troubleshooter. If somebody has a problem, I go in and try to fix it."

"Somebody? You mean anybody?"

"If I like them and they like me, and if I believe I can do them some good."

"So you scout out people with problems?"

Clearly uncomfortable talking about it, he shrugged. "Yeah, I guess you could say that. Like when I met Chase in Houston last year, I liked him immediately. It was mutual. He told me his company had bottomed out. I wasn't available to help at the time, but I didn't forget him. As soon as I was free, I went to Milton Point."

"Once a problem is solved—"

"To everybody's satisfaction . . ."

"You—"

"Move on to another one."

"No attachments."

"That's right."

"Ever?"

"Ever."

"Hmm."

She pondered the stretch of highway for a moment, suddenly feeling lonely and dejected. He disposed of things—trailers, pickup trucks—easily and with no remorse. When it was time to move on, he left people behind, too, without looking back. Sage wondered how many women he had left behind, women who had been in love with him.

The thought took the fizzle out of her effervescent mood. For the next few miles, she said nothing.

*   *   *

"There's a Dairy Queen up ahead." Sage pointed to the familiar red and white sign. "Let's stop. I'm starving."

"Sage, we stopped an hour ago because you had to go to the bathroom. Thirty minutes before that you had to have a Snickers bar or die."

"It's suppertime. Let's stop and eat, then drive all night."

"Okay. But with your stomach and bladder along for the ride, I'm afraid we'll never get to the valley."

They had made the Rio Grande Valley their general destination because there was so much agriculture in that region. They reasoned that cotton and citrus growers would be potential customers for their irrigation system.

The Dairy Queen was doing a thriving dinner business. They had to wait in line to place their order.

"I'm so hungry, I could eat a horse," she murmured while perusing the menu.

"Sorry. Not on the menu."

Undaunted by his teasing, she said, "I want a cheeseburger with everything. A large order of fries. A chocolate shake. And an order of nachos."

"With peppers?"

"Of course with peppers. What're nachos without peppers? Lots and lots of peppers."

That's when he kissed her. One second she was smiling up at him, smacking her lips in greedy anticipation of the spicy food, and the next, he was curving his hand around her nape and drawing her mouth up to his for a long, deep kiss that blocked out the racket of the restaurant. She tentatively rested her hands at the sides of his waist, then slid her arms around him and hugged him tight.

Harlan ended the kiss long before she was ready for him to. He gazed into her face for a moment, telling her with his eyes that propriety and not desire had prompted him to end it.

He draped his arm across her shoulders and pulled her close. She left one arm around his waist and reached up with the other to clasp his hand where it dangled over her shoulder. Sage thought that, to everyone else, they must look like a couple in love out on a casual date.

At that moment, she desperately wanted them to be.

When it came their turn to order, Harlan smiled down at her as he spoke to the waitress. "The lady wants an order of nachos with peppers. Lots and lots of peppers."

Sage gorged indelicately on the fast food. Food hadn't tasted this good to her in . . . She couldn't remember when food had ever tasted this good and wondered if Harlan's kiss had, in some mystical way, seasoned it.

"Want another cheeseburger?" he asked as she polished off the last bite.

Laughing, she blotted her mouth with the paper napkin. "No thanks, but it was delicious. It's been ages since I've had one."

"Didn't Don Juan ever take you to a Dairy Queen?"

"Travis?" Even saying his name sounded odd now, as though he had belonged to another lifetime. In a very real sense, he had. "The future Dr. Belcher wouldn't be caught dead in a fast food restaurant. For a while, he got on a health food craze and tried force-feeding me stuff like bean curd and tofu."

"Tofu? Is that a cousin to toe jam?"

She laughed until she was weak . . . and Harlan didn't even seem to mind that she was making a public spectacle of herself. In fact, he seemed to enjoy her laughter.

It was getting dark by the time they got underway once again. Her full stomach, general sense of well-being, and the monotonous growl of the car's engine made her sleepy. Before long, she was having a hard time keeping her head upright and her eyes open.

"Here," Harlan said, patting his right thigh. "Lay your head here and stop fighting it."

Warily, Sage stared at the notch of his thighs where his jeans were soft and faded and far from roomy. "I'd better not," she said uneasily. "You might fall asleep while you're driving."

He chuckled. "Having your head in my lap is one surefire way of keeping me wide awake." He laughed out loud at her startled expression. "I was only kidding. Come on." He patted his thigh again, and she couldn't resist. She lay down along the seat and gingerly laid her head on his thigh.

He swept her hair off her neck, exposing it briefly before covering it with his hand. His thumb stroked her jaw. "Nighty-night, Miss Sage."

"I won't sleep. I'll just rest my eyes for a minute or two."

He continued to idly stroke her neck, jaw, and earlobe.

The next thing she knew, he was nudging her awake. "Come on, Sage, sit up. My leg's gone to sleep."

Woozy, she sat up but seemed unable to open her eyes. "What time is it?" she mumbled. "Why are we stopped?"

"It's going on midnight. I stopped because the center strip was blurring into two. I'm sleepy and didn't want us to become a highway statistic. By the way, did you know you snore?"

"Shut up," she said grouchily, rolling her shoulders and rubbing her neck. "Where are we?"

"A nice, clean motel."

Because clean was an amenity, she was instantly suspicious. She forced her eyes open and looked around. The individual bungalows were limned with pink neon tubes. In the central courtyard, some prickly pear and a few oleander bushes struggled for survival around a swimming pool so murky a person could walk across it. The office of the complex looked sinister and dim behind a blinking blue star. A pair of longhorns were mounted above the door.

"Great. Texas's rendition of the Bates Motel. Norman Billy Bob Bates and his dead mother, proprietors."

TEXAS!
Sage

"This is a nice place. I've stayed here before."

"Somehow that doesn't surprise me."

"Sit tight. I'll see if they've got a vacancy."

"What, are you kidding?"

Moments later, he came back wagging a key. On the short drive from the office to the cabin they'd been assigned, she said, "Couldn't we stay in something luxurious, like a Motel Six?"

"We'll only be here for a few hours' sleep. All we'll be using are the beds."

"You're right about that. I'm sure not going to take a shower. From what I could see of him, the clerk was a dead ringer for Anthony Perkins."

The room had twin beds with a tiny, spindly table between them, and a chest of drawers. No telephone. No T.V. It was, however, warm and clean. Sage sniffed the sheets of the bed and, satisfied that they were sanitary, slid between them fully dressed.

She was too sleepy to take off her clothes. It was the first night of her life she had gone to bed without brushing her teeth, but she didn't care. All she wanted to do was sleep.

Harlan went into the bathroom. Seconds later she heard the water in the shower running. He was showering to spite her, she thought acidly. But there was a smile on her face. She was permeated with contentment. Strange, when she considered how inauspiciously this day had begun.

She'd left home with a man she'd known less than a month, riding in a broken-down pickup truck that had sold for scrap metal.

She'd cleaned out her bank accounts, which represented every cent she possessed, and it was a woefully meager amount.

She'd gorged on fast food without giving a thought to the high calories or low nutritional value.

She'd deserted everything safe and familiar and had embarked upon a quest that might yield her nothing except humiliation and animosity from her beloved family.

And she was spending the night in a sleazy motel room that had probably been the scene of countless illicit trysts.

Despite all that, her mind was at ease and she was smiling as she snuggled beneath the covers and plumped up the pillow beneath her head.

Harlan was still in the shower, singing a Rod Stewart song, slightly off-key. When he came out, would he lie down beside her and place his arms around her, or would he use the other bed?

She wouldn't mind if the other bed stood empty all night.

She had never felt happier.

"Sage, will you cut it out please? That's not helping our situation."

"I don't care," she blubbered, holding a damp tissue to her leaking nose. "I feel like crying, so I'm going to cry. Now leave me alone and let me do it in peace."

"We could have irrigated every parcel of land in south Texas with the tears you've cried. Maybe we should have tried to market them."

She glared at him through red, swollen eyes. "I'm really tired of your jokes about it, Harlan."

"Well, joking's better than bawling."

Two weeks on the road together without anything to show for it had strained their tempers to the limit. As they headed back on the same highway they had so optimistically traveled fourteen days earlier, Harlan's knuckles were white with tension as he gripped the steering wheel.

If he had a destination in mind, he hadn't informed her. She felt indifferent toward it anyway. They were just driving aimlessly, mile after mile, while she wept and he simmered. He seemed to be spoiling for a fight. Sage, feeling fractious herself, was prepared to give him one.

"You can't imagine how important the success of this trip was to me."

"I can guess," he shouted back. "You wanted to come home triumphant. You wanted your family's love and adulation."

"What do you know about family love?"

She saw a spark leap in his eyes, but he didn't

acknowledge the question. Instead he counterattacked. "You think you've got the whole damn world fooled, but I can see clean through you, Sage. You don't think anybody respects you. Well, you're wrong. You should have heard your family bragging to me about how hard and diligently you worked to earn your master's degree. Long before I met you, I was sick of hearing about you."

"They may talk about me, but they don't take me seriously. They never have."

"Maybe because you're always flouncing around and shooting off your mouth."

"Oh, thanks. I'm beginning to feel a whole lot better now that we've had this little talk."

He took his eyes off the road to study her for a moment. "You're in competition with your brothers, aren't you?"

"Of course not!"

"The hell you're not. Somewhere deep inside you, you're afraid you don't measure up to them, that compared to them you're second-rate."

"You're crazy."

"No, I'm right. Listen, Sage, you're a Tyler through and through. You've got the same rugged stuff inside you that Chase and Lucky do. It's just packaged differently. You've got grit and guts and integrity. You're a decent human being, and you're certainly not lacking in looks, personality, or intelligence."

"Then why did I fail to get one measly contract? Only

a few people would even talk to me. Several laughed in my face when I explained why I wanted an appointment."

"You didn't fail," he said with emphasis. "You did everything you could. You left every morning dressed up fit to kill, looking professional but still feminine. You practiced your presentation until you got it letter-perfect. Hell, every time I listened to you deliver it, I was ready to sign on the dotted line myself."

"Then why didn't one of those prospects we called on sign?"

"Bad luck. Bad economy. Neither of which reflects on anything you did or didn't do. Even the best fishermen using the best bait can't catch a fish if the fish simply refuse to bite."

She derived some comfort from everything he said. Secretly, she was persuaded that she had done her best. Through co-ops and agricultural associations she had gleaned a list of prospective clients. Together Harlan and she had systematically called on them. Their efforts had produced nothing, not even a prospect with good potential. She had done everything she had known to do.

She couldn't blame their lack of success on Harlan either. He had surprised her by wearing a necktie every-day. His explanation of the mechanism was articulate and thorough. He easily won the confidence of everyone they spoke to. People seemed instinctively to trust his opinion on a variety of subjects. He was a good ol' boy with a lot of smarts and a charm that wasn't cloying.

People liked him and he liked people. Very much like Laurie, he accepted people as they were and expected them to do the same regarding him. He made friends wherever they went. His need to develop friendships no doubt arose from his lack of a family.

But for all Harlan's affability, they were still leaving the valley empty-handed. It was their rotten luck that the farmers and fruit growers were suffering their own setback due to unseasonable freezes the previous year. The agricultural business was no healthier than the oil industry. The growers were worried about making ends meet this year. None was inclined to make an investment and increase his overhead, no matter how receptive he was to the product.

"Everybody agreed that we've got a terrific idea," Harlan reminded her now.

"Try paying bills with a terrific idea."

He hissed a curse. "So what do you want me to do? Take the next exit and head for east Texas? Are you giving up?"

"No. Absolutely not. That's the Harlan Boyd method of doing things. When the situation gets tough, simply disappear. Wash your hands of it and walk away."

"What the hell do you know about Harlan Boyd's method of doing anything?"

"Well, isn't that so?" she shouted, rounding on him. "Why does putting down roots and making a home like a normal person scare you so much?" It was a rhetorical question, so she didn't even wait for a reply. "I'm different from you. I don't slink away from my problems."

"No, you either avoid them by telling half-truths or hide them behind a smart mouth and highfalutin manner."

She glowered at him, then turned her head and stared out her window. The fields they passed were lying fallow. The dried, dead stubble of last year's crops lay in the furrows, waiting to be plowed under in spring.

Cultivation reminded her of irrigation, and irrigation reminded her of Harlan's invention, which could be the salvation of Tyler Drilling, at least until the oil business recovered. When it did—and she believed that it would— her brothers might turn the entire irrigation business over to her. It could be a subsidiary of the original company.

Before her imagination could run away with her, she bitterly reminded herself that their money was about to run out. Then she would have to return home not only defeated but penniless as well.

How long could Harlan and she stay together without murdering each other? The alternative was to make love again, and that was just as prohibitive. Some of her tears, she acknowledged now, stemmed from sexual frustration.

The closer their quarters, the more standoffish they were. The smaller the room, the wider the berth they gave each other. That avoidance hadn't been her choice. She'd taken her cues from him.

He hadn't kissed her since that night at the Dairy Queen. He didn't even hint that he might like to waste one of the beds in their double rooms. Their conversations revolved around the business at hand and lacked the double entendre teasing she had thought she despised but now missed. She was confused and disappointed.

Why hadn't he made one single pass in two weeks? Was he already preparing her for the day he would walk out of her life as unexpectedly as he had stepped into it?

Miserable over the thought, Sage propped her elbow on the ledge of the window and supported her chin with her palm as she gazed through the window at the passing landscape.

On the outskirts of Waco, they passed an extremely green, well-manicured field. There was pedestrian traffic on it and little white carts scurrying about. Triangular flags on skinny, swaying poles seemed to wave at her to get her attention.

She sat bolt upright. "Golf."

Chapter FOURTEEN

"*P*ardon?"

"Golf. Golf. *Golf*."

Harlan looked beyond her toward the golf course. "You want to stop and play a few holes?"

"Harlan, we've been fishing in the wrong fishing hole." In her excitement, she reached across the seat and gripped his thigh. "We've got the right bait, but we're not casting it in the right waters."

His blue eyes lit up with sudden understanding. "Golf courses."

"Yes. And . . . and planned communities where there's a golf course and homesites and lots of landscaped grounds."

"Upscale retirement communities."

"Health care facilities."

"Multidimensional industrial parks."

"Yes!" Unbuckling her seat belt, she launched herself against him, throwing her arms around his neck and noisily kissing his cheek. "We should be calling on property developers, not farmers. We need to see investors and contractors, movers and shakers."

"Do you want to head back to Houston?"

"Not particularly. Why?"

"Belcher. He would be a source."

She contemplated the suggestion for a moment, before vetoing it. "He's on the fringes. I want to go to the sources. Besides, I don't want to risk bumping into him after Lucky and Chase said their piece. My gut instinct tells me it was profane."

"I imagine your gut instinct is right. Then, where to?"

"Dallas."

"Why Dallas?"

"Because it's an expanding city with lots of areas just like we've been talking about."

"So's San Antonio. And Austin."

"But we're closer to Dallas, and it's closest to Milton Point. We can be there in a couple of hours."

Her excitement was contagious. With his easy grin, he said, "Buckle your seat belt," and depressed the accelerator.

He got them to Dallas in under two hours. While she was admiring the silver, mirrored skyline, he shocked her by pulling into the porte cochere of a hotel that outclassed the ones they'd been staying in by a million miles.

"What are we doing here?"

"I think we need to treat ourselves."

"You mean by staying here?"

"You're the treasurer. Can we afford it?"

"Probably not, but let's splurge," she said, her eyes dancing at the prospect.

"Let's eat at a fancy restaurant tonight. Cloth napkins, matching silverware, the works. Maybe go to the movies or something."

"Oh, yes, Harlan, yes. I can't wait."

"But tomorrow it's back to the salt mines, Cinderella," he cautioned.

"Now that we have a new plan of attack, I can't wait for that either."

"So I guess I grew up believing that I meant no more to my brothers than one of their sports balls, something to play with and kick around."

Her mood was reflective as Sage stared into the candle burning in the center of the small portable table. The hotel room was a palace compared to some they had recently occupied. In-room movies were available on the television set. The room-service menu was extensive.

The quarters had offered so many amenities that they opted to stay in. They were road-weary. Relaxing in the room had held much more appeal than dressing up and going out. They'd eaten a four course dinner served in their room. Now they were lingering over chocolates and coffee.

"I don't really feel competitive with them, Harlan. I just want them to recognize me as an essential part of the family and our business. I want to be more than their kid sister, the brat."

"I can understand your point." He peeled the gold foil off a disk of semisweet chocolate and placed it in his mouth to melt slowly. "But you've got to realize, Sage, that you'll always be the baby of the family, just like Chase will always be the oldest."

"This sounds like first year psychology."

"It is," he admitted on a short laugh. "I took it as an elective at A&M."

"Then your observations aren't based on personal experience?"

"No."

"No brothers or sisters?"

"No."

She fiddled with the slivers of bright foil she had removed from her own chocolates. She weighed the advisability of prying, but knew that if she didn't, he wouldn't voluntarily divulge anything about his past.

"I know your home life must have been rough, Harlan." She glanced at him across the candle's flame. His face remained impassive. "You don't have to tell me about it if you don't want to." She paused again, providing him an opportunity he didn't capitalize on.

"I don't want to."

She was disappointed that she hadn't yet won his confidence, but covered it by saying, "I'm sorry you had to bear the brunt of it alone. My family is my foundation. I can't imagine a childhood without my parents and boisterous brothers."

"You drew a lucky lot."

"I know," she conceded softly. "As aggravating as they can be, I love them very much."

"They love you too." Propping his forearms on the edge of the table, he leaned forward and drawled, "What's not to love?"

By the time she had finally left her long, hot bubble bath, their dinner had arrived. Rather than let it get cold, Harlan had insisted that she come to the table with her hair still wet, sans makeup, and wrapped in her no-frills terrycloth robe.

Now, as his eyes took a leisurely tour of her, he reached for her hand and pulled her to her feet, drawing her around the table toward him. He spread his knees wide and maneuvered her to stand between them.

Loosely clasping her hands at her sides, he nuzzled the spot where the lapels of her robe overlapped. "You smell good."

Her insides began to hum. After two weeks without so much as a mild flirtation, his touch was as shocking as an electric current. Still, she didn't want him to believe he could have her easily. Did he think all he had to do was crook his finger and she would come running?

"Harlan, what are you doing?"

"If you'd shut up long enough, I'd like to seduce you."

"That's not a good idea. You agreed to keep our relationship strictly business. And about what happened before, Harlan, I don't want you to think—"

" 'Bout the only thing wrong with you is that you talk too damn much."

He didn't stop her mouth with a kiss, but with a signal from his eyes that was just as potent. When she stared down into that smoldering gaze, the protests died on her lips, her insides turned to marshmallow, and her carefully arranged resolves scattered. He continued holding the stare as he untied the knot at her waist and parted the robe.

"Damn, Sage," he said when his hands slipped inside, "if I'd've known you were naked underneath this, I wouldn't have dawdled over my supper."

With his hands at her waist, he drew her forward and planted his open mouth in the very center of her torso. Her flesh jumped beneath the damp contact with his tongue. Reflexively, she rested her hands on his shoulders for support. She gripped them hard when he kissed first one nipple, then the other, idly flicking them with the tip of his tongue.

Sage moaned and almost lost her balance. He came to

his feet and caught her, holding her against his chest. "Unfasten my jeans."

His whispered urgency didn't induce her to hurry. Rather, she hesitated before timidly reaching for his fly. The top snap was easy. The buttons gave her some difficulty, especially since he was kneading her breasts and making love to her mouth with his chocolate-flavored tongue. He grunted with pleasure whenever her knuckles bumped against the rigid flesh behind the soft denim. Finally the last button was undone. She withdrew her hands.

"Thanks," he said, sighing his relief. "Will you take my shirt off, too, please?"

He had showered before she claimed the bathroom for her bubble bath. He had emerged dressed in the worn jeans that his lean body seemed made for and a white cotton T-shirt, stretched tight across his broad chest and shoulders.

Now, through the cloth, she could see that his nipples were distended. The sight of his bare chest never failed to elicit a response from deep inside her. She took hold of the bottom of his T-shirt and worked it up over the firm muscles, over the pelt of tawny hair, and pulled it over his head. His hair fell back into place, looking sexily mussed. Several strands dipped low over his brows.

"That's much better," he whispered as he drew her into an embrace that brought their bare torsos together.

The kiss lasted an eternity and gave Sage a mighty appetite for more of him. She moved against his chest, delighting in the tickling sensation of his body hair against her smooth skin. The contact aroused her nipples. He noticed it immediately and caressed them lightly, first with his fingertips, then with his lips, which continued to wander down her body.

He sat down in the chair again and kissed her belly, her navel, each prominent hipbone. Pulling back, he studied the patch of down between her thighs for several moments before letting his fingers play with it.

Sage's breathing and heart rate escalated. Everything grew dark around her, as though her peripheral vision were shrinking in scope until all that was highlighted were Harlan and her and the glow of the single candle.

When his lips touched that springy nest, she uttered a low groan and dug her fingers into his hair. The pleasure she derived from his sweet kisses was so exquisite it was almost unbearable.

Harlan dropped to his knees. Gently he separated the soft flesh with the pads of his thumbs, then did something wonderful to her with his mouth.

Her soft cry was one of desire mixed with doubt. Sensations, unlike any she'd felt before, skyrocketed up through her body into her head. And while they made her wildly ecstatic, the magnitude of the ecstasy frightened her.

She backed away from him and threw herself face-down across one of the double beds, burying her face in the pillow. Her fingers gripped the bedding because the sensations wouldn't stop. One by one, the aftershocks rippled through her. She couldn't stop making that breathy, choppy sound.

The mattress sank beneath Harlan's weight as he lay down beside her. He laid his hand on the back of her head. "What's wrong, Sage? What are you afraid of?"

She rolled to her back, still breathless, still flushed, still overwhelmed. But her pride was at stake. "I'm not afraid of anything."

"Then why didn't you let yourself climax?"

Embarrassed, she turned her head away. He caught her beneath the chin and brought it back around. "You were shimmering. You were on the brink. I could feel it. Why didn't you go with it?" His eyes demanded an answer.

"It startled me," she replied huskily.

"Didn't you and Travis ever make love like that?"

The thought was as appalling as it was unappealing. Vehemently, she shook her head no.

"That man's either an idiot or a fairy," he mumbled. "Why didn't you ever make love with Travis, Sage? With any man? I'm sure plenty have tried."

"Yes, plenty have tried."

"Then why?"

"I don't know, Harlan. Don't badger me about it."

He cupped her head between his hands. "Listen to

me. I've been struggling to keep myself decent around you for two weeks. It hasn't been easy. Just about everything you do, everything you say, each toss of your head and smile and expression makes me hard as all get out. Now, dammit, I think that entitles me to the answer to one simple question."

Sage was still very aroused herself. His erotic words didn't help her arousal subside. "It's not a *simple* question, Harlan. It's complex. I don't even know the answer myself."

"I've got a good guess. You didn't give a guy a chance to make love to you because you were afraid of being disappointing to your partner and disappointed yourself."

She gaped at him incredulously. "Where do you come up with this stuff?"

"You'd heard all the tales about your brothers' successes with women. You knew you couldn't compete in the romance department unless you turned into a bonafide slut."

"Talk about a double standard!"

"You're right. It stinks. But that's the way it is. So you decided that sex was one arena in which you wouldn't even try and be as good as they are."

"I have never even thought such drivel."

"I'm sure you haven't. It's all subconscious, but it's there. Well, listen to me." His hands increased their pressure around her head. He leaned over her, sliding one leg between hers, the denim feeling—impossibly—rough and soft at the same time.

"There's no one here but you and me, Sage. I haven't got a score card. You don't have to prove one damn thing to me. I already know you're sexy. I already know you make me hot and hard. I already know you'd burn, too, if you'd only let yourself.

"But if you say no, that's okay, too. I won't make any judgments one way or the other. You know I want you in the worst way, but it's up to you. What's it going to be? What do you want?"

"I want—" She faltered, unable to continue.

"What? Say what you were thinking. For once just be Sage, the woman, without worrying about what is expected of Sage Tyler, daughter to Bud and Laurie, and younger sister to Chase and Lucky."

She took several hard breaths, then said in a rush, "I want you to touch me."

"Where?"

"Everywhere."

"Be specific."

"You mean say the words?"

"I mean say the words."

She did. His eyes turned dark with sexual intensity.

"And?" he rasped.

"When you kiss me . . ."

"Yeah?"

"Be thorough with my mouth. Eat it up like it was your last meal."

"Sounds good so far," he whispered thickly. "Go on."

Sensuality pumped through her veins like a powerful narcotic. Her nerves were exposed and tingling deliciously. She felt high, exuberant, and marvelously alive.

"I want to run my hands all over your beautiful body. I want to hold you against me and squeeze the breath out of you. I want you to be inside me again, Harlan."

He whistled softly. "For a beginner, you talk damn good sex, Miss Sage."

Their first fiery kiss prompted her to put her brave words into action. She slid her hands into the seat of his jeans and cupped his buttocks.

Making a low, hungry sound, Harlan rolled to his side and shoved down his jeans, then kicked them off. His chest was rapidly rising and falling with each breath, but he left the next move to her.

Her eyes detailed his body. Curiously she touched his nipple with her fingernail. Harlan sucked in a sharp breath and held it but still didn't rush her.

She lowered her head to his chest and pressed her mouth over the projected bud, then pushed her tongue against it. He murmured her name and buried his fingers in her hair. She surrendered to every whim and brought to life the fantasies that she had been secretly entertaining for weeks. Her mouth danced across his chest, kissing randomly, nipping playfully, licking lightly, sucking softly.

The more she tasted, the greedier she became. Kneeling beside him, she rested her hands on the tops of his thighs and kissed her way over his ribs. She dipped her tongue into the fuzzy mystery of his navel.

He gasped her name repeatedly and knotted her hair around his fingers.

She nuzzled her face in the musky warmth surrounding his sex and glanced the smooth tip with her lips, then returned several times.

"I'm dying, baby," he moaned, dragging her up and sealing their mouths together around a wild, ravenous kiss. She ground her hips against his hardness. He lifted his head and hung it low over hers. "We've got to slow it down. We don't have to go this fast unless the hotel catches on fire. I don't want to hurt you again."

"You won't. Please, Harlan. Now."

For all her urgency, his entry was slow and gentle, yet firm. "You're so wet." He sighed, sinking into her. "Lord, you feel good."

"So do you."

They smiled at each other as he pressed even deeper. "Can you feel that?"

"Hmm, yes."

"And that?"

Closing her eyes, she murmured an incoherent yes.

"Good. Good. Now, draw your knees back. That's it. Ah, Sage."

In moments, he forgot to take his own advice against unnecessary haste. Sage didn't remind him, but eagerly met each of his thrusts. Emptying her mind of all else, she reveled in the thrilling sensations, returned them, relished each new one.

She drew him into her with her body and mind and soul until she couldn't tell that they were separate individuals.

When her extremities began to tingle in a way she now recognized, she didn't fight it, but clasped Harlan tighter. All her concentration centered on their joined bodies, on the friction and the heat and his pulsing, giving motions, until she dissolved in the sweetness and light of their mutual release.

Several minutes later, he would have slipped away from her. She whispered, "Don't go."

Without compromising their intimacy, he rolled to his side, bringing her with him until they lay face-to-face. "You talked me into staying."

Their smiling lips came together in a chaste, soft kiss before she nestled her face in his neck.

"Harlan?"

"Hmm?"

"Thanks."

"My pleasure."

She smiled against his warm skin. "Harlan?"

"Hmm?"

"Nothing. I was just saying your name out loud."

Drawing a deep, contented sigh, she closed her eyes and drifted to sleep.

*   *   *

The following morning when she came bustling through the door, he was lying on his back in bed with his hands stacked beneath his head.

"Well, you're finally awake," she said with a happy smile.

"Where'd you go? I was getting worried."

"I woke up early, simply bursting with energy. I waited for you to wake up, but when you didn't, I went out for donuts and scalding, black coffee just the way you like it."

She set the two white paper sacks on the table that was still littered with their dinner dishes and the candle which had burned down sometime during their night of lovemaking. They had napped and reawakened to make love so many times, Sage had lost count.

Moving to the bed now, she bent over him and kissed his forehead, where strands of pale hair lay, then his lips. Taking a corner of the sheet between her thumb and fingertip, she raised it and took a peek underneath. "Why, Harlan, you're naked! How uncouth."

"Is that a fifty-cent word for horny?"

"You went to college. You know what uncouth means."

"And you know what horny means. Come here." Snarling playfully, he grabbed her wrists and pulled her down over him. She put up only token resistance before melting on top of him, letting her body's softness conform to the hard strength of his.

"Again?" she whispered seductively. "I thought doing it too much could make you go blind."

"You only go blind if you don't do it enough."

"Oh, my. Well, we can't let that happen, can we?" she said, meshing her mouth with his.

Between fervent kisses, she wrestled out of her clothing until she lay stretched atop him, touching skin to skin, hairy to smooth, male to female. She registered momentary surprise when he slid his hands over her derriere onto the backs of her thighs and parted them, lifting her up slightly to straddle his lap.

"I don't know what to do," she told him with genuine anxiety.

"Yes, you do."

"Like this?" She executed a movement that made his eyes glaze.

"Yeah," he struggled to say, "exactly like that."

When it was over, she lay upon his chest, panting like the victim of a shipwreck washed ashore.

He folded his arms across the small of her back. His expression was soft and full of affection. "Who needs fantasies with you around, Sage?"

"You've fulfilled all of mine, too."

"All?"

"Well, there is one . . ."

He grabbed a double handful of her hair and lifted her head off his chest. "Well?"

"Can I wash your back in the shower?"

A slow grin spread across his sexy face. "Miss Sage, you can wash whatever your little heart desires."

*   *   *

Sage emerged from the bathroom first, leaving him to shave. Humming to herself, she collected her discarded clothes from around the bed and dressed again. She was removing the lids from Styrofoam cups of coffee when Harlan came out of the bathroom, hiking his jeans up over his hips.

"I'm afraid the coffee got cold," she apologized, handing him a cup.

"It was worth it. I'd rather have hot sex than hot coffee anytime."

She purred coyly. "I do believe you would."

He kissed her before taking a sip of the lukewarm coffee.

"The donuts are still fresh," she told him. "Have one."

She poked one into his mouth. He took a bite, then used the donut to gesture toward a pile of papers scattered across the table. "What's all that?"

"Before I went out, I skimmed the local business magazine we picked up in the lobby when we checked in. There were some impressive success stories in it, so I started compiling a list of potential clients."

"Very good," he said with approval as his eyes ran down her handwritten list.

With something close to idolatry, Sage was dreamily assessing his face when she saw his eyes fix on one of the names. He stopped his vigorous chewing and held the bite of donut in his mouth for several seconds before swallowing it.

"Strike the next to the last name." Abruptly, he tossed down the sheet of paper.

Sage picked up the sheet and read the name. "What have you got against Hardtack and Associates?"

"What difference does one name make? You've got another dozen companies listed there."

She looked at him with perplexity. Having set aside his coffee and the remainder of the donut, he was moving around the room restlessly, snatching things up, then setting them down just as quickly. She had never seen him behave this way. He was acting as testy as a caged animal.

"Harlan? Why has that one name upset you so much?"

"I'm not upset."

"Don't lie to me," she cried. "I can see that you are. Do you know something about Grayson Hardtack that I should be aware of?"

"Drop it, okay? Scratch his name off your list and everything will be all right. Just omit his name."

"Without a full explanation of why I should? Not hardly. According to the article about him, he's got a finger in every juicy pie in this city. He's exactly the kind of client we need."

He spun around to face her, his hands on his hips, his features taut and belligerent. "Save yourself the trouble. Hardtack wouldn't give you the time of day if he knew I was working with you. Believe it."

"Why?"

"That's my business."

"Do you two have an ax to grind?"

"You could say that."

"What kind of ax? What was the quarrel over?"

"Drop it, Sage."

"What kind of quarrel did you have with Hardtack?" she repeated insistently.

He gnawed on his lower lip for a moment. When he made up his mind to answer her, he spoke tersely. "For a while, I had something that belonged to him."

She gave the words plenty of time to sink in, but their meaning remained unclear. "You mean you stole something from him?"

Supremely agitated over her persistence, he raked his fingers through his hair. "I asked you to drop it."

"Not until I get an answer from you, Harlan. What did you have that belonged to Hardtack?"

His blue eyes turned brittle and cold. "His wife."

Chapter
FIFTEEN

*S*age nervously thumbed through the magazine without retaining a single word printed on any of the glossy pages. The suite of executive offices at Hardtack and Associates, Incorporated, was austere and ultramodern, decorated mostly in black and gray, with touches of maroon.

She glanced at Grayson Hardtack's secretary. The woman gave her another plastic smile. "I'm sure it won't be much longer, Ms. Tyler."

Her carefully outlined magenta lips barely moved. A gale wind wouldn't have disturbed a single lacquered strand of hair, which perfectly matched the color of the gray wall behind her.

"Thank you."

Sage was as jumpy as a cat. At any second she expected Harlan to come crashing through the black-lacquered doors and accuse her of double-crossing him. Because that was exactly what she was doing, she was all the jumpier.

After their argument two days before when he had dropped his bombshell about Hardtack's wife, they checked out of the luxury hotel and moved to one within their budget. Even though that budget was almost exhausted, Sage had rented her own room. She'd spent most of that day locked inside it, alone.

Hours of self-flagellation were behind the decision she had finally reached: She must put her personal feelings aside. The task she had chosen for herself had to take priority. Having arrived at that conclusion, she had marched to the door of Harlan's room and knocked.

He hadn't rushed to open it. In fact, he'd been deliberately slow about it. He pulled the door open, braced himself against the doorjamb, and waited her out, forcing her to speak first.

"I made some calls," she began coldly. "We have appointments with these people tomorrow morning." She slapped a list of names into his hand. He glanced through the list. Hardtack and Associates wasn't on it.

"Fine."

"Then you're still interested in working with me on this project?" she asked stiffly.

"You're the one who has spent hours sulking, not me."

"It just came as a shock that you had been involved with another man's wife."

He rolled his eyes and gave her a retiring look that made her furious. How dare he put her on the defensive? She wasn't the one who had an unsavory and suspicious past.

"That has no bearing on the here and now, on us," he said.

"You're wrong, Harlan. Everything in one's background is vitally important and relevant. Our pasts are what make us what we are."

He sadly shook his head. "If you believe that, then I'm not the guy for you, Sage."

In a matter of seconds, she recalled everything they had done together in bed, everything he had taught her to do, his coaching on how to draw the maximum pleasure from them both. The heat of embarrassment had made her face red, but she kept her eyes cool.

"How convenient for you to realize that now that I've already gone to bed with you."

She had stalked away and spent the night alone and miserable in her room, already missing him in her bed and hating herself and him because of it. During their appointments over the next couple of days, they behaved civilly toward each other and successfully suppressed the animosity between them. Each performed his part of the presentation as before.

From most of the vice presidents in charge of this or

that, they received a polite brush-off. They agreed to keep Tyler Drilling in mind and contact them at some unspecified point in the future, which would doubtfully ever come.

After another disappointing meeting that morning, they had returned to the motel at noon feeling disheartened and dejected. She had told Harlan, "Unless you need to go somewhere, I'd like to take the car this afternoon and see if I can find a place to have my hair and nails done."

He was instantly alert. "You always do them yourself."

"They're beginning to look like it." His eyes were as sharp as rapiers. She tried to keep her expression bland.

"Fine with me," he said at last. Before he left the car, however, he reached into the back seat and retrieved the portfolio carrying all his designs.

"G'bye."

"Bye."

Sage was blocks away before she reached beneath the front seat and removed the folder of copies she had made a week earlier while she'd had access to his portfolio. The drawings had to be greatly reduced in size, but were still legible. If Harlan decided to split, she didn't want to be left with nothing. Due to the most recent development, she was glad she had taken the precaution.

Luckily that hadn't been the only precaution taken that she now felt relief over. Harlan had been efficient and unobtrusive, but each time they'd made love, he'd protected her from getting pregnant.

Thinking about his sweet, passionate lovemaking brought tears to her eyes, which she blinked away before Hardtack's formidable secretary could see them.

It had come as no surprise to Sage that Harlan had been involved with other women. He received more than his share of smoldering come-ons and nonverbal invitations.

Everywhere they went, Sage was aware of the restless attention he generated in females. One of his disarming smiles could fluster an efficient cashier. One penetrating look could turn a cantankerous waitress into Miss Congeniality. One flirtatious wink could make even the most average-looking woman smile as radiantly as a beauty queen. Harlan Boyd definitely had an effect on the ladies.

Apparently Mrs. Grayson Hardtack was no exception.

Harlan had had an affair with her, probably while he was working for Hardtack. Hardtack had found out about it and all hell had broken loose. Sage was surmising, of course, but she was confident that his involvement with them was something like that.

What really hurt was that Harlan still felt hostile about it. Whatever had brewed between Mrs. Hardtack and him was still brewing as far as he was concerned.

Did he still care for the woman? If he didn't, why had he become so vexed? He could have laughed and said,

"You'd better go on that appointment alone, Sage. See, Mrs. Hardtack wasn't very discreet about her infidelities. Hardtack got sore and, well, you understand these things."

But he hadn't dismissed it as a fleeting affair without emotional entanglements. He had paced and flapped around like a marionette worked by an uncoordinated puppeteer. His personality had undergone a drastic change. For him to have behaved that irrationally, the affair must have been left unresolved.

How many affairs of the heart did Harlan have in his past that had been left unresolved? Dozens? Scores? Whatever the number, add one, Sage thought with biting self-criticism.

He had said he was a professional troubleshooter. She was just another problem he had spotted. She was a frustrated virgin whose ego had been badly bruised and was in desperate need of sexual awakening. If she had taken out a personal ad, she couldn't have publicized her problem more clearly.

Harlan, having the equipment and skill to solve her problem, had responded to her silent advertisement. He had introduced her to her own sexuality and released her from being uptight about expressing it. Now that she had demonstrated just how unrestrained she could be in bed, he would consider her problem solved and go on his merry way, ready to tackle another's dilemma.

She wondered if he would tell her good-bye, notify

her of his leaving. Or would she just wake up one morning and find him gone? Probably the latter. She couldn't envision him in a sad, tearful farewell scene. However it happened, it was going to break her heart.

She had fallen in love with the jerk.

"Ms. Tyler?"

She jumped and snapped to attention. "Yes?"

"Mr. Hardtack will see you now."

"Thank you."

She gathered her handbag and folder from the sofa and followed the secretary across an acre of polished marble floor, through a floor-to-ceiling door, into Hardtack's inner sanctum.

Its austerity was marginally relieved by Oriental rugs forming islands of pricelessness on the floor. A wall of windows afforded a spectacular view of the Dallas skyline. Having done her homework, Sage knew which of the buildings belonged to Hardtack. The immensity of his wealth and power intimidated her for a moment. What was she doing in this temple of commerce?

Well why not, a small voice argued back. Family pride asserted itself. She was a Tyler. The Tylers were as good as anybody.

Squaring her shoulders, she approached his desk and extended her hand. A graying, robust man, impeccably dressed in a business suit, partially rose from his chair and shook her hand across his desk.

"Hello, Mr. Hardtack. I'm Sage Tyler. Thank you for seeing me this afternoon on such short notice."

"Sit down, Ms. Tyler." While Sage was taking her seat, his secretary passed him a note card. He referred to it, then nodded at her. She soundlessly withdrew. "You told my assistant that you had to see me about something urgent and personal."

Hardtack was a man in his late fifties, with a wide chest and expansive belly, although it was more muscle than fat. His nose was large and bulbous and had the ruddiness of a man who enjoyed several bourbons spaced at intervals throughout the day. He had a quelling habit of peering from beneath his bushy gray eyebrows.

Sage, shocked by her own temerity, stated boldly, "I lied, Mr. Hardtack. I came here to sell you something."

He was taken aback by her candor. He studied her for a moment. Then he readjusted himself in his leather chair and, folding his hands over his stomach, chuckled softly. "Well, you've got guts, Ms. Tyler, I'll say that. What are you peddling? Has my subscription to *TV Guide* run out?"

Unsure how long his good humor would last, she gave him a tentative smile and spread open the folder on the edge of his desk.

"I want to acquaint you with a new sprinkler and irrigation system. I have the designs here."

He didn't even glance at Harlan's drawings. He didn't look at anything except the space between her eyes.

"Ms. Tyler, I'm a busy man. I've got an army of employees who handles that kind of thing for me."

"I'm well aware of that," she said quickly, sensing that he was about to toss her out. "But I've been seeing vice presidents and young executives for weeks. They're much more interested in staying within their present budgets than making an investment. None wants to rock the corporate boat in these troubled times, so no decisions are made.

"This time I thought I'd come straight to the top man, the one who signs the checks and ultimately makes the decisions anyway. I'm tired of being shunted from one subordinate to another."

For several ponderous moments, he stared at her, then he checked his wristwatch and said, "You've got five minutes." She pushed the folder toward him while hyping the sterling reputation of Tyler Drilling. A few seconds into her spiel, he interrupted her. "I'm familiar with your family's reputation in the oil business. Tell me what you're selling and why I should buy it."

"Have you awarded a contract for the sprinkler and irrigation system at Shadow Hills?"

Land-clearing had just gotten underway for the planned community several miles north of Dallas. Sage had read that, when it was completed, it would encompass several square miles, would have one eighteen-hole golf course, a nine-hole course, a polo field, a landing strip, a shopping area, a ritzy country club, as well as obscenely expensive homesites.

"Not to my knowledge," he told her.

"I would appreciate the chance to bid on the contract. We've got precisely what you need."

"Do you have references? Who else is using your system?"

"No one. If you buy it, you'll be our first customer."

She didn't want to commence her career with a lie. Even if she were so inclined, Hardtack would find out. She met him eye-to-eye, waiting for him to say he wasn't interested and signal for his secretary to usher her out.

Instead, he said, "I'm still listening."

Swiftly regurgitating everything she had heard Harlan tell their prospective clients, she explained the mechanics. "We can install above-ground sprinklers as well as lay underground systems. And we can do it a lot cheaper than any competitor because we've got the supplies, the pipes and pumps that went out of use when the oil market collapsed."

He studied the drawings for much longer than she would have dared hope. In fact, he studied each one at length. Without raising his head, he addressed her from beneath his brows. "Who did these drawings?"

"Our designer," she replied evasively. "My brothers will be in charge of all the installation and operation."

"Hmm."

Although she was curious to know if Hardtack would react as violently to the mention of Harlan's name as Harlan had to his, she didn't dare risk it. Hardtack was too excellent a prospect to take the gamble. A single contract with him could lead to many. He could lend Tyler Drilling's new enterprise more credibility than anyone.

That had been her primary reason for wanting to meet with him personally. The other had been that she wanted to see the betrayed husband.

"I'm keeping these," he said abruptly, stacking the drawings together.

"F-fine," she stammered. She would have to see that Harlan filed for a patent immediately.

"I'd like to look them over more carefully and speak with the project supervisor."

"Certainly."

"How can I get in touch with you?"

Her heart was knocking. After so many dismissals, she didn't trust her ears. "Then you're interested?"

"I'll be honest with you. A sprinkler system for Shadow Hills isn't one of the pressing problems on my mind right now. Someone within this corporation, an employee I don't even know by name, could buy one from a thousand different sources—"

"But none with our unique—"

"Save the sales pitch. I've heard it." He aimed his index finger at her. "I'm offering you a piece of free advice. Learn when to keep your mouth shut, Ms. Tyler."

"Yes, sir," she said meekly. Someone else had told her recently that she talked too much.

"What I'm saying is that I'm not as interested in your product as I am in you. It took guts for you to walk in here today. I like to reward people who take chances. I also admire people who don't sling bull, but tell it straight the first time." He checked his watch. "You're thirty seconds over your time limit. Leave your phone number with my secretary. Good-bye."

"Good-bye and thank you."

She stood up and confidently shook his hand. But as she turned to leave, she drew up short. Mounted on the far wall, the one she had been sitting with her back to, was a photographic portrait of a beautiful woman.

Deep waves of blond hair framed her lovely face. She was dressed in a sapphire sequin ball gown that looked tailor-made for her perfect figure. She was standing in the curve of a winding staircase, her bejeweled hand resting negligently on the carved bannister. Precious stones twinkled at her ears and throat. She looked extremely well kept.

"Who is that?"

From behind her, Hardtack replied, "My wife Marian."

Marian. "She's beautiful."

"Yes, she is."

Sage gave him a shaky smile, then hastened from the

office. After stopping at the secretary's desk and providing her with the company telephone number in Milton Point, she departed.

On her way to the elevators, she would have been skipping down the corridor, singing at the top of her voice, doing a gleeful little jig, if Marian Hardtack hadn't been one of the most beautiful women she'd ever laid eyes on.

Grayson Hardtack watched the young woman leave his office. He allowed time for her exchange with his secretary before speaking to the secretary himself from the intercom system on his desk.

"Get me Harry downstairs, please."

"Yes, sir. You're three-thirty appointment is here. Shall I send him in?"

"Give me five minutes."

"Yes, sir."

While he waited, he stared fixedly at the portrait across the room. He wasn't kept waiting long. The caller identified himself as Harry, one of the plainclothes security guards who patrolled the high-tech headquarters of Hardtack and Associates.

"Harry, there should be a young woman coming down any minute. Blond. Black suit. Pretty. Good legs."

"I see her, sir. She just stepped off the elevator."

"Follow her for a few days. I'll get someone to cover

your shifts here. I want to know where she goes, who she sees, and any background information you can dig up. Report back to me within seventy-two hours."

"Yes, sir."

He paid his people well and hired only the best. Confident that his directive would be carried out thoroughly and with utmost secrecy, Hardtack resumed his study of the designs. He could swear they had been drawn by a draftsman whose work he knew.

When his secretary escorted in his next appointment, he was still frowning over the sheets scattered across his otherwise immaculate desk.

Chapter SIXTEEN

"*S*age is coming home tomorrow," Chase said.

Marcie glanced up from her unfinished plate of lasagna. She and Chase were having a quiet dinner at home. Jamie was sleeping in a portable bassinet nearby. "Did you hear from her?"

"She called this afternoon from Dallas."

"I thought they were in south Texas, somewhere in the valley."

"Nothing happened there. They made a U-turn and went to Dallas with a different marketing strategy in mind."

He recounted to Marcie what Sage had told him. "She's excited about it. After being there for several days, she's compiled a list of six potential clients that are more than 'maybes.'"

"Then she's done some great work!"

"I told her so."

Marcie gave him a wide smile. "Good, Chase. She needs to hear that from you. Did she mention Harlan?"

"She's called us—what?—three or four times since she's been gone. This is the first time she's brought his name into the conversation. She asked if Lucky and I were going to beat him up if he came back with her."

"All things considered, I believe that was a fair question."

Chase frowned. There had been disharmony between them ever since their argument two weeks earlier. "You can't blame us for defending our sister, Marcie. We would have done it for any female member of our family."

"I admire you for feeling protective of us. But that's not the point. The point is that if Sage went to bed with Harlan, she did it of her own free will and doesn't need 'defending.' Lucky didn't ask anyone's permission before he fell in love with Devon, even though she was married at the time, legally if not technically.

"Lucky was appalled when you told him you were going to marry me. At the time, you were in a fragile state of mind and still very much in love with Tanya. From his perspective, he was giving you a sound piece of advice. Instead, you followed your heart and married me anyway. You trusted your instincts over his.

"Hell or high water or your own stubborn pride couldn't have kept either of you from falling in love with the women you fell in love with. Why should Sage be any different? She's a Tyler, too. She knows her heart and mind better than anyone else does. You have no right to interfere."

"We just don't want her to be hurt."

"Neither do I. But if she is, you couldn't have prevented it no matter what you did." She pondered the contents of her wineglass for a moment. "Do you think the incident with Harlan was isolated, or are they still sleeping together?"

"I got the feeling today that they haven't been. She referred to 'Harlan's room.' Whenever she mentioned him, it was in a business context."

"Hmm."

"You sound disappointed. Do you really think anything could come of that, Marcie?"

"Stranger things have happened."

"Spoken like a woman," he muttered with exasperation. "What does your woman's intuition tell you about him?"

"That he's very intelligent, more than he lets on. He's not afraid of hard work."

"I mean where women are concerned."

"Ah, where women are concerned." She steepled her index fingers and tapped her lips. "Well, as Devon said, much to Lucky's aggravation, he's sexy and gorgeous." Her eyes wandered to Chase's glowering face. "But not as sexy and gorgeous as you."

"Go on," he muttered, somewhat mollified.

"I think he must have lived through something very painful. He's still running away from it. Something or someone hurt him terribly. That's why he always stays on the fringes of any close group. He's personable, but guarded. An observer, but not an actual participant."

"I've noticed that too. Do you think a woman hurt him?"

"One can only guess."

"What would you guess?"

"I'd guess a woman."

"I thought so," he said unhappily. "I hope he's not punishing the entire female population, including Sage Tyler, for what one rotten female did to him."

"It could go either way." Chase looked at her quizzically, so she expounded on her theory. "That kind of emotional pain can either result in extraordinary cruelty or extraordinary sensitivity. I can't imagine Harlan being cruel, can you?"

"No. But who knows? We might not have seen him at his worst."

"Possibly, but you're overlooking a clue into his character."

"What?"

"He was the one worried about making Sage pregnant, right? Didn't you tell me that he admitted sleeping with her before anyone even accused him of it? That doesn't sound like a man without scruples who's out to break a woman's heart."

"No, it doesn't. Jeez," he said, running a hand down his face, "I guess we can't do anything more than sit back and watch the cards fall."

"Now you're catching on."

"So anyway, back to business. Where was I? Oh yeah, Sage said today that Harlan wants to come back and actually install a system. He wants to work out all the bugs before we get an order. My little sister must be quite a saleswoman," he said, smiling fondly. "Who would have ever thought she could take off like that and pull it all together?"

"I did," Marcie remarked staunchly.

"It appears that our first sale is imminent. I hope to hell it is. For everybody's sake." He set aside his empty plate and picked up his glass of red wine. "I haven't forgotten our deal, Marcie."

"What deal is that?"

He wasn't fooled by her nonchalance. "The deal we made when we got married."

"Oh, that deal."

Whenever he brought up this subject, she craftily maneuvered the conversation around it. He wasn't going to let her do that this time. "You bailed us out, Marcie, and I haven't forgotten it. Without your money—"

"*Our* money. It became yours when we got married."

"It was your money. Money you worked hard to earn. I told you when we got married that I intended to pay back every red cent. So far, I haven't been able to. But if we land one of these big contracts that Sage was prattling about today, you'll get your money back."

Leaving her chair, she circled the table and sat down in his lap. "Do you think I care, Chase?"

"*I* care."

"Your integrity is admirable. It's just one of the millions of reasons why I love you. And always have. Ever since kindergarten."

She bent her head and kissed him meaningfully. When they finally pulled apart, she said softly, "The payoff on my investment has been tremendous, Chase. Look at all I got in return. A healthy, beautiful baby boy and a husband who loves me."

"Well, I'm your husband and I love you. Though sometimes I'm intimidated by your computer brain and totally baffled by your quirky logic."

"Think how bored you'd be otherwise."

"Bored? With you? Never." He slid his hands beneath her sweater. "Hmm. You always feel so warm and soft." Her breasts were heavy with milk. He fondled them gently. She kissed his ear, following the rim of it with the tip of her tongue. "Please, Marcie," he groaned. "Have pity. Cut it out."

"Are you getting hard?" she whispered teasingly.

"*Getting* hard? I've been miserable for weeks."

"Then don't you think it's time we did something about that?" She reached for his fly and unfastened it.

His eyes swung up to hers. "You mean . . . ?"

"Um-huh."

"Green light?"

She closed her hand around him and smiled seductively. "It doesn't get any greener than this."

"You look like the cat that just swallowed the canary," Lucky commented as his brother entered the office the following morning.

Chase was humming. His step was springy. He poured himself a cup of coffee from the automatic maker and turned with the cup raised in a toast. "To love and marriage."

Lucky laughed and raised his own coffee mug.

They hadn't yet finished their coffee when they heard a car pull up outside. Chase glanced through the window. "It's Sage and Harlan." He gave his younger brother a stern warning. "Stay cool."

Sage came in first, followed by Harlan, who looked reluctant and unsure. Sage gave Chase a hard hug. "It's so good to be home! Milton Point never looked so wonderful. I got a lump in my throat when we drove through downtown."

All her remarks so far had been addressed to Chase. She turned. "Hi, Lucky." Smiling and forgiving, she crossed the office and hugged him too. "How's your arm?"

"It's okay," he said laconically. His arm was still riding in a sling. "Good to have you back, brat."

Chase stepped forward and shook hands with Harlan who was still standing near the door. "Have some coffee."

"No thanks. We stopped a couple of times between here and Dallas." Warily, he looked at Lucky, then moved toward him. "I'm sorry as hell about your arm. I didn't want anything like that to happen."

"I threw the first punch, but I figured you had it coming."

"Well you figured wrong," Sage said, intervening before tempers began to fly again. "Can we please forget all about it? We've got much more to deal with than my personal relationship with Harlan and whatever ramifications it might have." Bashfully, she added, "You'll all be greatly relieved to know that I'm not pregnant. Now, shall we talk shop?"

"Sounds like a good idea," Chase said, drawing up a chair for her. "Show us what you've got."

For the next hour, she filled them in on the results of their trip, detailing their failures as well as their successes.

"Harlan and I are convinced that this is our market."

"These are the people with the money," he contributed. "Even if they don't have it, they know how to get it from people who put together deals."

Glancing over the list of potential clients, Lucky whistled. "These are the head hogs at the trough, all right. I'm impressed."

"For a while there, it was looking grim," Harlan admitted. "We weren't getting anywhere with anybody.

Then, the day before yesterday—wasn't it, Sage?—things started turning around. The folks we contacted began listening and were much more receptive."

She tugged on a strand of her hair. "It was getting rid of the split ends that did it."

"You lost me," Chase said, looking befuddled.

"Inside joke." She waved her hand as though clearing the air. "All the companies on this list are ripe for a follow-up call. Our next step is to have a lawyer draw up a standard contract, so that if we do get a call, we'll be prepared to negotiate. Before leaving Dallas, I had Harlan file a patent application."

"Under whose name?"

Harlan's spine stiffened as he aimed a hard look at Lucky. "Tyler Drilling Company. I may be a despoiler of young women, but I'm not an embezzler."

"Just checking."

Chase held up his right hand in a gesture of peace. "Relax, you two." He turned to Harlan. "How do we stand on the machinery itself?"

"I'd like to lay some pipe and give it several run-throughs. I know that pump will work, but we should have one setup in case somebody wants to see it in operation. 'Course it still needs a timer that can be computed—"

"Lucky can help you with that," Chase said. "Tell him, Lucky."

"While you were gone, I scouted out several possibilities. Turns out that an old buddy of mine just got into the computer business. He's real hungry right now and eating his overhead. I think we can swing a good deal with him if we buy in volume."

"Fantastic!" Sage exclaimed.

"Meanwhile," Chase said to Harlan, "several of the old crew are on standby and chomping at the bit to go to work. We've got a few cleared acres out at the ranch you can play on. Just tell us when you're ready, and I'll show you where to dig."

"I'm ready, but I need transportation."

"Where's your pickup?"

"It expired in Austin," Sage told them as she stood up, zipping her portfolio closed. "We gave it a proper burial. Come on, Harlan, I'll drop you in town. Chase, who's Marcie's business attorney? I'd like to consult with him about a contract as soon as possible."

Chase wrote down the lawyer's name for Sage. They gave Harlan several tips on where he might find a dependable, but inexpensive, used pickup and warned him against the dealerships where he was certain to get ripped off. Then the brothers stood on the office porch and watched the couple drive away.

"She seems all right," Lucky remarked.

"Yeah, she seems fine."

"It took guts for him to come back with her."

"Hmm."

"You've gotta respect a man with that much character."

"As Marcie pointed out last night," Chase said, "we would never have known he'd slept with Sage if he hadn't told us himself."

"Unless she had gotten pregnant."

"Thank God that didn't happen."

"Thank God," Lucky repeated.

"They're talking strictly business now."

"Strictly business."

"I guess that whatever was between them is all over."

"Guess so."

They watched the car round the bend and drive out of sight.

"So," Lucky asked, "what do you really think?"

"I think they've got the hots for each other and are fighting it for all they're worth."

"Yeah," Lucky bleakly agreed, "that's what I think, too."

Harry, the security guard, entered Hardtack's office unannounced. It was early in the morning, before anyone else's business day had begun. His boss habitually arrived well before daylight, working at his desk while there was no one around to interrupt him. This was one interruption he wouldn't mind.

"What have you got?" Hardtack asked. He extended his hand to receive the envelope he expected the guard to have, which he did.

Hardtack pried open the metal brads and dumped the contents onto his desk. The guard was a lousy photographer, but the people he had captured on film were clearly identifiable. He had caught the couple several times, always together. Hardtack wasn't surprised by what he saw, but he was careful to screen his reaction from his employee.

"Are they lovers?" he asked.

"Tough to say, Mr. Hardtack. They shared a room at one hotel, then moved the next morning to another one. They had separate rooms there."

"Interesting. Go on."

"She paid their bills at both places in cash."

"Where are they now?"

"They left town yesterday morning. I followed them to Milton Point. They're both staying at the family home there."

"So she's legit?"

"Very." He summarized for his boss all the information he had gleaned about Tyler Drilling. It coincided with what Hardtack already knew.

"They've been having a rough time the last few years, but their reputation is above reproach. The number two son—they call him Lucky—had a run-in with federal agents a few years back. An arson charge."

Hardtack's head came up quickly. He glared at his employee from beneath his brows, demanding specifics. "Turned out to be a bum rap. The arsonists are in prison. Oldest son's first wife died in a car crash. It was an accident. Currently both are married with families.

"The girl in the picture has just earned a master's degree from the University of Texas, Austin. Never married. Involved for a while with a Travis Belcher from Houston. Affluent medical family. Nothing shady. Laurie Tyler, their mother, a widow for more than five years, recently married the county sheriff, an old family friend."

"Can't get much more respectable than that," Hardtack said with finality. The guard took his cue and began backing out of the room. "Thank you, Harry. I'm sure you made all your inquiries with discretion."

"Absolutely, sir."

"You'll be compensated and reimbursed for your expenses. See my secretary later in the day. As usual, I'll depend on your confidentiality."

"Sure thing, Mr. Hardtack."

Once the security guard had withdrawn, Grayson Hardtack studied the pictures more closely, spending several minutes pondering each one.

It was Harlan Boyd, all right, no mistaking that.

Had he sent the Tyler girl? Or was it a contrivance she had conceived? Was her intention to sell him a sprinkler system or blackmail him? What? Or was it all merely a bizarre coincidence? Was she totally innocent of the hornet's nest she had stirred up?

He raised his head and gazed at his wife's portrait

across the stately chamber. These unsettling questions needed answers he had to hear for himself. He couldn't send an emissary in his place. He would have to find out what was afloat, even if it resulted in an unpleasant confrontation.

Depressing a button on his panel telephone, he got an outside line and punched in a sequence of numbers. When the telephone on the other end was answered, he barked an order.

"I want the Learjet ready to fly to Milton Point first thing tomorrow morning."

Hanging up, he went back to studying the fuzzy photographs, particularly the handsome visage of the man who had broken his wife's heart.

Chapter SEVENTEEN

*S*age's horse limped toward the parked pickup. "Hi." She threw her leg over the saddle and dropped to the ground.

Harlan was sitting on his heels studying a connection in the pipe that had recently been laid. He pushed his hat back on his head and looked up at her. "What's up?"

"I was sent to get you. Somewhere along the way, I think my horse picked up a pebble." Using the caution she'd been taught, she stepped behind the gelding and raised his right rear hoof, securing it between her knees. "Hmm. Sure enough."

A small rock was caught between his hoof and the horseshoe. "I don't think I can get it out without the proper tool." She patted the horse's rump consolingly. "You'll have to give me a ride back," she told Harlan.

"No problem. It's quitting time anyway. Getting dark. I'll only be a minute."

While he applied a wrench to the faulty connection, she walked around the pickup, kicking the tires as she'd seen her brothers do, but having absolutely no idea what purpose was served by that strange, masculine maneuver.

"This wreck looks as bad as its predecessor," she observed out loud.

"Beats walking."

After tying her horse's rein to the bumper, she let down the rusty tailgate and hopped up on it to sit down and wait. It was a moderately mild evening. The sky had already turned dark enough to see the moon.

She removed her riding gloves and unbuttoned her jean jacket. Her horseback ride had loosened her ponytail. Wispy strands of hair drifted across her face with the merest hint of wind.

"Who sent you to get me?" Harlan stood up, peeled off his leather work gloves and slapped them against his thigh to knock the dirt off before tucking them into the hip pocket of his jeans. When he smiled at her, she was glad he didn't know about her secret interview with Hardtack.

Because his trailer was still parked behind a filling station in Austin, he was staying in the house. He and Lucky weren't yet to the backslapping stage, but were working at being friends again. Everyone's focus was on their common goal. Personal feelings had been temporarily suspended.

Well, not all personal feelings, she mentally amended. Harlan and she kept up a pretense of pure professionalism, but she remembered their lovemaking all too well. At night she tossed restlessly and sleeplessly and wondered if he found it just as impossible to sleep.

She hadn't deluded herself. He wouldn't be staying much longer. Once he drew his commission from their first contract, he would leave. Money meant nothing to Harlan. He wouldn't stick around, waiting to profit on bigger and better contracts.

He would have achieved his goals. Tyler Drilling would be back on its feet and prospering. Although she was no longer sexually repressed, she wouldn't be included in any of Harlan's plans for the future. The sooner she started getting over him, the better.

That didn't stop her from loving him. The sight of him in his hat and boots and vest, looking just as he had the first time she saw him on the Belchers' veranda, had painfully increased her yearning and completely obliterated the reason for her being there until he reminded her of it.

"Oh, yes, Mother and Pat called from town," she blurted out. "They're due home any minute."

"No kidding? How do they sound?"

"They were jabbering like magpies, neither making much sense. Like newlyweds, I guess."

Harlan chuckled. "That's good."

"Devon insisted on having everybody out to supper to hear all about their trip."

"All about it?"

"The stuff they can tell." Her insides responded warmly to his naughty inflection. "The boys are picking up babyback ribs from Sammy's Smokehouse. Marcie's bringing baked beans. Devon's making potato salad. I baked a batch of brownies before I left."

"I'm impressed."

"Don't be. I used a packaged mix and prechopped nuts."

"What can I bring to supper?"

"Just yourself. Devon was afraid you'd stay out here working and miss the party altogether, so she sent me to get you."

He sauntered forward, moving to stand directly in front of her. "I'm glad she did."

Her resolution to begin withdrawal procedures evaporated in the heat of his gaze. She missed being with him day and night. She even missed his annoying penchant to tease. She missed his kiss, his touch, and ached to have them again.

Damned if she'd let him know that though.

"Well," she said, scooting forward so she could jump from the tailgate, "I guess we'd better get on our way."

Before she could deflect his hand, he pulled the loose rubber band from her ponytail and plowed his fingers through her tumbling hair. His mouth was hot and masterful as it covered hers. She returned the kiss for several seconds before pushing him away.

"Harlan, I'm still mad at you."

"And the madder you get, the better you look. Put that energy to good use and kiss me like you mean it."

She did. For one thing, she couldn't resist meeting the challenge in his eyes. For the other, she was dying to gobble him up. She threw her arms round his neck and arched her body into his.

Awkwardly, keeping their mouths cemented, he climbed into the pickup's bed, dragging Sage with him. Once he was sitting against the cab, she lay on her back across his lap and reached for his mouth with her own.

"Damn, Sage, I gotta breathe sometime," he said, finally tearing his lips free.

"You said for me to kiss you like I meant it. I only did as I was told."

"That's a switch." Grinning, he whisked his thumb over her moist lips. "You're the damnedest woman I ever met."

"Half the time I don't know whether to slap you or kiss you."

Chuckling, he parted her faded Levi's jacket and lowered his head to nuzzle her breasts. She tugged his shirttail from his waistband far enough to get her hands underneath it and onto his bare skin.

His lips caressed her breasts through the weave of her

sweater. Breathlessly she said, "I could kill you for doing this to me."

"What, this?" He rubbed his open mouth over her nipples.

"No," she sighed raggedly, "for making me want you when I can't have you."

He continued kissing her through her sweater while he unfastened her jeans. He pulled down the zipper and slid his hand inside. "I almost wish there was."

"What? You almost wish there was what?"

He placed his hand low on her abdomen. "A baby."

She drew a sudden breath of chilly air and lay very still within his embrace. "Don't lie to me like that, Harlan Boyd. You'd run like a jackrabbit."

He squinted one eye, as though considering it. "No, I think that might give me a damn good reason to stick around." He gazed down at her tousled sexiness. "Not that you're not reason enough, Sage," he added hoarsely.

"I know you've had lots of women. You've left them by the dozens." Beneath his shirt, her fingers curled into his chest hair and pulled tight. "Sage Tyler is going to be the one you find hard to leave and even harder to forget."

"You're right about that." His fingers probed her intimately, finding her soft and moist. Gruffly he added, "You're going to be hell to leave and impossible to forget."

*   *   *

Looking flushed, flustered, and windblown, they arrived at the ranch house just as everyone was convening in the dining room. Sage was immediately smothered in Laurie's embrace.

"Oh, I'm glad to see you looking so well. Doesn't she look wonderful, Pat?"

"Sure does. Like her old self."

Laurie set her daughter away from her and gazed into her face. "You finally got the sparkle back in your eyes and the color back in your cheeks. Whatever you're doing has been very good for you."

"I, uh, well, I've been working very hard. And I went riding out to get Harlan. M-my horse picked up a pebble, so I rode back with him in his truck. We, uh, we left the windows down. Then when we got back, we had to take care of the horse before coming inside." She paused for breath. "Welcome home, Mother, Pat. How was your honeymoon?"

Chase, who had been closely observing his sister and Harlan, cut his eyes toward Lucky, who was also watching the new arrivals with ill-concealed suspicion.

"We put the ribs in the oven to keep them warm," Chase said. "I'll get them."

"I'll help." Lucky instructed Devon to get everybody seated, then followed his brother from the dining room.

When they were alone in the kitchen, Chase posed a silent question with one arched eyebrow.

Lucky nodded soberly.

* * *

"I love you, Sage."

Her eyes flew open as a hand closed over her mouth. She panicked for an instant before recognizing Harlan who was bending low above her.

Beneath his hand she tried to ask what in the world he was doing sneaking into her room in the middle of the night. The words came out a garbled mass of un-formed syllables.

"Shh! If Lucky catches me in here with my hand over your mouth, he'll skin me alive and ask questions later." She frantically bobbed her head up and down. "Okay, so lie still and listen." He lay down beside her, but kept his hand cupped firmly over her mouth.

"Did you hear what I said? I love you, Sage. You're exasperating as hell. Bullheaded. Impetuous. A spoiled brat. A frequent liar." She glared at him murderously. His white smile showed up in the darkness. "But you're also a hell of a lot of fun, as exciting and unpredictable as whitewater. You kiss like a high-priced call girl, and those brownies you baked for supper weren't the worst I've had.

"What I'm leading up to is, if—and that's a big if—if I asked you to marry me, would you say yes?"

Lying perfectly still, she stared up at him over the back of his hand. Someday, she thought irrationally, she would be able to tell her grandchildren the crazy man-ner in which their grandpa had proposed to her.

Slowly, she nodded her head.

"Aw, *damn*!" he cursed. "I was hoping you'd say no. Then I could just thank you kindly for your time and a couple of terrific rolls in the hay and be outta here once Tyler Drilling was turned around.

"Now . . ." He made a regretful sound and shook his head. "Since you've said yes, that means we've each got some heavy thinking to do. I guess you love me, too, huh?"

She nodded.

"I'm not what you want, Sage."

She nodded, making guttural protests.

"I'm not ever going to be a society doctor who drives a fancy car. I'll never be city slick. What you see is what you get."

She nodded vigorously.

"But you wanted the other and all the trappings that went with it."

She shook her head no.

"You know how I live. I mean, I wouldn't ask you to live in the trailer. We'd get a house around here somewhere, but it wouldn't be a mansion like Belcher's." His eyes probed hers. "I wouldn't stock our house with things we didn't need just to impress the neighbors."

She shrugged.

"But I promise you this." He scooted closer, half covering her body with his. His voice turned soft and sexy. "I'd be faithful to you, Sage. I'd make good love to you every night. And sometimes during the daytime, too. I'm not squeamish when it comes to making love. I do it all, baby. Whatever you want. There's nothing I wouldn't do if it made you feel good."

She swallowed visibly.

"When I left for work every morning, you'd know that you were the most important thing on my mind. Not making a buck, not chasing a dollar, not getting ahead of the next guy."

The fingers of his free hand slid up into her hair, then closed into a fist next to her head on the pillow. "You'd better give this careful consideration, Sage. You're an executive in a company that's on the brink of busting wide open. You would be marrying the hired help."

She rolled her eyes as though saying, "Oh, please."

"What the hell do you know? You're just a bratty kid."

She shook her head.

"You're smarter than I am."

She shook her head again.

"Prettier."

Another shake of her head.

"Sexier."

A vehement no.

"Yeah?" he asked, pleased. "Well, softer, anyway."

He ducked his head and used it to work the covers off her shoulders. He kissed her there, then on her collarbone, then lower, moving the linens down as he went. When his lips reached the top curve of her breast, he raised his head.

"Are you naked under there?"

She nodded her head yes.

"Lordy." He paused as though weighing his options. To help him make up his mind, she shimmied her shoulders until the covers slipped down to reveal her breasts.

Groaning, he asked, "Do you think they'd know if we—"

She shook her head.

"Okay, then. But you've got to promise not to make those little hiccupping noises you usually make."

Using only one hand, he stripped off his jeans, his only article of clothing, and slid between the sheets beside her. Sighing, he curved his arm around her waist and drew her against him. His sex was pressed full and strong between their bellies.

Sage shuddered at the sensations that coursed through her. Her heart overflowed with love and happiness. She rocked her body against his invitingly. Bracing himself above her, he leaned over for a kiss. Only then did he remove his hand.

"You can open your mouth now," he whispered.

She did . . . in order to receive his tongue. As they kissed, he gathered her beneath him. Effortlessly, he slipped into her warm center. The loving was smooth and easy, creating no more havoc than butter melting, with the smallest motions and minimal sounds, only the rustling of their naked bodies among the linens. He stretched into her, reaching higher than before because love propelled him.

His hands covered her breasts, rubbed them, petted them. He stroked her thighs. When the momentum reached the breaking point, they clasped hands on either side of her head and held onto each other until long after the climax had subsided.

Finally he eased off her and brushed his lips across her dewy forehead. "I don't want to say good-night, but I've got to."

"Don't go," she whispered, ensnaring her fingers in his hair.

Tenderly, he kissed her lips. "You know I have to."

"Don't go." Her hands slid beneath his waist.

"Ah, Sage, baby . . ."

"Don't go."

He didn't go until dawn when she finally slept peacefully beside him. Then he slipped from the room as silently as he had come in.

"Good morning," Sage chirped as she entered the kitchen the following morning. Though the weather was inclement, her mood was positively sunny.

"Hi." Devon was spooning baby oatmeal into her eager daughter's rosebud mouth. "Coffee's ready. Help yourself."

"Thanks. Where is everybody?" Sage asked casually.

"He left about thirty minutes ago."

Sage turned away from the counter and gave her sister-in-law a sharp glance. There were teasing green glints in Devon's eyes. "He said he'd be working on the system all day."

"In this weather?"

"That's what he said." Sage joined her at the table.

"Sleep well?" Devon asked with phony innocence. She was barely suppressing her laughter.

"I take it you know."

"Um-huh."

"Does Lucky?"

"No. I wasn't spying on you, Sage. I swear. I happened to wake up and went across the hall to check on Lauren."

Swamped with embarrassment, Sage cast her eyes downward.

Devon reached for her hand and squeezed it. "You love him, don't you?"

"So much it hurts."

"I know what it's like."

"Do you?"

"Absolutely."

"Then you don't think I'm cheap or trashy for letting him sneak down the hall and climb into my bed?"

Devon gave her a smile that was tinged with sadness. "How can you even ask me if I judge you? The first night I met your brother we made love."

The two women smiled at each other with complete understanding. "When people find out," Sage said, "they're going to think I'm crazy. I just came out of a near engagement to Travis."

"If I had let public opinion bother me, I would have stayed married to a convicted felon, ruining my life and Lucky's in the process. Marcie would tell you herself that people were shocked when Chase married her. She didn't let that stop her."

Devon tightened her grip on Sage's hand. "You have to go with your instincts, Sage. Follow your own heart. Do what's best for you and Harlan. To hell with what an outsider thinks about it."

Sage laid her hand over Devon's. "Thanks." Before they could yield to the tears that threatened, the telephone rang. Sage sprung up to answer it.

"Hi, Lucky. Devon's right here. Need to talk to her?"

"No, actually I'm calling you." His voice was laced with excitement. "One of your prospects came through. He's on his way now to talk terms. Chase said for you to haul tail over here to the office. Is Harlan around?"

"He told Devon he was going to work in the field all day."

"Too bad. Chase wanted him here, too, but said for you not to waste time rounding him up."

"Who is it, Lucky? What's the client's name?"

"Hardtack and Associates. Big, bad Grayson Hardtack himself flew in to negotiate the deal."

Chapter
EIGHTEEN

*T*he silver Mercedes limousine looked odd parked outside Tyler Drilling Company between a company truck and a pickup. To keep out of the rain, the uniformed chauffeur was sitting behind the wheel. Disinterested, he barely gave Sage a glance when she alighted from her car.

There was no sign of Harlan. She sent up a little prayer of thanksgiving that he had been unavailable when Grayson Hardtack put in this unexpected appearance. It was still a close call, however. She prayed they could conclude their business quickly, and she could contrive some sort of explanation before she saw Harlan. Her legs were rubbery as she went up the steps and pushed open the door.

From across the room, Hardtack said, "Hello, Ms. Tyler."

Sage froze on the threshold. The blood drained from her face. Her brothers, expecting her to be effusively glad to see their guest, looked at her with puzzlement, but she simply could not move or speak.

Her eyes had immediately been drawn to the woman. Sitting quietly in a scarred, scratched straightback chair, she looked as out of place as a masterpiece in a paint-by-number box.

Her clothes, makeup, hair, and the way she held herself were impeccably correct. The back of the chair had been draped with a white mink coat, its pastel satin lining facing out. A pair of kid gloves, which perfectly matched her mauve shoes and suit, were lying in her lap along with a matching handbag.

The breathtaking portrait in Hardtack's office hadn't even done her justice. She was more than beautiful; she was exquisite. Although, Sage thought with a tiny grain of gratification, Marian Hardtack was older than she had expected her to be.

Sage finally regained her composure. She moved inside and extended her unsteady right hand to her client. "Good morning, Mr. Hardtack. It's so nice to see you again."

"Likewise. This is my wife, Marian. Marian, Sage Tyler."

"Hello, Mrs. Hardtack." The woman raised her well-manicured hand. Surprisingly, it felt soft and warm. Sage would have expected it to feel cool. Mrs. Hardtack was so immaculately groomed that, by comparison, Sage felt tacky and disheveled, though there was certainly nothing wrong with her own grooming and attire.

Mrs. Hardtack's smile was warm, too, and that came as another surprise. Her expression was gracious, a tad curious, and as gentle as her voice. "It's a pleasure to meet you, Ms. Tyler."

Sage wondered if she would think so if she knew who she'd been sleeping with the night before.

Remembering her manners, she asked, "Did my brothers offer you coffee?"

"They did, but we drank several cups on the flight over," Hardtack said.

"Oh, you flew from Dallas. I thought . . ." She gestured toward the door.

"The limo? It's only hired for the day to get us around Milton Point." Hardtack resumed his seat. "Let's get down to business."

"While we were waiting on you," Chase said to Sage, "we showed Mr. Hardtack the contract our attorney drew up."

"I think you'll find it's standard," she said.

Hardtack grunted noncommittally. His wife said nothing, but Sage was uncomfortably aware of her unwavering stare as she sat down in the chair Lucky brought for her.

"We guarantee all the parts on the machinery for five years."

S A N D R A   B R O W N

"That's at least three years longer than most companies guarantee either their equipment or their work,"
Lucky said. "We firmly stand behind both and are
willing to put our reputations on the line to guarantee
them."

Sage had never seen her brothers looking so intense
or well behaved. They realized the importance of making a sale to Hardtack. Using his name as a reference
would give them instant credibility. Additionally, because he had so many business interests, one job with
him could lead to several.

"As I told your sister the other day," he said, speaking to Chase and Lucky, "I can get a sprinkler system
anywhere. She sold me on herself. She piqued my
interest in your small company. I wanted to come over
and personally meet the rest of the family."

He leaned back in his chair. "You know, not everybody in the oil industry is suffering these days. If you
know where to get operating capital, there's still money
to be made."

Chase's Adam's apple slid up and down. Sage could
tell that Lucky was having a hard time keeping his
exuberance in check. She hoped he wouldn't leap up
and execute one of his infamous backward flips.

Chase said, "We've got a crew standing by, and every
man in it likes hard work." Sage was proud of him. He
was showing his interest without groveling.

"Glad to hear that," Hardtack said. "I like knowing

where I can find expert drillers." He slapped his thighs. "I think this visit has been well worthwhile for everybody, hasn't it?" Looking toward Sage, he said, "I'll have my project supervisor for Shadow Hills contact you. You'll be working directly with him from here on."

He was halfway out of his chair when she asked, "When can we expect the deposit?"

He dropped back down and peered up at her through his eyebrows. Chase and Lucky looked as though lightning had just struck them. They gaped at her, their expressions a mix of incredulity and anger.

"Deposit?"

"That clause is on page three of the contract, Mr. Hardtack. We require a ten thousand dollar deposit, payable immediately upon retention." Her heart was making a racket against her ribs, but she didn't flinch from Hardtack's intimidating stare.

"I'll send you a check by messenger tomorrow. Will that do, Ms. Tyler?"

"Splendidly."

Her brothers slumped with visible relief. Sage, trying to maintain a cool, professional demeanor, glanced at them. Chase gave her a subtle thumbs-up signal. Lucky winked.

"Thank you for taking such a personal interest in this, Mr. Hardtack," she said with a big smile. "Working together will be—"

"Before we shake on it," he said, interrupting her and

ignoring her extended hand, "there's one thing I want to know."

Her heady, jubilant flight had been short-lived. Her ego-boosting success stalled, then went into a spiraling nosedive. She lost oxygen on the descent. She awaited the inevitable crash.

"The drawings you left with me had distinctive traits I believe I recognize," Hardtack said. "Was the draftsman Harlan Boyd?"

For a moment her ears roared. She was certain that, had she been standing up, her knees would have buckled. She might have fainted.

The realization of all her aspirations came down to one simple question. Success or failure hinged on her answer. Equivocating would mean an enormous contract with one of the most influential men in the state. It would mean the end to Tyler Drilling's years-long financial struggle and virtually guarantee future prosperity for her family and their employees.

Her ingenuity would get partial credit for bringing it about. She would have won the admiration and confidence of her brothers, proved herself to be a knowledgeable and capable businesswoman, not just their kid sister.

She was a master at avoiding the truth. She didn't lie, exactly, she merely skirted the truth when it wasn't convenient. Hardtack had asked her a pointblank question that required either a yes or no answer. This was one question she couldn't dodge. Somewhat to her surprise, she found she didn't want to.

Even if Lucky and Chase hadn't been looking at her strangely, wondering why the cat had suddenly got her tongue, surely ready to correct her if she told a fib, she confronted Grayson Hardtack, prepared to tell the truth.

Gazing up at her from beneath his shelf of heavy brows, he was an intimidating presence, but she faced him squarely and opened her mouth to speak.

"Yes, I did the drawings. You knew that before you asked her."

Heads turned in the direction of the open doorway. Harlan was standing on the threshold, rain water dripping off the brim of his hat. He was wearing a bright yellow slicker, but his boots and his jeans from the knees down were wet and muddy.

Lucky and Chase seemed baffled, as though they had missed the first two acts of a mystery play and were getting in on the denouement.

Sage recoiled from Harlan's expression. It matched the one he'd assumed when he first saw Hardtack's name on the client list she had compiled. She wanted to go to him with a sound explanation for why she had betrayed his wishes, but his belligerent face and stance kept her rooted where she was.

It was impossible to gauge what Hardtack was thinking.

The woman's reaction, however, was swift and baldly honest. She shot up from her chair. Her gloves and expensive handbag slid from her lap and fell unheeded to the floor. One pale hand, decorated by Tiffany's, found its way to her chest, which was rising and falling rapidly.

"Harlan." His name was expelled on a faint breath. Then she repeated it with more stamina. Finally she cried it joyfully. "Harlan, darling!" She rushed across the room, throwing herself against him, regardless of what his wet slicker was doing to her fine, designer clothing.

He fell back a step to regain his balance and awkwardly placed his arm around her. "Hello, Mother."

"The bottom line is, Harlan is loaded with a capital *L*."

The entire Tyler clan was gathered in the kitchen, as if tom-toms had notified all members of the family that there was a crisis afoot.

Sage, chopping onions for the pot of chili simmering on the stove, kept her back to them. Since Lucky was the best storyteller, he held the others in thrall.

"We're talking rich. Learjet rich. Limousine-and-driver rich. College-grants and museum-loans and getting-hospital-wings-named-after-you rich." He shook his head in disbelief. "To look at him, you never would guess, would you?"

"I'm confused," Laurie said. "Does the wealth belong to Harlan or Mr. Hardtack?"

"Both. See, Harlan's father Daniel Boyd and Hardtack were business partners. They made millions in commercial real estate and went from there. Daniel died of a heart attack like that," Lucky said, snapping his fingers. "Hardtack bought his interests from the widow, Marian. About a year later, he married her."

"How do you know all this?" Marcie wanted to know. She switched Jamie to her other shoulder. Chase, seeing that she was getting tired, took his son onto his own shoulder.

"It all came out during the shouting match," he said. "At first we weren't able to keep up. Gradually, the more they said, the more we were able to piece together."

Sage raked the chopped onions off the cutting board into the chili pot. With her sleeve, she blotted tears from her eyes and wiped her runny nose. The onions gave her a good excuse to cry.

She had felt so smart, so smug. She thought she had pulled together a big deal, a granddaddy of a deal, a Mount Everest of a deal. Instead, all she had really done was alert Hardtack to Harlan's whereabouts.

That was the only reason he'd flown his private jet to Milton Point and rented a limo for the day. He hadn't come to negotiate a deal with insignificant Sage Tyler, but to track down his wayward stepson.

"I take it that Harlan didn't cotton to the idea of Hardtack marrying his mother," Pat said, rolling a matchstick to the other side of his mouth.

"Hardly," Lucky replied. "Apparently Harlan and his daddy were very close. When he came home from school—he was at Saint Edward's in San Antonio at the time—and they told him that their marriage was a done deal—"

"A *fait accompli*," Marcie said.

"A what?"

"A done deal," Devon told her husband impatiently. "Get on with the story."

"Harlan accused them of carrying on behind his daddy's back *before* Daniel died. He made the same accusation today. That's when Mrs. Hardtack collapsed into a chair and started bawling something terrible. She kept saying, 'You're wrong, Harlan. You're wrong. I loved your father. How could you ever think I was unfaithful to him?' "

Laurie was automatically sympathetic. "I think Harlan was being too hard on her."

"He was fifteen years old!" Sage spun around and confronted them all. "Don't you realize how protective a fifteen-year-old boy feels toward his mother, especially if she loses her husband? Harlan's reaction was perfectly normal. He felt like Hardtack was usurping his position as head of the household."

Having had her say, she turned back around and began cutting up chili peppers, wielding the butcher knife with a vengeance. What weight did her opinion carry? None. She had made a fool of herself again, bragging about the contracts she was going to get for the company. Hardtack hadn't been interested in the merits of her sales technique.

Lucky continued. "Harlan probably was off-base, but, as Sage said, he was looking at it through the eyes of an adolescent."

"A child grieving for his lost parent and feeling betrayed and deserted by the other," Laurie said, ever fair and ever the sympathizer. "That was a no-win situation for them all, wasn't it? How tragic."

"Harlan resented Hardtack for trying to have everything that had belonged to Daniel Boyd. He judged his mother as a Jezebel. So he split," Lucky said. "He hasn't gone back since. Which brings us to today. When Sage showed Hardtack the drawings, he recognized Harlan's technique."

"How?" Devon asked.

"Unbeknownst to Harlan, Hardtack and Marian have been keeping track of him all this time, though they never interfered in his life. They'd seen his work before."

Chase said, "Hardtack admitted to having Sage followed after she left the drawings with him."

"Oh, my goodness," Laurie said.

The blade of the butcher knife hit the chopping block with a solid *thwack*. Sage was outraged at the thought of being followed and photographed by a private investigator. It seemed so sleazy. She didn't care how many zillions Hardtack was worth, he had his nerve!

"Hardtack pulls a lot of strings," Lucky said. "When he says jump, legions of folks ask how high. Anyway, he verified that Harlan was our draftsman, figured it was time to confront his prodigal stepson face-to-face, and brought Marian along for the showdown."

"He tricked her into coming? She didn't know?" Marcie was aghast at the thought.

"No, she knew. She was anxious to get a glimpse of her son, since she hadn't seen him in fourteen years."

"To his credit, Harlan treated his mother kindly," Chase told the group. "He let her paw him, his face, his hair. You know how mothers do when they haven't seen their kids for a while. They kissed each other and hugged for a long time. It was Hardtack he felt the animosity for."

"So his feelings haven't ameliorated with maturity?" Marcie asked.

"Apparently not," Lucky replied. "He accused Hardtack of taking it all—his partner's business, his partner's money, his partner's wife."

"Strong words," Pat remarked.

"Well, Hardtack was doing his share of shouting, too. He told Harlan that he could think anything he wanted to about him, but he staunchly took offense at Marian being accused of adultery. I got the impression that the tough old buzzard really loves her.

"He claimed that every penny belonging to Marian and Harlan is right where Daniel Boyd left it—in trust, earning interest at an astronomical rate. He said, 'Why don't you stop acting like a snot-nosed kid and claim your inheritance. It's time you assumed some responsibility.'

"Then Harlan said, 'I don't want my inheritance. Not if it could turn me into a money-grabber like you. Screw it and screw the ball and chain that go with it.' "

"Lucky!" Laurie remonstrated. "The children."

"Mother, I'm editing as I go. Harlan didn't say 'screw.' Then Hardtack said that Harlan had no sense of responsibility whatsoever and never would amount to anything except a bum and a drifter. That's when Sage piped in and told Hardtack that Harlan was the most responsible person she had ever met."

All eyes moved to her. "Sage, I commend you for defending our friend," Laurie said, "but it really wasn't your place to interfere."

She swung around. A piece of meat was skewered to the tip of the butcher knife. "It *was* my place. I have every right to stand up for Harlan. He's going to be my husband."

Their exclamations ranged from total disbelief to happy surprise.

"Does Harlan know that?" Lucky asked.

"He asked me to marry him last night."

Lucky came out of his chair. "When last night? Where was I?"

"You were sound asleep."

He looked hard at his wife. "Devon, I knew you were keeping something from me. Do you know something I should know?"

"Sit down, Lucky. You're upsetting Lauren."

"She's right, Lucky, sit down," Chase barked. "If you fly off the handle, you'll only make things worse."

"And if you fight him again, I'll break your arm myself this time," Sage declared.

"I thought you broke your arm when you tripped against a trailer hitch," Laurie exclaimed.

Lucky ducked his head sheepishly.

Chase sighed and said to Laurie, "He tripped and fell against a trailer hitch during a fistfight with Harlan over Sage's virtue. We were afraid she might be pregnant."

Laurie gasped and reached for Pat's hand. The sheriff's expression was thunderous. "Can't you young'uns ever behave yourselves? We leave town for a few weeks, and everything goes to hell in a handbasket."

"Is there more?" Laurie asked, looking pained.

"Not really," Lucky said. "Except that Hardtack didn't back out of his deal with us despite his shouting match with Harlan."

A door slammed upstairs.

"Shh, here he comes," Chase whispered.

In the sudden silence of the kitchen, Sage held her breath. No one had seen Harlan since his stepfather had called him a 'sniveling little sonofabitch,' whose damned stubborn pride was breaking his mother's heart. That's when Harlan had slung open the door of Tyler Drilling's office and stalked out.

Sage had plunged after him, but he was already out of sight by the time she reached her car. She had driven home through a blinding rain, hoping to see his pickup parked out front. She had sobbed with relief when she turned into the lane and saw it there.

But then she had lost her nerve. Instead of rushing upstairs, she and everyone else had allowed him privacy to sort through the upsetting events of the morning. After years of running from it, he had been forced to confront his unhappy youth. He would need space in which to grapple with it.

Now they could hear his boots on the stairs, then in the dining room as he made his way toward the kitchen. Everyone pretended to be occupied, but Lauren was the only one actually moving. She was blowing slobbery bubbles against her mother's cheek.

He stepped through the doorway, his eyes seeking out Sage immediately. She gave him a tentative smile, which collapsed the instant she spotted the duffel bag in his hand.

"I'll be leaving now. I cleared your room out. You can have it back."

The announcement left them stunned. Chase was the first to recover his speech. "You're leaving?"

Harlan stepped forward and shook hands with Chase. "I liked you the first time we met in Houston last year. I like you even better now that I've gotten to know you. Good luck."

He moved to Lucky and clasped his left hand. "Sorry again about your arm. I didn't mean to do it. You're a hell of a guy."

To them both he said, "Everything checked out this morning. With those new computers, the pumps'll work like a charm. You'll find all my drawings in the file cabinet in the garage. Using them as guidelines, your people shouldn't have any problems with the layout and assembly."

"We hate to see you go, Harlan," Chase said quietly.

"It's time I did." He glanced quickly at Sage. "Past time."

"But what about your commission? How'll we know where to send your checks? If some of these contracts that you and Sage worked on together pan out, you'll be due a lot of money."

He gave a dismissive shrug. "I've got enough cash to last a while. If I need the money, I'll contact you."

They knew he wouldn't. Even as he said it, he was backing out the door. "Devon, Marcie, take care of those sweet babies. I'm gonna miss them. Pat, look after Laurie. She's a darlin' lady."

Laurie stood up and extended her arms toward him in a maternal gesture. "Harlan, please."

"Bye, y'all." He pulled on his hat, ducked out the door and disappeared.

Sage gaped at the empty doorway for the space of several seconds, aware that everyone was trying desperately hard not to look at her with pity.

Before she had time to think about it, she dashed after him. Dodging furniture like an expert swordsman, she charged through the rooms of the house, bolted through the front door, ran across the porch, and leaped over the steps. Heedless of the cold, pelting rain, she caught up with him as he tossed his duffel bag into the cab of his pickup.

Grabbing hold of his sleeve, she spun him around. "Where the hell do you think you're going? You can't just walk out on me like this!"

"Get back inside. You're gonna get soaked."

"I don't care if I get wet anymore than I care if you're a Texas Donald Trump or as poor as Job's turkey. I want you, whether you come garbed in riches or standing buck-naked."

On her headlong flight from the kitchen, she had forgotten to discard the butcher knife. She shook the blade at the end of his nose. "I learned something about myself today. I'm a person to be reckoned with.

"At first, I thought that Hardtack had come here strictly to find you. Then about thirty seconds ago, it occurred to me that he didn't have to sign a contract with us to locate you. Once his investigator had sighted us together, he could have circumvented us and gone straight to you.

"So that means he *was* sold on me just as he said. I sold him on Tyler Drilling. I didn't get that contract because of you, but in spite of you.

"Oh!" she ground out. "You've been accusing me of avoiding the truth, when you've been living a lie for years. It's time you stopped avoiding who and what you are, Harlan. It's time you reconciled your differences with Hardtack, if not for your own benefit, then certainly for your brokenhearted mother's.

"And another thing, you can't make love to me and propose marriage and then hightail it out of here, Harlan Boyd. How dare you even try? How dare you embarrass me in front of my family right after I announced that you had asked me to marry you?

"This time I'm not going to swallow my pride and hide my hurt feelings like I did with Travis. This one counts. This time I'm going to kick and scream and pull temper tantrums and lie down in front of your truck and whatever else it takes to keep you.

"You boasted of never leaving a job unfinished. Well, last night you promised to remain faithful to me and make me happy. That's a job that's going to last for the rest of your life.

"You can't accuse me of wanting to marry you for your money either. Because when you asked me and I said yes, I didn't know you had a nickel. I loved you then as much as I do now. So haul that duffel bag out of that truck and march it right back upstairs. You're not going anywhere without me."

Rain was streaming down her face. Her clothing was plastered to her. Her hair clung to her face and neck in wet clumps. But she was impervious to it all.

In his adorable drawl, he asked, "Are you gonna poke me with that butcher knife if I don't?"

"I might. You're going to marry me if I have to kill you first."

Muttering curses and ruefully shaking his head, he gazed out over the sodden landscape. When his gaze came back to her, he laughed. Reaching out, he dug his hand into the waistband of her slacks and jerked her against him. Wresting the butcher knife from her hand, he tossed it away. It landed with a splash in the nearest puddle.

"I've got a lot of money," he said for starters.

"So what?"

"I'll never let it own me, Sage. Don't count on my changing my attitude toward it."

"The only thing I'll count on is your not changing your attitude toward me."

"What's my attitude toward you?"

"You love me. You adore me. You're addicted to me. You'd die without me in your life. I make you hot and hard and happy."

Laughing, he cupped his hands beneath her bottom and lifted her up. She wrapped her legs around his hips. He pivoted slowly while the rain fell on them. "You're crazy, but you're right."

"On which point?"

"All of the above."

"Then kiss me like you mean it."

When they finally broke apart, he glanced warily toward the front of the house. "Damn, Sage. If you don't quit kissing me like that, we'll have to start the honeymoon right here and now."

She bit his lower lip. "That's the general idea."

EPILOGUE

"*H*arlan, wake up. It's time."

He snuffled and buried his face in her hair. "I'd love to, baby, but I'm beat. Can you wait till morning?"

Sage laughed softly and removed his questing hand from her breast. "I don't mean it's time for *that*. It's time to go to the hospital."

He sat bolt upright in bed. "You mean the baby?"

"I've been having contractions for the past two hours."

"Two hours! Damn, Sage. Why didn't you wake me up?"

"As you said, you were beat. You really shouldn't have driven home from Louisiana tonight."

"If I hadn't, where would you be now, huh?" He shoved his legs into his jeans and stood up in one fluid motion.

He'd been in the neighboring state overseeing a rig

Tyler Drilling had leased to a new oil company headed by his stepfather. When he had called at dusk to say he was coming home, she had discouraged him from making the trip that late in the day. Now she was glad he had insisted.

"I've been away from you too long, baby," he had said.

"It's only been two days."

"That's way too long."

Recalling the fervency behind his words made her smile as she reached for the nightstand telephone. "I'll call the doctor."

"Where's the damn suitcase?" he asked, plowing through the clothes hanging in the closet. "Good thing you already packed it. Where is it?"

"It's in the other closet." She asked the doctor's answering service to notify him that she was on her way to the hospital and hung up. "Harlan, calm down. We've got plenty of time. My water hasn't even—Uh-oh!"

"What?" His head popped out of the closet.

"My water just broke."

Cursing liberally, he wrapped her in a blanket and carried her out to the car. "Breathe," he commanded, even though his own breathing was unsteady. "Remember to breathe the way they taught us in class."

He tucked her into the passenger seat and ran around the hood, his open shirt flapping.

"Button your shirt," she told him as they pulled away

from the house that Marcie had sold them, waiving her commission as a wedding gift.

"Why are you worrying about my shirt at a time like this?"

"I don't want all the nurses drooling over your hairy chest, that's why."

At a traffic light he stopped only long enough to hastily fasten the buttons, then sped through the red light. "You're going to get a ticket," she warned.

"I've got connections at city hall."

"Not for long. Pat's retirement party is next week. Oh, Harlan, I can't miss the party!"

Laurie had redecorated Pat's former bachelor pad from the foundation up, turning it into a dollhouse of a showplace. She loved living in town where she was close to all her friends and activities. For all practical purposes, they were still on their honeymoon. It was difficult to say which of them was more besotted.

"If necessary, they'll postpone the party," he assured her. Reaching across the car interior, he laid his hand on Sage's stomach. "He's early, isn't he? Why's he early? You don't think anything's wrong, do you?"

"Nothing's wrong. He's just anxious to meet you. I've told him so much about you," she said gently, covering his hand with her own.

The tires squealed when he pulled up to the emergency room. Not even waiting for a gurney, Harlan scooped her into his arms again and carried her inside.

Once they were officially checked in, a nurse said, "The doctor will need to see her alone for a few minutes, Mr. Boyd, then you can join her."

"Call everybody," Sage shouted over her shoulder as she was wheeled away.

By the time the family had been notified, he was able to join her in the labor room. He put on the scrub suit that was required.

"Definitely your shade of blue," Sage remarked once he was properly gowned.

"Always the smart aleck. Never knows when to keep her mouth shut." He bent over her, his eyes suddenly turning serious and misty. "Damn, Sage, I love you."

"I love you too." She gripped his hands. "I'm kind of scared."

"You?"

"Yes. And you know I wouldn't admit that to anyone except you. Stay with me, Harlan."

"Forever, baby. You can count on it."

Huffing and puffing and calling her OB a heartless, male chauvinist pig, she was wheeled into the delivery room. Minutes later, with Harlan's assistance, she gave birth to his son. The good-natured doctor lifted the squirming, squalling infant into the father's waiting arms.

"Congratulations, Mr. Boyd."

"Call me Harlan," he said absently as he laid his son on Sage's breast.

"Oh, he's beautiful," she whispered in awe. "Look, Harlan, at what a wonderful baby we made."

It was almost an hour later before they were finally left alone with their son. The nurse had warned them they couldn't keep him long before he needed to be returned to the nursery.

Sage fingered his cap of blond fuzz. "He's got your hairline, Harlan. Your nose."

"My penis."

"Oh!" she exclaimed. Then, giving him a sultry smile, she added, "Not hardly." They laughed together softly, then kissed. "Did you call everyone?"

"They'll descend on the nursery as soon as the hospital staff will let them in. The hospital ought to give us a family discount, as much business as we're giving them."

To everyone's delight, Marcie had announced that she was pregnant again, even though Jamie wasn't even a year old. Her biological clock was running out, she had said. Her business was prospering even though she only worked part-time, so she could indulge her maternal instincts. Chase and she were fabulously happy.

Devon's column had been syndicated to several out-of-state newspapers. Lucky and she were talking about having another child, although he swore he couldn't possibly sire another one as delightful as Lauren. In the same breath, he said he sure would have fun trying though.

Tyler Drilling almost had more business than it could

accommodate. Between the two separate entities, they kept their trucks rolling from city to city. Until a few weeks ago, Sage had been at the helm of the irrigation business, coordinating schedules, soliciting new clients, and managing the office, which had been added onto and was now staffed with two secretaries.

"What about Marian and Grayson?" Sage asked her husband now. "Did you call them?"

"Mother flipped out. They're flying over in the morning."

Sage reached up and affectionately stroked his cheek. Thanks to her peace-making attempts, Grayson and Harlan were civil to each other. There was still some turbulence between them over Harlan's refusal to become Grayson's business partner. It was a point they constantly disagreed on, and always would. But mother and son had been reunited, and that was the most important thing.

Harlan had admitted to Sage that he had carried the wounds of adolescence into adulthood. He never really believed that his mother had been unfaithful before his father's death or that Grayson had done anything unscrupulous. It was simply easier to blame them for his father's death than to focus his anger on something he couldn't combat.

Grayson, with his brusque personality, was such a departure from the easygoing man who had fathered Harlan, that the boy couldn't accept him. Sage patiently explained to him that Grayson didn't treat Marian in the same manner he treated a business rival.

"I'm certain he loves your mother very much."

"I suppose he does. But after Mother married him, I started thinking of money as something evil," he had told her in an attempt to explain. "With enough money, someone could assume control of other people's lives. I wanted no part of it."

In the last few months, he had begun to dip into his inheritance, but only because he hated to see it lying in waste when so many people could use it. He was quietly philanthropic. The substantial donations he made to diverse organizations and charities never knew from whom the staggering contributions came.

"Why didn't you just give it away before?" Sage had once asked him. "For instance, when you saw Tyler Drilling was in trouble, why didn't you just give the money to Chase?"

"Because money alone wouldn't have solved the problem. Not in the long run. Besides, I liked getting involved and having to use my own resources to work out problems. Folks don't accept charity too well, but unless you're dealing with fools, they're usually open to fresh ideas. I left them with the satisfaction of knowing that they'd worked through their difficulties themselves. If I'd signed a check, they would have missed that personal gratification. So would I."

He still wore jeans older than most graduating high

school seniors and drove a pickup that Sage threatened to shoot and put out of its misery if it broke down one more time. He claimed it still had some good miles left in it.

Now, gazing up at him with love, she said softly, "They asked me how to fill in his birth certificate. I told them his name is Daniel Tyler Boyd."

"Daniel," he repeated thickly, tears shimmering in his eyes. "Thanks, Sage. I like that." He swallowed hard and cleared his throat. "I can't get over how much he weighed. To be so premature, seven and a half pounds is a lot, isn't it?"

She moistened her lips and pulled her lower one through her teeth. "Actually, Harlan, he's not all that premature."

"You told me your due date was in early November."

"That's what I told you, yes. The fact is, Daniel's right on time."

"But this is the first of October. That would move his conception back to early January."

"Um-huh."

As clarity dawned, his eyes connected with hers. "Why you little liar. You were pregnant all along. It happened that day in the trailer, right? You lied and said there was no baby."

"I didn't exactly lie. When I said there was no baby, the jury was still out. I couldn't have you and my brothers at fisticuffs, could I? I certainly didn't want you to marry me out of obligation or pity. So, yes, I denied that there was a baby when, in fact, Daniel was already developing fingerprints."

Harlan stared at her for a moment, absolutely incredulous. Then he threw back his head and laughed. Daniel frowned against his mother's breast.

"Well, I'll be damned," Harlan whispered. He took the baby's tiny hand and rubbed it between his fingers. "Did you hear that, Daniel? Your mama really pulled one over on me this time."

Then he buried his free hand in Sage's hair and lowered his lips to hers. "You're the damnedest woman I ever met, Miss Sage. Kiss me like you mean it."